WHAT THIS MYSTERY IS ABOUT

... A fat, perfect joint
... Midlife crises
... A Gibson SG
... Fresh-squeezed orange juice
... The girl who got away
... An eclectic after-hours club
... Julie Andrews
... Local television news
... Breast reduction surgery
... Grilled cheese sandwiches
... The Berlin Wall
... A gruesome murder-suicide
... One VW Beetle after another
... A girl's gun
... Skipping the light fandango
... Voice mail hell
... eBay
... Naked neighbors
... A high-speed chase
... A biker bar
... A shootout at the beach
... Cookie tins full of photographs
... A hideaway in the desert
... A ten-foot-tall peace symbol

PEOPLE THIS

Joe Portugal
TV commercial actor, lapsed musician, and perpetual
stumbler over dead bodies

Gina Vela
Joe's best friend, former and present lover,
an interior designer by trade

Squig Jones
A shrimp of a guy who never outgrew the sixties

Robbie "Woz" Wozniak
Squig's pal, something of a psycho,
wielding a mean electric bass

Darren Chapman
He had what it took to make Joe feel old

Frampton Washington
A shadow of his former self,
he gave up the drums for a slide rule

Bonnie Chapman
Three-hit wonder, record company executive,
and the girl Joe wishes he'd shtupped

Toby Bonner
Ace guitarist, Bonnie's recording partner,
unseen in twenty years

MYSTERY IS ABOUT

Deanna Knox
She needed Joe for something—she just wasn't sure what

Detective Kalenko
He knew Joe's history, and told him not to repeat it

Alberta Burns
A good cop, who took one in the leg

Aricela Castillo
The kid was all right, but she did her best to hide it

Ronnie from Arkansas
She may not have been a real blond,
but she was the real deal

Harold "The Horse" Portugal
He decided it was time to let his son in on a secret or two

Mott Festerling
Cradle robber, couch potato, and part-time drug dealer

Hoss, Buck, and Pam
The boys hung out at the joint
where she and her cleavage tended bar

Vinnie Mann
Only two things mattered to him—
rock and roll was one of them

ONE LAST HIT

a Joe Portugal mystery
by Nathan Walpow

UGLYTOWN
Los Angeles

First Edition

UGLYTOWN AND THE UGLYTOWN COIN LOGO SERVICEMARK REG. U.S. PAT. OFF.

Library of Congress Cataloging-in-Publication Data
Walpow, Nathan, 1948–
One last hit / by Nathan Walpow.
p. cm.—(A Joe Portugal mystery.)
ISBN 0- 9724412-0-4
1. Portugal, Joe (Fictitious character)—Fiction. 2. Los Angeles (Calif.)—Fiction.
3. Bands (Music)—Fiction. 4. Musicians—Fiction.
I. Title.
PS3573.A4478 O54   2003
813'.6—dc21   2002155083
CIP

Find out more of the mystery: UglyTown.com/OneLastHit

Printed in the United States of America

10 9 8 7 6 5 4 3 2 1

Dedicated to the memory of John Entwistle

Why can't we have eternal life, and never die?

"It is not hard to compose, but it is wonderfully hard to let the superfluous notes fall under the table."
—Johannes Brahms

ONE LAST HIT

GET YOUR MOTOR RUNNIN'

A Little Is Enough

The relic in the next seat wore a threadbare Quicksilver Messenger Service T-shirt. His long blond hair was parted in the middle. His muttonchops were impeccable. His eyes were red, his pupils huge.

"Hit?" he said.

I checked on Gina. She was pumping her hand in the air, yelling "dude looks like a lady" at the top of her lungs.

Back to my new buddy. "Sure," I said, plucking the fat, perfect joint from his grimy-fingernailed hand. I took a toke, handed it back, said thanks.

"Anytime, man," he said, nodding sagely. He nestled the jay between his lips, inhaled deeply, closed his eyes. His head bobbed along half a beat behind the music.

I hadn't had any dope in a year or more, and this stuff hit me right away. A stupid grin stole over my face. I got lost in the bass line, the tinkle of the hi-hat, the interplay between the guitars. It was groovy, man.

The song ended. Tyler went into a rap about the band's early days in Boston. Gina turned to me. She frowned, looked in my eyes, leaned in and sniffed. "Somebody gave you dope."

"Take me to an Aerosmith concert, you suffer the consequences. It was just one hit."

"And you're high as a kite. You're such a lightweight."

The band broke into "Big Ten Inch Record." Gina watched Tyler's every move. When the song was over she said, "How can a guy so ugly be so sexy?"

"It's the clothes."

"You think?"

"If I wore clothes like that, I'd have women all over me."

She smiled. "Dream on," she said.

Halfway through "Jaded" I felt a nudge. Another offer I couldn't refuse. When I went to give back the joint the guy nodded in Gina's direction. I held it out in front of her. "You've been offered some."

She thought about it. She rarely indulged, maybe twice in all the years I'd known her. Finally she shook her head. "I'm driving," she said.

I gave the jay back. Leaned in close so he could hear. He smelled like a hemp factory. "She's driving," I said.

"Me too. Back to Fresno. Gonna see 'em there again tomorrow night. I've seen 'em a hundred and four times."

"Really."

"Yup."

It took me a second to come up with an appropriate response. "Far out," I said.

"Far *fucking* out."

He held out a fist. I punched it with my own, turned to watch the show. Tyler was giving the mike a blow job. Ah, rock and roll.

•

We stayed at Gina's place. I crashed while she was in the bathroom. She woke me and had her way with me. When she rolled off she said, "That was transcendent."

"I don't think I've ever heard you use that word. I don't think I've ever heard anyone use that word."

"Well."

"You were fantasizing about Steven Tyler, weren't you?"

"What? No way."

"Gi. You don't have to lie about it. It doesn't bother me."

"It doesn't? I mean wouldn't?"

"Nope. Actually, I was fantasizing about the singer in the opening act."

"You thought she was sexy?"

"Yeah."

"She's young enough to be your daughter." Five seconds passed. Ten. "How did you know?"

"The way you were watching him."

"How was I watching him?"

"Like a mongoose watching a cobra." Not quite what I was looking for. Clearly the dope hadn't quite worn off.

"You think I looked like a mongoose?"

"It was a metaphor. Simile. Whatever."

"Oh." Another few seconds passed. Her fingers idly stroked my stomach. "What is a mongoose, anyway?"

"I think it's like a fat weasel."

Her fingertips glided south.

"Here's what I think," I said.

"What do you think?"

"I think it's time to break out my SG."

She gave me an odd smile. "That's your electric guitar, right?"

"Uh-huh."

Her hand diverted from its course, left me altogether. She sat up. "I think you should." She reached behind her, grabbed a pillow, laid it against the headboard, leaned back into it.

"But you don't think I will."

She was bouncing around, searching for the perfect position. "I didn't say that."

She didn't have to. I knew what she was thinking.

Every time we saw live music, I relived my dream of being a rock star. Not someone like Steven Tyler or Joe Perry, Aerosmith's more flamboyant guitarist, strutting around the stage with my outlandish shirt unbuttoned to my *pupik*, acting like I was a generation younger and getting away with it. I just wanted to be like Brad Whitford, the other guitar player. One of the guys in the background, making music I liked with people I liked, being the target of some small degree of adulation.

A couple of years back, I'd gotten as far as pulling my old Epiphone acoustic out of the closet, and since then I'd played it every two or three days. I'd gotten to the point where I was at least competent, with occasional flashes of, if not quite brilliance, at least minor luminosity. The fingertips on my left hand boasted a fair set of calluses. I could play most of *Tommy* by heart.

But the next step—the Gibson SG—was a whole 'nother kettle of fish.

"I've been thinking about the AARP," I said.

"Nice segue."

"When I was at Austin and Vicki's yesterday, Austin mentioned he'd gotten his invitation to join."

"No way Austin's sixty-five."

"They come after you when you're fifty. It was creepy, he said. The letter came right on his fiftieth birthday."

"So?"

"So it got me thinking. In a year I'm going to get a letter like that."

"And two years after that I will too. So what?"

"So I started thinking about my life."

"You never think about your life."

"I am now."

"And what are you thinking about it?"

"That I haven't really done anything. I'm nearly fifty and I still don't know what to do with my life."

"The old midlife crisis."

"I suppose." I sat up, leaned my own pillow against the headboard, positioned myself next to her. "Tonight reminded me what I want to be when I grow up."

"A rock and roll star."

"Maybe not a star, but in a rock and roll band. And seeing Aerosmith—hell, those guys are older than I am—made me think I should go for it. Unless it's the dope talking."

Her hand gripped mine. "So go ahead."

"Just like that?"

"Just like that."

"You're humoring me."

"You've talked about this ever since I've known you. Even twenty years ago, you would jabber about your bands when you were a kid, especially that first one when you were living at that place in the Hills, what was it called again?"

"The Platypuses."

"Right. Them. When you'd talk about them your eyes would light up. And your eyes hardly ever light up that way about anything else."

I thought about it. "Here's what I'm afraid of."

"What?"

"I'm afraid I'll find out I'm terrible, and this dream of mine that I've sublimated for so long will be impossible, and then what?"

"You're a really good guitarist. I've heard you enough times."

"I'm okay. And electric is different."

"How?"

"It just is." I heaved a sigh, reached over to the nightstand for water. "I don't even have an amplifier."

"What happened to your amplifier?"

"I sold it. I figured I'd never need it again, so I sold it."

"But you kept the electric guitar."

"No way I could ever part with that."

"So you buy an amplifier."

"I guess."

"Not, I guess. You do it. End of story. Now go to sleep. I have clients in the morning."

"Okay."

"Promise me you'll follow up on this."

"I promise."

"Good." She kissed me good-night, laid her pillow and herself down. A while later thinking got too hard, and I did the same.

•

I spent the next morning shuffling plants at the Kawamura Conservatory. When I got home I found three messages from Elaine on the machine, each more peeved than the last. She had a Toyota audition for me at three-thirty in North Hollywood. Where the hell was I?

Elaine's my agent. Also my cousin. Also, for a few years on

either side of 1970, my housemate. I called back, soothed her feathers, explained again why I didn't have a cell phone, no-not-even-a-beeper. I made myself presentable and around two headed up to North Hollywood. An early start, but you never knew about the traffic.

There wasn't any. I got there at twenty to three. I stashed the car at the industrial park where the casting people had their offices and walked back to Lankershim to amuse myself until audition time at Rico's Recycled Records.

The eight-track player in my '72 Datsun had nearly made it through the millennium. When it finally gave up the ghost I was stuck with a clutch of eight-track tapes and no way to play them. Gina went on eBay, found a portable player, and surprised me with it on my birthday. A week and a half later it ate the Electric Light Orchestra. Gina said it was time to move up to CDs. We compromised on a cassette player.

I replaced some of my eight-tracks and made cassettes of a few LPs. But I was stuck without Splinter. They were George Harrison protégés who had an album called *The Place I Love* that made my ten-best-of-the-seventies list. Until that afternoon, the only copy I'd ever seen was the eight-track cartridge gathering dust in my spare bedroom.

I found the LP in the miscellaneous *S*s, right between Azalia Snail and Salloom Sinclair *&* The Mother Bear. I pulled it out. $5.99. Seemed fair. I slid the album out of the jacket, angled it to the light like I knew what I was doing.

Someone said, "Good band."

He was about my age, and very small. Not a little person, but a couple of inches shorter than Gina, and she's a shrimp. He had a long dark ponytail and a receding hairline. Not a pretty combination. He wore jeans and a T-shirt from the Jefferson Airplane reunion tour. You don't see many of those, unless you happen to be rummaging through my dresser.

I said, "You've actually heard of these guys?"

"Course I have. Hell of a group. And George, shit, he played better guitar on this than he did on his own albums." He shook his head. "Poor George. I really miss him."

"I know what you mean."

"It's like, when John died, it was, you know, he was killed, but George—I mean, even though he was sick, he was old. Well, not old exactly, but—you know what I mean, right?"

"Sure."

"So it's like, what do they call it, the end of an era, and—"

"Yo, Squig," someone behind me said.

"Yeah?"

I turned to see who was there. The face raised a rogue memory.

Back in '97 there was a bank robbery in North Hollywood, not terribly far from the record store. Couple of guys came bursting into a B of A branch, armed to the teeth and wearing body armor. The law showed up, and a huge gun battle erupted, with hundreds of shots fired, ending with one of the robbers bleeding to death on the pavement because somehow the cops never got around to calling an ambulance. I've seen pictures of him, lying there with his hands cuffed behind his back while his life leaked out.

The man in front of me had the same look in his eyes as that bank robber. Like everything bad that ever happened to him was your fault and he was ready to exact his vengeance. Like he would give your well-being about as much thought as that of a cockroach that crawled into his breakfast. Middle-aged, with slicked-back thick black hair, and a scar that started at the outer tip of his left eye and went down an inch, then jagged toward his nose, like a backwards *L*. He had shoulders like a linebacker and a lot of muscles everywhere else.

He held up a cassette, waving it at us. "Blue Cheer," he said. His voice was rough, like he was getting over a cold. "*Outsideinside*. I have it?"

The short guy—Squig—shook his head. "Don't think so." Back to me. "Like Blue Cheer?"

I dropped my voice. "Not really. A little … primeval for me."

"'Primeval.' I like that. I can't stand 'em either. But he likes that shit."

He moved across the aisle, to the beginning of the alphabet. "There's a Long John Baldry I've been looking for forever."

I reinvestigated the *S*s until I felt someone standing behind me. I turned around. It was the Blue Cheer guy. One hand held three cassettes. The other, a gun, directed at my midsection.

I managed a wild-eyed scan of the record shop. The counter guy was on the phone, with his back to us, checking a rack against the wall. A crewcut chick with a Daffy Duck tattoo on her shoulder was at the import rack, also facing the other way. No help there.

"There's no need for that," I said to the Blue Cheer fan. It didn't seem very persuasive, but I'd heard it in a Dana Andrews movie just a couple of nights before.

"For what?" the man with the gun said.

"Shooting. Blood. Me dying."

He didn't see it that way. His finger tightened on the trigger.

Bang.

Getting in Tune

I clutched my hands to my stomach. Reflex, really. There
wasn't any good reason to do so. No searing pain wracking
my guts, no dawning realization that I'd never see Gina
again, no pitching face-first onto the chipped linoleum. Just
a ringing in my ears. And a memory of a sound I hadn't
heard since I was a kid.

I took a good look at the gun. Snatched it out of his hand.

A toy. I hadn't seen one like it in years, decades maybe.
Cheap chrome plating, flaked off in spots so you could see
the gray plastic underneath. SIX-GUN impressed into the
part you wrapped your hand around. The kind of toy I used
to play with when I was a kid. You would put a cap under
the hammer, and when you'd pull the trigger the cap would
go off. You could run arround terrorizing the neighborhood. Good clean fun.

"A toy," said Squig.

"I figured that out."

"For my kid," said the linebacker. "Found it at the swap
meet."

"Nice," I said. "Mind telling me why you were aiming it
at my stomach?"

He smiled. "Why not?"

It didn't matter that it was a toy. I didn't like him pointing it at me. I'd had a couple pointed at me over the last several years. "That was an asshole stunt."

"Scared you?"

"Yes, you scared me." He was still scaring me. That smile was like the clown's at a funhouse.

He took the gun from my hand, stuck it in a pocket, turned to Squig. "Guy can't take a joke."

Squig shrugged. "A lot of guys can't take your jokes."

The best course of action seemed to be to get out of there. I headed for the door.

"Hey," Squig said.

Visions came. A real gun turning up, me shot in the back. Or being pummeled senseless by his friend. I kept going.

"Hey!" More insistent.

I stopped, still facing the door. "What?"

"You forgot your record."

"I don't want—"

"Record like this, you don't want to pass it up. Next time it could be gone."

I turned to face him. He was holding the LP out.

"Come on. You want it. I promise, he won't pull any more shit. Will you?"

The wacko was rooting through another bargain bin. "Nah," he said. "I'll be a good boy."

Maybe I'd overreacted. Maybe they were harmless. Just a couple of aging drugged-out hippies.

I went back, grabbed my album, went to the counter and paid for it. Shoved the change in my pocket and hustled for the door. Went out, back to the industrial park and my audition. I said my three words—"best deal ever"—six or eight times until everyone was satisfied, got in my car, and drove home. I kept checking the rear-view, but I didn't see anything I shouldn't have.

•

Gina came over that night, made something out of a pack of noodles and the random vegetables in the fridge, got us stuffed. I told her about the record store episode. She shook her head and said, "This town."

"That's deep."

"You want philosophy, sleep with Ayn Rand. What's happening with your electric guitar?"

"I haven't had—"

"Excuses, excuses."

"Tomorrow. I promise."

"Cross your heart?"

"Cross my heart. And hope to die."

Had I known what reviving my music career was going to lead to, I probably would have left out the last part.

•

The next day I got as far as lugging the SG out of the closet, giving it a few swipes with a polishing rag, playing a few chords. I hadn't picked it up in three or four years, hadn't played it seriously for several times that. I was surprised how close it was to still being in tune. Or maybe the un-amplified sounds were too thin to tell.

I stuck it back in the case, and instead of returning the case to the closet I left it in the corner of my bedroom, next to the acoustic. Over the next few weeks I opened it a couple more times and checked the guitar over. That was as far as I got. Gina asked me every four or five days if I'd looked for an amplifier. Each time I said something lame. I was waiting for a sale, or something equally insipid. Each time she'd roll her eyes. She rolls her eyes better than anyone else I know.

Then my birthday came along. Gina took me to Divino, an Italian place in Brentwood, tonier than our usual joints. After we ordered Gina gave me my card. I opened it, said the appropriate things, put it aside. Then she gave me my present. A gift certificate from Guitar Matrix for two hundred dollars.

I looked up. "What's this?"

"What does it look like?"

"But—"

"Look, Portugal, it's pretty clear you're never going to get off your own ass with this electric guitar thing. I decided you needed a jumpstart."

"This is a lot of money."

"I've got a rich new client." She's an interior designer. Most of her clients have money up the ying-yang.

"But—"

"No buts. You will use that to buy an amplifier and whatever else you need. By the end of the week. *Comprende?*"

"Yes."

"Good. Now put it away and enjoy your meal."

•

I managed to stall all the next day. And the one after, until about two in the afternoon, when I went to Trader Joe's for peanut butter and apple juice and spent thirty-seven dollars on stuff I'd had no idea I wanted. On the way back KLOS played "Cowgirl in the Sand." It was still going when I got home. I sat in the truck and listened to all ten minutes and three seconds of it. When it ended I went inside and dug up my gift certificate.

•

Guitar Matrix is in Culver City, on Sepulveda Boulevard
north of Braddock, between a *botanica* and a camera repair
place. I got a parking spot across the street and sat staring at
the front window. Then I got out and dumped a pair of
quarters in the meter and went inside.

The place was wall-to-wall with instruments and amps
and everything else you needed to make music. A couple
of customers, a couple of salespeople, engaged in earnest
discussions. I was the oldest person in the store.

I wandered around like a yokel. I recognized some of
the brands but had never heard of most. I gawked at an
array of effects pedals and rack gear with purposes I hadn't a
clue about. Finally a frizzy-headed kid in a Limp Bizkit
T-shirt took pity and asked what I needed. I told him my
story. He asked how much I wanted to spend. I told him
about the gift certificate. He said he had just the thing and
started to tell me about it. I stopped him and said I trusted
his judgment.

He went in the back and came out with a Fender
Frontman. It had seven knobs and three jacks, which
seemed like plenty. He plugged it in, hooked up a
Stratocaster, played a couple of riffs that I'd never be able to
duplicate. I told him it would do fine. He said it listed for a
hundred and seventy bucks, and they were supposed to sell
it for one forty-five, but in honor of my resurrected music
career he could knock off another ten. I didn't know if he
was playing me, and I didn't care.

He unplugged and asked if I needed a cable, which I
did. I also got some picks, a few sets of strings, a new strap,
a QuikTune guitar tuner, and ninety-three cents change.

I took everything to the truck and got in. I sat there wondering what the hell I thought I was doing. Then I remembered ...

Guitar and Pen

There was always music at Mark and Ginger's sanctuary for troubled teenagers, the radio or the record player or the newfangled eight-track someone had picked up somewhere, likely off the back of a truck. We'd listen to Jefferson Airplane and Steppenwolf and the Animals and all the rest. The Beatles, of course. And my favorite, the Who.

We had a band of our own too. We went through names once a week. Canvas. The Purple Horde. Then one day our keyboard guy, little Lenny Jones, got loaded and went to the zoo. He came back and said he had the perfect name for the band. The Platypuses. Everyone loved it. I said I liked it, but wasn't *platypi* the plural of *platypus*, and they all looked at me like I was crazy.

From that day on we were the Platypuses. Besides Lenny we had Robbie Wozniak on bass, Frampton Washington on drums, Toby Bonner on vocals and lead guitar, and me on rhythm. Our other singer was a girl named Bonnie Morgenlender. We used to joke that if Bonnie married Toby she'd be Bonnie Bonner.

•

I played for two hours that afternoon. There were so many songs to choose from. All the Neil Young and early Beatles, the Airplane, the Kinks, the fabulous oldies by one-hit wonders. And of course the Who. When I was a kid, Pete Townsend was my hero. Because his style was built around chords, and so was mine, such as it was.

Over the next few months I played at least an hour a day. I surprised the hell out of myself. I was getting damned good—good enough that the idea of being in a band, one people would actually pay to see, crossed the line from fantasy to possibility.

•

A quiet morning in May. I lay in bed with "My Generation" running through my head. When it wouldn't stop I got out the SG, plugged it in, began playing. Singing too, if you can call it that. I kept the volume low, so I wouldn't disturb the Clement clan next door. I wasn't concerned about the extended family of wackos on the other side. They'd been waking me up for years with all manner of mysterious noises.

I played for an hour, then went out to the greenhouse for my rounds. They didn't take long. The plants, the cacti and other succulents I'd been so crazed about the last several years, had lost much of their appeal. It made me vaguely uneasy. The only passion I'd developed since I grew up—not counting Gina, and who knew if calling that a passion was appropriate—was losing its hold on me. It was like I didn't have room for the plants and the music.

I went in, showered, fed the canaries. Went to make breakfast and turned up nothing but a bag of oranges I'd bought from a wizened woman on a street corner. I needed starch. So I went to Trader Joe's. I managed to get out with only six unplanned purchases.

When I got home, company was waiting. They were on the front patio—the Jungle, I sometimes call it, because it's overrun with plants—on my wicker chairs.

I considered driving to the police station. But, hell, a man's house is his castle, right? I cut the engine, got out, started toward the house. What were they going to do, kill me right there in front of little Suzy Clement, who was Big-Wheeling on my front sidewalk?

Maybe they would. And little Suzy too.

Too late to consider that. I continued up the walk. Squig was writing in a small book. The linebacker was holding a glass up to the light, like he was trying to spot something swimming around inside. Another glass sat at Squig's feet. A third waited atop an old milk crate. The glasses were mine, green ones I'd won at the County Fair many years back. They were filled with an orange liquid. I didn't even want to consider what this all meant. I was sure I'd locked the door when I went to TJ's.

It wasn't a book Squig was writing in. It was a *TV Guide*. He looked up. "What's a four-letter word for *wiseguy*?"

"Wahl," I said.

"Wall?" He fingered my stucco.

"Wahl. W-A-H-L. Ken Wahl, he was in the show. Mind telling me what the two of you are doing here?"

Painstakingly, using a pen, he wrote in the name. "Thanks," he said, and stuck the pen in the pocket of his denim jacket. He picked up his juice, sipped it, said, "You don't know who I am, do you?"

"You're some character I met in a record store who's stalking me."

"I was at Mark and Ginger's."

I shook my head. "I would remember if there was a kid with a name like Squig there."

Columbo-like, he clapped his hand to his head. "Right. That's why you're not remembering." To the other guy: "That's why he's not remembering." But the other guy was more interested in the daddy long-legs clambering up the wall.

"What's why I'm not remembering?" I said.

"My name. I wasn't Squig then. I was Lenny. Lenny Jones."

I'm a Boy

It was 1968, the summer after the Summer of Love. I was fifteen and always finding new ways to get into trouble. My father was in San Quentin. My mother hadn't the foggiest idea what to do with me. One day everything came to a head. I think it had something to do with leaving my shoes on the dining room table, but maybe that's just a story I made up to impress some girl and grew to believe.

While my mother was at the market I found a laundry bag, shoved some stuff in, grabbed my precious SG and my little amp. I left a note saying I'd call soon. I toted everything up to Culver Boulevard, caught a bus to La Cienega, transferred to a northbound, took it to the end of the line at Santa Monica Boulevard. I schlepped up the steep hill to Sunset. I was breathing hard by the time I got there. Even then I was in lousy shape.

I crossed to the north side, stopped, looked both ways. Walked west, toward Gazzari's and the Whisky. Went into Ben Frank's, one of my favorite places on earth. I ordered a burger and a Coke and wondered what to do next.

A man slid into the other side of the booth. He had long thick dark hair, a five o'clock shadow, a leather jacket. "What's happening?" he said.

I figured he was a shark, preying on lost little boys and girls on the big bad Sunset Strip. Before long he'd have me selling hash and getting buggered. But when he offered to pay for my lunch and take me somewhere to crash, I went with him anyway. Because this was the real world, not my Beaver Cleaver neighborhood. I wanted to experience it. I thought I could handle the trouble when it came.

So I got in his shiny Sunbeam convertible and let him drive me up to a weird compound up above Sunset. Five buildings, lots of strange nooks and crannies and corridors, one big room with a high ceiling and stained-glass windows. There were a couple of dozen other teenagers around, boys and girls, black and white and everything in between. He showed me to a big bedroom with half a dozen cots, told me the one in the corner was free, said pot was okay but nothing stronger, and disappeared.

I had it all wrong. This guy—Mark Gray was his name— had spotted me at Ben Frank's just like he'd spotted dozens of starry-eyed kids before me, and knew if he didn't grab me someone vile would. Just like had happened to him a dozen years before up in San Francisco.

He was able to provide for us because his old lady Ginger had inherited a million dollars. They bought a deserted monastery and turned it into a place for kids to stay when living at home became too hard. For as long as they needed it. Some were there a year, two, three. Some as little as a week.

When September came Mark and Ginger got me enrolled in Hollywood High. Then my mother died, and four months after I'd left I moved back to Culver City.

Four months of heaven. Because I was in the Platypuses.

My first and best band. With, among others, a shrimp of a kid named Lenny Jones.

•

I was ready to believe him. I was willing to accept that some cosmic force had gotten me back to my guitar right before I ran into a guy from the best band I'd ever been in. Then I remembered that he and the other guy on my front patio, the creepy one still staring at the wall, were drinking orange juice out of glasses they'd gotten from my kitchen.

"You broke into my house," I said.

Without diverting his attention from the bug, the scary guy broke into a grin. Not the funhouse one. It made him look not quite so terrifying. "It wasn't much. I could've done it in my sleep."

"It wasn't a compliment."

"You know, you ought to get some better locks on that door. Anybody could—"

"Wait. I didn't *have* any orange juice. I had oranges, but I didn't have any orange juice." I was having trouble with my thought processes. I had to verbalize everything.

"We squeezed it," Squig said.

"Right. You squeezed it. In my kitchen. What were you doing in my kitchen? What were you doing in my *house*?"

He head-gestured to the other one. "He had to take a leak. So he saw the oranges sitting in the kitchen, and we found the squeezer and squeezed juice. Hope you weren't saving the oranges for something. And don't worry, we washed the squeezer." He picked the third glass off the milk crate. "Here, this is yours."

"Will you *stop* with the orange juice already?"

"Okay, man, don't get all trippy on me."

I looked him over. If he was Lenny Jones, he'd put on weight since back in the day. Who hadn't? I tried to recall the Lenny I'd known, tried to overlay that face on the one in front of me. It didn't work. "How do I know you're really him?"

"Hey, I'm not anyone anybody would want to make believe they were." He put down "my" glass of OJ. "I mean, it's not like I'm gonna walk into some fancy restaurant and say, hey, I'm Squig Jones, and they're all gonna treat me like a king."

"If you're really him, tell me—" I searched for something one of the kids in the band would know. "Tell me what we used to call Bonnie Morgenlender."

The other guy quit monitoring the creepy-crawly long enough to swap looks with Squig. Neither said anything.

"I thought so. You guys are *so* full of shit. Now get off my—"

"Course I remember," Squig said. "The one with the—" He held his hands out palms up and bobbed them up and down, like he was trying to guess the weight of a couple of cantaloupes.

"Yeah," I said. "That's the one."

"Course I remember what we used to call her. We called her Bumptious Bonnie Boobs."

•

Bonnie Morgenlender was one of my two best friends at Mark and Ginger's. She was a year older than me by the calendar, several emotionally. She would give me pep talks when I was feeling down because Toby could play guitar ten times better than I could. I would play cheerleader when she was bummed because her parents were such assholes and she thought she could never go home. It was weird for me having a girl as a friend. But somehow it worked out. Though every once in a while she would smoke too much dope and start hanging on me and telling me I looked like Jean-Paul Belmondo. I didn't know who he was, but I got the feeling she thought he was sexy.

Bonnie had giant breasts. Our bass player Robbie started calling her Bonnie Boobs. Our drummer Frampton, a fat black kid, added the Bumptious because she could be loud and pushy when she wanted to.

Of course, we only called her Bumptious Bonnie Boobs behind her back. I felt kind of bad when I said it, because we were such good friends, but that didn't stop me. I was a teenager. What did I know about appropriate behavior?

Wait a minute. Our bass player Robbie …

•

I looked the thuggy one over. Squinted. Closed my eyes, opened them, squinted some more. "Robbie Wozniak?"

He tossed me a look like he was disappointed in me. "It's about time." Then it was back to the daddy long-legs.

Lenny Jones. Robbie Wozniak.

Not that IDing them made me feel a whole lot better about them tracking me down and helping themselves to my produce. "Why didn't you tell me who you were that day at the record store?"

"Woz wasn't ready," Squig said.

"What the hell does that—Jesus. It wasn't a coincidence running into me there, was it?"

"Not exactly."

"Not *exactly?*"

"Okay, we were following you."

"What in God's name for?"

"We wanted to check you out. Catch your vibe."

"Experience my aura?"

"Nah, we didn't ... oh, I get it. That was a joke."

"None of this is a joke. Stalking people is not a joke." There were too many questions. I grabbed the first one that surfaced. "How'd you find me in the first place?"

"You're in the phone book. We got a Thomas Guide. The phone book said Madison Avenue in Culver City, and we looked in the Thomas Guide, the part where they list the streets and it tells you which page, and—"

"I'm familiar with the process."

He looked upset. Like I'd made him feel bad. That made *me* feel bad. What the hell?

"Sorry, Lenny, I didn't mean to shut you up."

He flashed a smile that I imagined I remembered. "It's okay. But call me Squig, okay?"

"Sure, whatever. What is it about me you had to check out?"

"Woz wanted to make sure you weren't a narc before we—"

"A narc? Me a narc? Where'd you get a stupid—"

This elicited a glare from Robbie Wozniak.

"Where'd you get an idea like that?"

"Those people you got arrested," Woz said.

A friend was killed a while back. The cops suspected me. I stumbled on the real culprit. A year later, something similar happened. I was a three-day wonder in the paper and on TV. Six-day, altogether. Three times two.

"The people who got arrested were murderers," I said. "You're not murderers, are you?"

Woz was back to watching the wall. I didn't see the daddy long-legs anymore. Maybe he was having a flashback too. The acid kind. Or maybe I'd imagined the bug. Or maybe I'd fallen down a rabbit hole and was in Wonderland.

"Guys? You aren't, are you? Murderers?"

Woz finally returned to Earth. He stared at me, sighed, shook his head. "A guy's gotta be careful. Know what I mean?"

"Not really, but I'll take your word for it. So did I pass?"

"Course you passed," Woz said. "You didn't pass, we wouldn't've come back to see you."

"And I still don't know what for. So will one of you please tell me what the hell's going on here?"

"Figure it out."

"Figure what out? Excuse me if I'm a little thick here. People burgling my house tend to fuck up my head."

"It's simple, dumbshit," he said, "We're getting the band back together."

Fiddle About

We were together for three months, Lenny and Robbie, Bonnie and Toby, Frampton and me. Then we got our first gig. It was in a little club off the Strip, half an hour, opening for some hotshot new group. We all got excited when we heard that Monte Freeman was there. He was the head of Hysteria Records, and he was there to see the band we were opening for.

It turned out he hated them. But he loved us.

No. What he really loved was Bonnie and Toby.

•

"The Platypuses," I said. "You're getting the Platypuses back together."

"Yeah," Squig said.

"Any particular reason?"

"It's time."

"That's mighty heavy, Squiggy, but it doesn't tell me shit."

He flinched. "Don't call me that, okay? Not with the -gy part."

"Squig, then."

"You guess how come I'm called that?"

"Something to do with *Laverne and Shirley*, I suppose. So besides it being cosmic, is there—"

"One day some asshole starts calling me Squiggy, which is dumb because Lenny and Squiggy are two different guys, right?"

"Can't this story wait? Because right now I—"

"So the shitheads I'm hanging around with, they pick right up on it, and all of a sudden they're all calling me that. Only some other prick leaves out the -gy part one day, and sure enough the rest of them go along with that too. And after I hear people calling me that enough times, I say the hell with it, if they want to call me that, it's fine with me."

"Are you done?"

"Uh-huh."

"Glad to hear it. Why'd you guys decide to get the band together now?"

"We didn't," Woz said.

"I *am* down a rabbit hole."

"Bonnie did."

I opened my mouth. Shut it. Opened it again. Nothing would come out.

"Look at him," Woz said. "Like a fucking fish. I always knew he wanted to ball her."

I said, very quietly, "Bonnie's in on this?"

"I just told you, dickhead, she's the one getting the whole thing together. Hey, Squig, take a look at this guy. Is he spacing out or what?"

•

A couple of nights after our one and, it turned out, only gig, Bonnie got me alone and said she and Toby were leaving the next morning. Monte Freeman liked them so much that he wanted them to cut a record, and he was going to have them live at his place in Brentwood until things broke for them. Then she looked at me with tears in her eyes and told me that he didn't want the rest of the band. That he had some other musicians he wanted to use. I said he just wanted to ball her. She said, why's he bringing Toby too? I said, he wants to ball him too.

Back then, most of us still thought homosexuals all dressed in funny clothes and went around talking like girls. Neither of which Monte Freeman did.

Bonnie and I looked at each other and cracked up. Then I put my hands on her shoulders and said what was happening, the band being split up, wasn't her fault. She stopped laughing and looked into my eyes like I'd never had them looked into before. Then she was kissing me. And I was kissing back. It was my first time with tongues. I didn't know such a thing existed.

I was a virgin. All those girls at Mark and Ginger's, and they all just wanted to be friends. I was dying to lose my cherry. But I didn't have a rubber. And some renegade noble impulse wouldn't let me have sex with Bonnie without one. Maybe it was the result of an awkward talk I'd had with my father before he went up the river. Maybe it was that I knew Bonnie was sexually experienced and I was afraid I'd make a fool of myself.

Bonnie wanted to do it anyway. I said no. She wrestled me onto the sofa and rubbed my crotch. I couldn't help myself. I fondled her bumptious breasts. And came in my pants.

I was mortified. Bonnie was sympathetic. She said we should try again. I said I really didn't want to get her pregnant. She said there were other things we could do. I vaguely knew what she was talking about. I was too embarrassed to find out for sure.

After a while we both fell asleep on the sofa. At some point she got up and left. I pretended to still be asleep. I never saw her, nor Toby, again.

•

"Yo. Joe. You with us here?"

My turn to return to Earth. I looked from one to the other. I wasn't sure which had spoken. "I was just remembering some things."

"Yeah," Woz said, "And I know what two of them are."

"Hand me my OJ." Squig stood and got it for me. I took the vacant seat and drank down half the juice. Stalling. Not knowing where to go next. Squig kept shifting his weight from one foot to the other, like the conversational vacuum was eating at him. Finally Woz said, "Frampton's already in."

I half-looked at him and said, "Frampton Washington?"

"You know anyone else named Frampton?"

"There's Peter Frampton—"

"You know Peter Frampton?" Squig said. "Far out."

"No, I don't know Peter Frampton. It was just an example. Of someone else named Frampton. What's he up to these days? Our Frampton, I mean."

"Lives near the Marina," Woz said. "Got a wife's twenty years younger'n him and a couple of kids. Works in El Segundo. Some kind of engineer. We went over to his house a while back. He answers the door, we think we're in the wrong place."

"How come?"

"He got skinny," Squig said.

"No way."

"Like a fucking toothpick," Woz said.

"You never know," I said. A semi sequitur. I was still thinking about Bonnie. Trying to figure out why I was all shook up over a woman I hadn't seen in over thirty years.

"He's like you," Squig said. "Just got back to rocking and rolling."

That brought me around. "How'd you know I just got back to it?"

He looked over at Woz, who wasn't ready to help. "Just something we figured out." Clearly a lie. Maybe when they were in the house they took a look at my amp and found the manufacture date.

I didn't feel like pursuing it. "And what about you guys? You just get back to playing?"

"Uh-uh," Squig said. "We been playing all along. Together."

"Squig's my best friend," Woz said. I couldn't tell if he was serious.

"We live together," Squig said. "I mean, not live together like a guy and his old lady live together, but we live in the same house. Have for … how long's it been, Woz?"

"A fucking long time," Woz said.

Squig nodded. "A fucking long time. We been in and out of a lot of bands. Some were pretty good. But you know what?"

"Yeah," I said. "I think I do. None of them were as much fun as the Platypuses."

"You got it," Woz said.

•

After I left my sanctuary, after my mother died and I blamed myself, I moved back home. I wasn't sure why. I just knew I had to. Elaine, who's a few years older than me, wasn't getting along with her parents, and she moved in with me, serving as a sort of surrogate mother. During that time, in the five years until she got married and left, I was in and out of a dozen bands. I didn't last in any of them. They never had the vibe that banging around in the music room at that spooky old monastery had. The music might have been as good, maybe better, but it didn't matter. I always found something wrong, something to get me out.

Over the next four or five years my interest in making music petered out. I got into acting, if you can call what I do that. The guitar went into the closet, as did the acoustic I'd left behind when I ran away. I sold the amp. And things stayed like that until my neighbor at the Aerosmith concert offered me a joint.

•

"Aren't we forgetting something?" I said.

"What do you mean?" Squig said.

"Toby."

"What about him?"

"Rumor has it that he's dead."

"You believe everything you hear?" Woz said.

"No. But, and correct me if I'm wrong here, no one's seen or heard from him since 1980 or so."

"Yeah, well …"

"You guys know something I don't?"

"Yeah. We know a lot you don't."

"About Toby, dumbshit."

"Hey, Squig. Guy called me a dumbshit."

"About time," Squig said. "You been calling him all sorts of stuff."

"Okay, guys," I said. "Spill."

"We're not supposed to," Squig said.

"Says who?"

"Bonnie."

"Then maybe I need to talk to her."

"Maybe you need to ball her," Woz said.

I turned on him. "Get this straight, *Robbie*. I have no interest in screwing Bonnie or anyone else except my girl-friend." Gina hated the term, I wasn't fond of it either, but it was convenient. "If I go along with this insane idea, it's because I want to be in a band again, not because of Bonnie. Got that?"

Woz smiled. The first real, somewhat-warm smile I'd seen out of him. "Hey, Squig," he said. "I kind of like this guy." He looked right at me. "I thought you were kind of a pussy, but you got some *cojones* after all."

"That's right," I said. "I got as many *cojones* as anyone."

Young Man Blues

Squig said they were getting together that night to jam at Bonnie's house in the Hollywood Hills. I hadn't jammed with anyone in twenty-five years. The concept was exciting. Also scary as hell.

After Woz drove them off in a cool old Barracuda, I stayed on the porch and tried to process what had just happened. I should have felt more upset, more violated, at them breaking into my house and squeezing my oranges. But I couldn't. Too much else to keep my mind occupied. I was, maybe, going to be in a band again. And not just any band. The best band I'd ever been in.

Then there was Bonnie. My male friends, admittedly not a huge sample, have all had one woman they wish they would have slept with. Not the great love who got away, though everyone seems to have one of those too. But the one they wished they'd nailed, for the pure carnal joy of it. Mine was Bonnie. Over the months after she left Mark and Ginger's, as she zoomed to fame and just as quickly back to obscurity, I berated myself hundreds of times for not screwing her when I had the chance. After I moved back home I kicked myself less often, but she was always there in my mind. Maybe if I'd been getting any I would have forgotten her faster. Maybe not.

Even as I got older, I'd get that little twinge once or twice a year. That little voice in the back of my head that said, You blew it, Joe, you could have balled a super chick with humongous tits back when you were fifteen, and you didn't. And you can't ever fix that.

Now, suddenly, three decades later, I was going to see her again. It made me a little queasy. It made me feel like a teenager.

•

At nine-thirty—we music types kept late hours—my SG and I showed up at the address Squig gave me. The amp stayed home. He'd said there'd be plenty of amps.

Squig had told me that after Bonnie's singing career went south she stayed at Hysteria Records, switching from artist to employee. She'd been there ever since, working her way up to president, changing her name somewhere along the line from Morgenlender to Chapman.

Being a record exec must have paid well enough. The place was huge. Three stories, lots of windows, a facade enveloped in ivy and creeping fig. Giant split-leaf philodendrons and a jumbo schefflera out front, along with half a dozen towering palms. A couple of mil at least.

I rang the doorbell. It echoed somewhere beyond the door. Eventually I heard footsteps inside. I held my breath. The door opened.

A man of around thirty stood there. A bit shorter than me, green eyes, dark hair needing a trim. "You must be Joe," he said.

"Yes."

"I'm Darren. Bonnie's son."

"Hello."

"Planning on coming in?"

"Oh. Right." I moved inside.

"Something the matter?" he said.

"I didn't know Bonnie had a son."

"No reason you should." He shut the door behind me. "Something wrong with that?"

"Of course not. It's just—nothing."

He knew it wasn't nothing, and maybe he knew what it was … that there's nothing better than meeting your childhood friends' adult children to make you feel old.

If he did know, he didn't let on. "They're in the back," he said. "Come." He turned and walked off across the parquet. I followed, taking stock. The furniture was the kind you see in architectural magazines. The art looked expensive. The plants were low-maintenance.

We went through the house and out the back. A path cut across a patch of ground cover to a guest house. Light leaked out around the curtains in the front windows. Someone was practicing drumrolls inside. I followed Darren in.

The front was a kitchen and a small living area, neat, spare, functional. A red-eyed basset hound lay in front of the sofa, languidly guarding the premises. An open door led to the back, where the drum sounds were coming from. Frampton was in there. I wondered who else was.

Squig and Woz were. They stood in front of a Fender Bossman. Off to its side were a couple more amps, another Fender and a Marshall. In front of them, a synth setup. One keyboard said Yamaha, one Roland, one Korg. They were surrounded by pedals and racks and dozens of patch cables. Three mics waited atop chrome stands. Darren headed for a closed-in area in the corner. It had a big glass window, behind which a console sat bristling with knobs and sliders and lights.

Frampton sat behind a minimal drum kit. I assumed that was who it was. No way I could reconcile this stringbean with the blob of a kid I knew back in the day.

He put down his sticks, rose, moved out to greet me. "Joe?"

"Frampton?"

"The same."

Then he was laughing, a big, genuinely pleased laugh, a laugh that brought back a summer of no worries, abundant dope, and all the music in the world.

Instant Party

"Where's Bonnie?" I said.

"What did I tell you?" Woz said. "That's all he's interested in."

"Hey, putzface, she's part of the band. Why wouldn't I expect her to be here?"

"Putzface?"

"Sorry. Best I could do on short notice."

"Putzface. I like it. Care if I use it?"

"Be my guest. So where is she?"

"She's at her office," Darren said. He'd crept up behind me. "Got a problem with one of her acts. Singer got caught with a fourteen-year-old."

"Things never change."

"They do a little. This fourteen-year-old was a boy. Anyway, she should be here within an hour."

I walked over to the drums. "Nice kit. New?"

"Uh-huh," Frampton said. "Just got back into playing a couple of months ago."

"I heard."

"You too, right?"

"Pretty much. Electric, anyway. Liking it?"

"What do you think?"

"I think we ought to make some music."

"I agree." He turned to Squig and Woz. "Guys?"

I opened my case and took out the SG. Squig said, "Same one?"

"Uh-huh."

"Right arm."

"Out of state."

"Farm out."

"Farm *fucking* out," I said.

•

We all plugged in. Darren went back in the booth. "He going to record this?" I said.

"If you don't suck," Woz said. He had a Fender Precision bass. The strap had skulls on it.

Squig flicked a couple of switches on the Yamaha. "'96 Tears,'" he said. He diddled another switch, fingered a couple of chords. You would have sworn he was playing a Farfisa.

Frampton picked up on it right away. Woz joined in. They got as far as "too many teardrops for one man to carry on." Squig stopped and looked at me. "What's happening?"

"I don't know it."

"Everybody knows '96 Tears.'"

"I don't. But just give me the chords and I'll be fine."

He looked at me and frowned before turning to Woz. "You know where the book is?"

"Yeah." Woz took off the bass, laid it lovingly on a metal stand. He went behind the amps and reappeared holding a beat-up volume labeled "Hits of the Sixties Fake Book" and a music stand he'd no doubt liberated from some high school band room. While I set up the stand he flipped open the book, turned some pages, squinted. "Fuck." He went to his amp, took a pair of black-framed eyeglasses off the top, put them on, returned, checked again. "One forty-two." Shuffled the pages, put the book on the stand. "Here."

"One, two, three, *four*," said Frampton, tapping a cymbal, and he and Squig were Farfisa-ing away again. Woz traded the glasses for his bass and joined them. I looked at the book. The chords were easy.

Squig sang lead. The rest of us contributed *ooooh*s. The guitar part wasn't much, but I screwed up a couple of times. Nerves. Mostly I just strummed along. During the part about me being on top and you looking up, I did some single-string doodling, approximating what I remembered from the record. It wasn't great, but it wasn't miserable.

We did "A Whiter Shade of Pale" next, with Frampton on vocals and Squig closing with a classical organ flourish. Then "Born To Be Wild," which was hot during the Platypuses' first incarnation. Everyone contributed vocals. After that, a dozen more. Somewhere along the line I realized no one thought I sucked, and I relaxed. Then I really got good.

Squig said, "Let's try 'Time Is On My Side.' You know that one, Joe?"

"Not anymore," I said. "It in the book?"

"I don't think so."

"Sure it is," Woz said.

"No, it's not."

"Is too."

"Is not."

"Is too."

"Not this again," Frampton said. "You believe these jokers, Joe?"

"Yeah," I said. "I believe it. And I love it."

"It *is* kind of a kick," someone else said.

She was standing in the doorway. And though I hadn't recognized the others, I would have known Bonnie Chapman—née Bonnie Morgenlender—in an instant.

Behind Blue Eyes

Monte Freeman had them cut a single first, as Bonner and Bonnie, with some studio musicians. "Loves Me, Loves Me Not." One of their singer-songwriters had put it on an album that went nowhere. Monte Freeman thought it was perfect for Toby and Bonnie. The first day they played it on KBRK phones started ringing. Two weeks later it was number one in L.A. Three weeks after that, number two in the country, with only "Hey Jude" keeping it from the top.

They made an album, named after the single. The LP reached number three. The next single, "Fakeout," made the top five. The one after that, "Like Velvet," number two. There was a tour, backed by a bunch of guys who didn't play any better than we did but looked a whole lot hipper.

Squig and Woz, Frampton and me, we watched all this happen with mixed feelings. Happy our friends had made it, bummed that we didn't get to go with them. No one blamed Bonnie and Toby. Even at that tender age we knew how carnivorous the record business was.

Bonner and Bonnie started work on their second album. A week in, Bonnie got tonsillitis. When she recovered, she couldn't sing. Some freak of medicine, the doctors said, only happened once in a hundred thousand cases. It might get better eventually. It might not.

I read about it all in the paper. Then Bonnie became old news, and I lost track of her. From then on, she was just a lost opportunity, a late-night fantasy, a much-missed friend.

•

"It's good to see you too, Joe," she said. She walked across the room, with the basset hound at her heels, and hugged me. Her scent was flowery, sweet, fresh.

She let go, held me at arms' length. "You look good. Kind of like Jean-Paul Belmondo."

"Never heard of him."

"Funny boy."

"You look pretty good yourself."

Her hair, so long, so blond when we were kids, was shoulder length, darker, tinged with gray. Her face had filled out. There were smile lines, crow's-feet by her eyes. Her blue eyes were greener than I remembered, a not-quite-natural shade, contacts probably. Her earrings were small gold hoops, her necklace a simple chain. Her suit was dark blue, almost black, her blouse bright white. She was taller than I remembered. Probably the heels. Bonnie in heels. There was a lot I'd have to get used to.

"I see you all the time on TV," she said.

"My bug commercials." I'd practically made a career out of them. Olsen's Natural Garden Solutions. Good insects that eat bad ones. People recognized me on the street. I got to do booth gigs in malls. Whoopee.

"Yes. And your detective adventures."

"Fortunately," I said, "my detective career seems to have run its course."

"Has it?" She turned to Woz, looked him a question.

"He's cool," Woz said.

"Good." Back to me. "Woz has become a very suspicious type."

"So I've seen."

"But he plays a hell of a bass."

"So I've heard. Just now."

"You've all been playing for a while."

"Yeah, for …" I looked at my watch. Nearly two hours had passed. "For a while."

"You ready to sing a few, Bon?" Squig said.

"Know what, boys? I'm really not. It's been a long, miserable day, and I'm just not up to it. I'm so sorry. And anyway, this was good, right? Gave you boys a chance to work together without some chick singer getting in the way. Right now, all I want to do is change into some comfortable clothes and find something to eat. Can we try again in a couple of days? Maybe this weekend."

Mumblings of assent.

"Good. Then why don't you all pack up and call it a night." She passed a dazzling smile around the room and went out. We straightened up, packed our instruments, went back to the main house. Darren and the basset hound followed at a respectful distance.

Bonnie waited at the front door. She gave the other three a quick hug on their way out. When my turn came she said, "Stay for a bit."

Woz turned and leered.

"Night, Woz," Bonnie said, and closed the door behind him. "What was that all about?"

"Woz is convinced I only agreed to this reunion because I have the hots for you."

"And do you?"

"I'm pretty much over it."

"Pretty much, hmm? Well. Go in the kitchen. Through that hall. I'm going upstairs to change."

The basset hound followed me into the kitchen. Lots of stainless steel, stained wood, glass. Recessed lighting in the ceiling, terra cotta tile on the floor. The pooch meandered to a doggie bed in the corner and lay down. I leaned against a counter and waited. Darren showed up, got a Coke from the fridge, vanished. A little after that Bonnie came in, wearing a T-shirt advertising a band I'd never heard of, sweatpants, and slippers. She opened the refrigerator, bent down, popped back up. "Want anything?"

"Just something to drink."

"I have some fresh-squeezed orange juice."

I stifled a giggle. "That'll do."

She took cheese, a tomato, and a jar of mustard from the fridge, and bread from the cupboard. "Grilled cheese. Sure you won't have one?"

"Well …"

"I'm making you one."

The T-shirt fit more snugly than her suit. She caught me looking.

"Reduction surgery," she said. "Back in '88. Men gawking all the time. Backaches. Who needed it? And I couldn't even think about going to the gym."

"I—"

"Don't be embarrassed. All the boys had the same reaction. Speaking of my breasts, there's something I ought to tell you."

This explained everything. She had breast cancer and wanted to cut a record before she died.

"I knew about Bumptious Bonnie Boobs," she said.

Well, *that* was a relief. "How come you never said anything?"

"Because it was funny, you all thinking you had this silly secret from me. But enough about my boobs." She got out the orange juice, poured a couple of tall glasses, brought me one. "A toast. To renewal."

"To renewal." *Clink.*

She went to work on the sandwiches. Amiable silence filled the room. I sampled my juice, then said, "Nice place."

"It keeps the housekeeper employed."

"Doing your part for the economy, you big music biz muckymuck."

She nodded. "And you? You're making a living acting?"

"More or less. I still live in my folks' house, so I don't have to worry about rent."

"You live with your parents?"

"God, no. My mom died around the time you were becoming a rock and roll star. My dad's still around, but he lives with some other old folks in the Fairfax district. What about yours?"

"Long gone, thank God. I never saw them again."

She finished making the sandwiches while we got the grand tour of each other's careers. She made a hell of a grilled cheese. It was actually grilled. None of that toaster oven stuff. She topped up the OJ and we brought everything to the dining room.

I took a bite. It was right on. You have to use the good cheese. "When did you become Bonnie Chapman?"

"'72."

"A child bride."

"A very stupid one."

"How long did it last?"

"Four years. By that time people in the industry knew me as Chapman, so I didn't change it back. About the only good thing to come out of that marriage is not having to spell out Morgenlender every time someone asks for my name."

"And that's where Darren came from?"

"Yes."

"It's weird, you having a grown son."

"Think how it must be for me."

"He live here?"

"Yes."

"How come?"

"It's convenient."

"For you, or for him?"

"Both of us. I like having him around, he likes being around." She made a vague gesture. "The place is so huge, we can go for days without seeing each other."

"What's he do?"

"He's between careers."

"What was the last one?"

"Musician. He sang with a band."

"He any good?"

"Pretty good. Not great."

The phone rang. She got up, answered, listened. Her expression turned hard. "Tell the mother to go fuck herself." More listening. "No. She wants to sue us, let her sue us. We'll win."

She slammed the phone down and took her seat. "Do you know how many music legends are into kid-fucking?"

"All of them?"

"Just about."

We finished our life stories. She told me about Hysteria Records, more about her short-lived marriage, and how she'd gotten the house in the divorce and had never gotten around to finding someplace more her size. I told her about my theater days and the commercial work since. She asked about wives and children. Informed there'd been none of either—"no kids that I know about, hee-hee"; being with her was turning me back into a teenager—she asked if I was "with anyone." I told her the Gina story: How we were briefly lovers back in the eighties, how we'd run into each other years later and become best friends, how we'd taken the relationship to the next stage. Or the old stage. Some stage, anyway.

"What about you?" I said.

"No one at the moment. I'm a living, breathing cliché. Married to my job."

We'd both had enough history. "Why get the band together now?" I said.

"Two things. One of them's middle-aged angst."

I nodded. "I had a suspicion."

"You too?"

"Uh-huh."

"Feeling older. Missing the stuff of my youth. Hitting fifty."

"You hear from the AARP?"

"Those bastards. Right on my birthday."

"Say no more. What's the other thing?"

"I got my voice back."

"When?"

"Six months ago."

"How?

"Serendipity. There was an article in the *Times* health section on menopause and—why that look?"

"It's just weird. Last time I saw you you were sixteen, now you're dealing with menopause."

"I'm not there yet, thank God. Anyway, I opened up the paper to finish the menopause article and right next to it was one about voice restoration. There are all sorts of advances going on. So I called Julie Andrews, who—"

"You know Julie Andrews?"

She smiled. "Quite well, actually. You going to let me tell this story?"

I grinned and said yes.

"The article said she was a big restoration advocate, and I got the scoop. A couple of months later I had the procedure."

"Which worked."

"My singing voice isn't the same, the register's lower and my range is limited, but it's workable." She shook her head. "Fact is, it's better than half the chicks on the Hysteria roster." She popped the last bit of sandwich in her mouth. "One morning the idea of getting the band together came to me, and it wouldn't go away."

"You started tracking people down."

"Squig and Woz, I didn't have to. I ran into them ten, twelve years ago, and keep in touch. Every once in a while I get to throw them a crumb. A backup gig, something like that. As for you and Frampton, you're both in the phone book. So there wasn't any tracking involved."

"Did Woz have Frampton under surveillance too?"

That raised a smile. "No. Only you had that honor. I mentioned one day how I'd read in the paper about your crimebusting, and Woz got paranoid and said he had to check you out."

"A guy's gotta be careful, he told me."

"Evidently you passed muster."

"Has he been watching me this whole time?"

"Why would you think that?"

"It just seems a little weird that he and Squig accosted me in a record store a couple of months ago, but I didn't hear anything else till now."

"Oh, that. I got all hot to get the band together, and we found you and Frampton, and then I got cold feet. I thought it was such a dumb idea. So I let the whole thing percolate, and then a couple of days ago I woke up and couldn't figure out why I was waiting. I called the boys again, and Woz offered to clue you in, which in retrospect probably wasn't such a good idea."

"What's his story, anyway?"

"The tough guy act? Part of it's just his public persona. Some of it's earned. He's been busted a few times. Nothing very serious. A dope bust here and there, a disorderly conduct or two. Though he did once shoot up someone's car."

"Did you know they broke into my house?"

She grimaced. "Woz was rather proud of it. They break anything?"

"No. If they hadn't told me I wouldn't have known about it. I guess lock-picking is among Woz's skills. Anyway."

"Yes?"

"We've talked about you, me, Squig, Woz, Frampton."

"Mm-hmm."

"What about Toby?"

"What about him?"

"Nobody's seen him in twenty-five years. Most people think he's dead."

"He's not dead. At least, I don't think so."

"What, you've found him hidden away somewhere? Having nightly jam sessions with Jim Morrison, Gram Parsons, and Elvis?"

"No," Bonnie said. "I haven't found him." She leaned in closer and caught my eyes. "You're going to."

Fallen Angel

Toby Bonner was my other best friend at Mark and Ginger's. We'd sit around, and he would show me tricks on the guitar. No matter how much I screwed up, he stayed with me until I got whatever we were doing. He had a Triumph TR4—he was a little older, old enough to drive—and one day he took me to a secret hideaway he had out in the desert. As far as I knew no one else ever had that honor.

He arrived at the Greyhound station in Hollywood from some little town in Wisconsin, and within two days got mixed up with some sharks who drugged him up and let him loose on Santa Monica Boulevard. Mark rescued him from the nasties, and his Les Paul from a pawn shop, before much damage was done to either.

Toby's guitar playing was simply amazing. I would sit in awe as his fingers flew up and down the fretboard. He coaxed incredible sounds from his ax. A lot of kids could play a million notes a minute. Only the rare one like Toby could make it sound like the music of the gods. To top it off, the boy could sing.

Then Bonner and Bonnie happened. And ended with Bonnie's tonsillitis. After she stopped singing, Toby finished that second album with a new girl singer. They barely charted. Toby and Hysteria Records agreed to a parting of the ways. He signed with a smaller label and put out one more album. The music was harder, more bluesy, a power trio in the Cream mold. The record tanked.

Ten months later, Toby got hooked on heroin. No need to cover the next several years. You've heard that kind of story before.

He cleaned up his act in '76 and started booking gigs in clubs around town. Whenever I saw in the paper that he'd be playing, I'd vow to go see him. Somehow I never made it. He put out a final album, this one on a label no one had even heard of. It got a rave review in *Creem*, an adoring paragraph in *Rolling Stone*, and miserable distribution. I looked all over but never found a copy.

After that, Toby dropped off the radar. Rumors flew. He was a subsistence farmer in South Dakota. He'd taken a vow of silence and was in a monastery in the south of France. He was at Jonestown but got out the day before the massacre.

Eventually people lost interest. The rumors stopped floating.

MTV did a feature on him in '84. Their conclusion: He was most likely "jamming with Janis and Jimi."

•

"There was a sighting," Bonnie said.

"Really."

"He showed up at a club with his guitar, plugged into someone's amp, and played a set."

"What club?"

She pushed away from the table, stood, began clearing the dishes. "I don't know."

"Who saw him?"

"I don't know that either. It's all know-a-guy-who-knows-a-guy stuff. A lot of people in the industry have heard the stories."

"A lot of people have seen Elvis too."

"I know this sounds stupid. But I just have a feeling about it."

"Cosmic, man."

She smiled. "You could call it that. But what could it hurt to look into the stories?"

"It probably couldn't, unless you look in the wrong places."

"I don't get you."

"A couple of years ago several people I trusted turned out to be murderers."

"I know. So?"

"So it's made me leery of going around poking into other people's business."

"The only person's business you'd be poking into is Toby's. If he's dead, it doesn't matter. If he isn't, we can at least tell him what we're up to."

"What if he's alive, but doesn't want to be found? Which, given that he hasn't been seen in twenty-odd years, seems a likely possibility."

"If he doesn't want to be found, why did he show up somewhere to play?"

"You really think he did?"

"I really do."

"That old cosmic bit again."

"Yes."

"Why does it have to be Toby? There are a million guitarists in this town. You could use someone else."

"Would you want me to use someone else instead of Squig?"

"I guess not."

"Instead of Woz?"

"Jury's still out on that one."

"Instead of *you?*"

Pow, right in the dream. "No."

"Of course you don't. The whole idea is to get the original band together and … shit, Joe, I can't put it into words. Can't you just file it under Cosmic and let that be enough?"

"Please. Enough with the cosmic already."

She sat down opposite me. "Don't you think there's a reason you and Frampton started playing your instruments again right around when I got this lamebrain idea?"

"Coincidence."

"You really think so?"

I really thought so. At least ninety percent's worth. "Okay," I said. "Let's assume it's worthwhile looking for Toby. There are a lot of people in L.A. who'd be better than me at finding him. All those private eyes you're always seeing on TV."

"Fictional characters, Joe."

"There must be real ones."

"We have to do this ourselves. Within the group."

"Why?"

"We just *do*. Damn it, Joe, haven't you ever done anything that wasn't entirely logical?"

"Not since I turned you down back in '68."

"Bullshit."

She was right, of course. Everyone does things against their better judgment because they refuse to accept that they're dumb ideas. Like picking up my electric guitar again just short of the half-century mark. And thinking I could be in a rock and roll band, one that actually made a record. "What if I find out he really is dead? What then? Do we give the whole thing up? Find someone else to play lead?"

"We'll cross that bridge if we come to it."

The basset hound got up, yawned, and came my way. He waited patiently by my chair. "What's he want?" I said.

"His ears scratched."

I did my duty. He seemed to like it. "What's his name?"

"Papa Cass."

"Why—"

"Don't ask."

I looked down at Papa Cass. He gazed up at me. Damn, his eyes were red.

Still playing with his floppy ears, I looked across the table at Bonnie. "I'll see what I can dig up."

"I thought you would," she said.

HEAD OUT
ON THE HIGHWAY

Daily Records

It was nearly one when I left. Bonnie and Papa Cass walked me out. Just outside the door Bonnie said, "Wait. I almost forgot." Papa Cass gave me that look again. I gave him some more of the ear treatment and asked him what was happening. He wouldn't say. Canaries notwithstanding, I'm not real good with animals.

Bonnie came back out and handed me a cassette. "Give it a listen, okay?"

"Okay."

We reached the truck. A short, tight hug, and the two of them headed back. The front door snicked closed. I got in the truck and turned on the radio. Stuck the cassette in the slot but didn't push it all the way in. I wasn't ready.

I was tuned to Arrow 93. They were playing "Stairway to Heaven." They run it once an hour whether they need to or not. I switched to KLOS where I could hear "classic rock that really rocks." It was Jim Ladd's slot. I started down the hill and listened to him meander. By the time I hit Sunset, Jim had decided some music was in order. My friends from Aerosmith. "Just Push Play."

"Good idea," I said, and gave the cassette a shove.

Nothing but tape hiss for ten or fifteen seconds. Then

the electric sitar intro to "Loves Me, Loves Me Not" blasted from my cheap speakers. I adjusted the volume.

Thirty years later, it still sounded fresh. Some songs are like that. "Time Won't Let Me." "Satisfaction." You hear them a million times, they still kindle that thrill of the new.

Except I hadn't heard this one a million times. Not this version, anyway. The electric sitar was richer, fuller. The rest of the instruments were subtly changed. Bonnie's voice was different. More mature. Like listening to Madonna now versus the Madonna of "Like a Virgin." Except Bonnie could sing in the first place.

Verse one, chorus, verse two, chorus, bridge, verse three, chorus, fadeout. Bonnie's voice, clear, strong, sweet. The piping oboe near the end, stolen from Sonny and Cher.

It wasn't better than the original. It wasn't worse. It was just different.

Another song came on, one I'd never heard before. That Farfisa organ tone I'd heard Squig create a little while ago. An acoustic guitar, strumming simply. Bass and drums. And that new voice. The "Different Drum" theme, two lovers who were having a great old time, but one of them knew it would never work out. The organ dropped out on the chorus, leaving that simple guitar and that still-so-pure voice.

The song drew to a close. I waited for more tunes. There were only the two. The second was good, but it needed something. It needed some lead guitar. It needed Toby Bonner.

•

In the morning I walked to the Culver City library. They had computers there to provide Internet access to Luddites

like me who didn't have their own. I sat down at one of the
screens, between a couple of nine-year-olds who looked like
they hadn't seen the sun in months. I did what Gina said
should always be the first step in looking for something on
the Internet. The obvious thing. I typed in *www.bonnerand-
bonnie.com.*

The screen filled. A big photo of Bonnie and Toby,
similar to the one from their album cover, hovered over a
black background. Underneath it said CLICK TO ENTER. I
clicked and entered. More black background, more yellow
lettering. It was hard on the eyes. In the upper right a
picture kept morphing from Bonnie to Toby—the 1968
versions—and back again. The verbiage said who Bonner
and Bonnie were, why they were worth caring about even
now, what happened to them. Whoever ran the site had
decided it was cool to refer to them as B&B. B&B this, B&B
that, B&B the other thing. It didn't work for me. If you live
in Culver City, B&B is a hardware store.

There was a fan club. A mailing list. A bulletin board. I
checked out the last, feeling tawdry, paging through the
scrivenings of people with too much time on their hands,
ones who named their daughters Bonnie and their sons
Toby, ones who were upset over the exclusion of "Loves
Me, Loves Me Not" from the VH1 list of the hundred
greatest pop songs of the century. Several begged B&B to
resume their careers. I wondered how they'd react if that
happened.

I turned up a few Toby sightings. Someone had seen him
in a 7-Eleven in Helena, Montana. Somebody else found
him working at a muffler shop in Atlanta. And there was a
grainy picture from 1989, a couple of dozen ecstatic people

chipping away at the top of the Berlin Wall, with an outline drawn about one of them. IS THIS TOBY? someone wanted us to know, in three-quarter-inch letters in a typeface straight out of Star Trek. I suppose it could have been. It could have been Elvis too. Or Amelia Earhart.

I pushed away from the keyboard, thinking. Another youngster, this one a girl, same age, same pale complexion, said, "Are you done?"

"Not yet."

"You look done."

"I said I'm not. Go away. Why aren't you in school?"

"It's spring break." Followed by an unsaid "you dumb-shit."

"Kids on spring break are supposed to be outside. Go outside. Play soccer or something."

She stomped away, and I slid back up to the keyboard. There was a page of links. One was to the official Bonner and Bonnie page. I took a look. It was a perfunctory appendage on the Hysteria Records site. I went back where I came from.

Next up: A reissue of Toby's first solo album on Rhino Records. The CD had come out a year back. It was a special edition. They made just 1500, which had all been sold. There was a note to try eBay. I wasn't that far gone yet.

I visited a few more sites but didn't find anything very interesting. More sightings. The amazing revelation that Bonnie Morgenlender, teenage rock star, was now Bonnie Chapman, record company president. They had a picture of her at the Grammys, shepherding one of her acts. I wondered if he liked little boys.

I decided to try one more and give the little brat the computer. I went down the list. I came to Toby's Minions.

It seemed worth a click. It came up. It was astounding. It wasn't quite clear what Toby's Minions thought he was, but the words "second coming" came to mind. They thought he was going to "return to us" in the year 2007, bringing kindness, joy, love, and happiness to all. It was touching, in a way. They seemed so damned sincere. Like they really believed Toby was out there in Montana or Atlanta or Berlin, waiting for the appropriate time to come back and save us all.

I'd had enough of the site and enough of the Internet. I slipped from the chair and the pale girl immediately took my place. "It's about time," she muttered. I frowned, she doled out a phony but endearing smile, and I went out the automatic door.

•

I walked home, picked up the truck, drove to Guitar Matrix. I'd been back a few times to buy picks and strings, and to indulge my desire for a wah-wah pedal. I found Dex, the kid who'd sold me the amp and everything else.

"Joe, dude," he said. "What's up?"

"Got a question."

"Shoot."

"You ever hear of Toby Bonner?"

"Course I have. Guy's a god."

"Even after all these years, he's a god?"

"Gods are immortal."

"You think he is? You think he's still alive?"

He shrugged, and the mask of cool dropped away, and he was just a kid with dreams to spare. "Could be. I mean, no one's ever seen him dead, have they? And I heard he showed up at a club a little while back, and played a set."

"I heard about that."

"It would've been something. Can you imagine seeing Toby Bonner play?"

"It would be something, all right."

"Can you imagine playing *with* him? I could die after that."

Yes, as a matter of fact, I could imagine playing with him. Because a third of a century ago I had. "You don't happen to know the name of the club where he played, do you?"

"No. Some after-hours place, I think."

"How long ago?"

"I don't know. A while back."

"Define 'a while.'"

"Couple of weeks, maybe? I'm not really sure."

"And you don't know the name of the place?"

"Nah. The dude who told me, he's kind of hard to get anything out of. I'm not even sure he remembered the place. Kind of fucked up, you know?" He mimed smoking a joint.

"Then why did you believe what he said about Toby Bonner?"

"I never said I believed it. I just said I heard it."

"How do I find this guy?"

A flicker of suspicion. "How come you want to find him?"

Great. The kid thought I was a narc. First Woz, now him. I leaned in, elbow on the counter. "I used to know Toby when we were kids. I'm trying to hook up with him again."

"You knew Toby Bonner?"

"That so hard to believe? Chances are you know some-one who'll be famous someday. You just don't know it yet. Or maybe it'll be you who's famous."

I hit a nerve. A goofy smile stole up his face. "Yeah. Maybe I will." He came back to earth. "You can find Mott at Da Capo just about any night."

"Mott? Like in Mott the Hoople?"

"What's that?"

That's the trouble with kids. They're so young. "A group in the seventies. 'All the Young Dudes,' that kind of thing. Where's Da Capo?"

"Hollywood Boulevard, a couple of blocks east of Vine."

"Thanks."

"No problem. Look, I gotta get back to work now. If my manager sees me standing around like this—"

"Sell me some strings, then."

"The flat-wounds, right?"

"You got it."

•

I paid Dex, thanked him again, walked out into the sunlight. It was another groovy Southern California day. I caught the 405 north, got off at Sunset, drove east to Amoeba Music in Hollywood. Supposedly the biggest record store in the world. They'd have Toby's stuff if anyone did.

The place was big as a football field. Half the floor was filled to the gills with used albums, the other with CDs old and new. Plus cassettes along the walls, with hundreds of framed posters and other rock esoterica hanging above them. I saw things I hadn't seen in thirty years, at astonishing prices.

A few dozen people were browsing. Most already had an album or two or six picked out. Little kids like the ones at the library, a couple of ancient black men, an obese woman in a nurse's uniform. All intense or enraptured or wrecked.

I went to the LPs and found the *B*s. Bonner and Bonnie had their own divider. There were six copies of *Loves Me, Loves Me Not*, the album, one of them the U.K. version with the shiny cover. I already had the American and I didn't need the British, even if it did include their cover of "Needles and Pins." There were also two of the second album, the one with the ersatz Bonnie. $2.99 and $3.99. I took the cheap one.

They also had a couple of copies of Toby's first solo album, with the power trio, and one of the last, the one I could never find. The former were $4.99 each. The latter must have still been scarce. The cover was worn, the name Bobby Bastone written in green ballpoint grade-school handwriting on the back, and it still went for $13.99. I pulled the record out, tilted it toward the light. Last time I tried that Squig and Woz showed up. This time no one did. I added it and one of the $4.99s to my stash.

I went back to the As and started going through semi-methodically. I found an LP by Earth Opera, another eight-track I'd never replaced. And one by Fat Mattress, the group put together by Noel Redding, Hendrix's bass player. Their first album was fabulous. This one would probably suffer from sophomore suck, but for ninety-nine cents I could take a chance.

I picked out a Manfred Mann and a Nazz. When I hit the *S*s I spotted another copy of the Splinter album. It was $1.99. It added it to my hoard. You can never have too many copies of your Splinter album.

My bladder gave a call. I asked where the bathroom was. The answer was the burger joint across the street. I put my goodies on a card and held my water till I got home. While

I was relieving myself I flashed on Woz picking my lock and standing right here doing the same thing. I wondered if he washed his hands when he was done.

Woz. What a character. Squig. Another strange soul. Frampton. Bonnie. The rest of the band. Of *my* band. The concept hadn't fully taken hold. Even so, I was a lot more excited about it than I'd ever been about acting.

Excited? I was fucking euphoric. I was in a band.

But only if I could find someone who hadn't been seen in over twenty years.

•

That night Gina and I were going to a play, then staying at her place. In the morning she'd be flying to San Francisco for a couple of days at an interior designers' confab. I called and told her about Da Capo. She wanted to go. I mentioned her trip. She reminded me her flight wasn't until eleven, and that was that.

I hung up, sorted through my Amoeba finds, decided to pull the first album down from the shelf. They played the singles all the time on K-Earth and The Arrow, but I hadn't heard the rest in fifteen years. The record was excellent, with perfect singing and guitar work throughout.

The second LP, the one finished after Bonnie lost her voice, didn't suck. That was as far as I could go. It wasn't throw-across-the-room bad, but if I never heard it again I wouldn't care. The fake Bonnie wasn't within miles of the real one.

I put on Toby's first solo album next. I listened to half a song, raised the needle, and went looking for my headphones. They were in the canaries' room, in the same box as my eight-tracks. I set them up and settled on the couch.

The power trio was a far better showcase for Toby's guitar skills than the pop-flavored songs Bonner and Bonnie did. On every song there was something to perk my ears up. His singing was better too, stronger and more confident.

Somewhere along the line I checked the writing credits. The two instrumentals were credited to Toby alone. The others, all except one, to Toby and Spencer Sommers, the bass player. That last to Toby and Dee Knox, the chick drummer.

The phone rang while I was switching to the final album. It was Squig. "What's shaking?" he said.

"I was listening to the first Toby Bonner solo album."

"I been listening to Blue Cheer. We got Black Sabbath next. You find him yet?"

"I found all his albums. It's a start."

Nothing.

"It's a joke, Squig."

"Oh. Funny."

"You're high, aren't you?"

"How'd you know?"

"The odds were with me."

"Want to come over and do a jay?"

It was tempting. "Where do you live?"

"We got a house on Leland."

"Where's that?"

"Hollywood. Off Cherokee."

If it had been closer … "Think I'll pass."

"How about tonight?"

"What's tonight?"

"Me and Woz and Frampton are going to sit around remembering stuff."

There was yelling in the background. Squig said something, the other person said something. Squig got back on. "Woz says if you have any Grand Funk Railroad you should bring it."

"I don't. And I can't make it tonight. I'm going to a play."

"A play?"

"You know, actors on a stage, that kind of thing."

"What about after?"

"We're going to a club."

"Which one?"

"It's called Da Capo."

"Cool place. I saw Spencer Davis there a while back. Who's on tonight?"

"I don't know. But supposedly Toby showed up there one night, and I'm looking for a guy who's supposed to have seen him."

"What guy?"

"Named Mott."

"Like Mott the Hoople?"

"Yeah. Gina and I are going and I'll see if I can track him down, or maybe someone else who saw Toby."

"Your old lady."

A good a term as any. "Yeah. My old lady."

"Cool. Hey, tell you what. We'll round up ours and meet you there."

"I don't think—"

"It'll be a groove. The Platypuses and their chicks. Just like old times."

"In the old times I didn't have any chicks. I don't remember you having any either."

"Just like old times, only better. What time?"

"Ten, eleven, something like that."

"Far out. See you later." And he was gone.

"Far *fucking* out," I told the dead phone.

•

I put on the second and last Toby Bonner solo album. It was just him and his guitar with simple bass, drums, and occasional piano backing. Eleven songs. On all but two he was playing acoustic, something I'd never heard him do before. It was absolutely gorgeous. Some of the picking sounded classical. Some was like flamenco. Some was like nothing I'd ever heard in my life.

His voice had changed, maybe as a result of his trip through heroin hell. It was rougher, more world-weary. It fit the songs perfectly. Four of them were old blues things. There were six originals, each more heart-rending than the last. The finale was just Toby and his acoustic doing "A Whiter Shade of Pale." It made me want to cry. He sounded like he was skipping the light fandango on the night the world ended.

Love Is Coming Down

The play that night featured my old acting pal Joe Parlakian. He'd been trying to get me to join his theater company. The show was in a storefront on Willoughby in Hollywood. There were thirty or so seats, half of them filled.

It was a mediocre play, but Joe was damned good. He transcended the material, that kind of thing. Gina and I hung out afterward, doling out congratulations. Joe invited us to coffee. I begged off, citing my previous plans. We shook hands all around. Joe held onto mine and asked if I'd given any more thought to joining their company. I said I'd found another outlet for my creative urges and told him about the band.

He shook his head. "Rock and roll. It will wear off. Then you'll come join us."

"I don't think so."

"We'll see." He gave me an all-knowing smile, let go my hand, strode off.

I turned to Gina. "What about you? You think it's going to wear off?"

"I hope not," she said.

"Why's that?"

"Because," she said, "you're going to look *fabulous* in leather pants. "

•

It's a shame Love, with their inspired blend of rock, folk, jazz, flamenco, and psychedelia, never made it big. Their third album, *Forever Changes*, constantly shows up on best-of-all-time lists, even though practically no one has heard of them. After that one they lost the muse, mutating constantly, the only constant being a demented genius named Arthur Lee.

He'd gone to jail in '96 on weapons charges, but according to the guy collecting nine-buck covers at Da Capo, he'd just been sprung. The buzz was that he was going to make an appearance, which was appropriate, given that *Da Capo* was the title of Love's second album.

We stepped through a dark alcove lit only by a blacklight that made Gina's bra glow through her shirt, and into a room with Fillmore posters on the walls, lava lamps on each table, baby boomers in every seat. The waitresses wore tie-dye shirts and bell-bottoms. The bartenders were dead ringers for Chad and Jeremy. Or maybe it was Peter and Gordon; I never could keep them straight. A Byrds tribute band was on-stage, complete with Prince Valiant haircuts, granny glasses, and twelve-string. They were well into "Eight Miles High."

We craned our necks, looking for a table. Something hard poked the small of my back. "Don't move," came a gravelly whisper.

I froze. But only for half a second. Then I relaxed and glanced over my shoulder. "Hey, Woz."

He was wearing a paisley shirt, open most of the way,

with a large pewter cross dangling between his pecs. He was clearly disappointed that I'd sussed him out. But his eyes brightened when they alit on Gina. On her breasts, more specifically. "Hey," he told them. "You must be Joe's old lady."

"I'm up here," she said.

"Huh? Oh. Sorry."

I sniffed. Eau de marijuana. "You got a table?" I said.

"Yeah. Come on." He sneaked another peek at Gina's chest and led us into the throng.

"Another boob man," Gina said.

"We all are," I said.

They had two round tables pushed together. Squig, also in retro costume, sat with his arm around a fortyish willowy blond. When he saw us he jumped up. His friend unfurled herself too. She was half a head taller than he.

"Joe," he said. "You made it."

"Yup," I said. "Though I didn't know proper attire was required."

"No big. This is Chloe."

"Gina." We shook hands all around. Chloe's was like ice.

Frampton was there too, with his wife June, an Asian woman thin as he was, and, as Woz has said, a couple of decades younger than Frampton. We got through that round of introductions before I noticed the last person at the table, the proof that Woz was indeed a breast aficionado. Hers were astounding. They brought to mind the old commercial: so round, so firm, so fully-packing her blue leather minidress. She had long auburn hair and great teeth. Her name was Goldie, and she was, we found out within fifteen seconds of meeting her, a professional psychic.

As we got settled a waitress came over. Gina and I ordered beers and some of the others asked for refills. The band was working on "The Bells of Rhymney." They had the sound down, all right, the jingle-jangle, the nasal harmonies. I listened to a couple more songs before excusing myself and making my way to the bar. In the movies the bartender was always on top of everything. I waved to get someone's attention.

Chad or Jeremy or Peter or Gordon came over. He was between twenty and fifty and had a blond bowl-over-the-head do. "What can I get you?"

"Information. I'm looking for a guy named Mott."

"You're not the only one."

"What's that mean?"

He nodded toward a lissome redhead sitting alone at the other end of the bar. She was running a stirrer through a glass of something blue.

"His old lady. He took off a couple days ago with another chick. She was like seventeen. Deanna over there would love to get her hands on him."

"Thanks." I laid down a couple of bucks, moved along the bar, stood behind her. The red hair which had looked so good from across the room was brittle and frayed. "Excuse me."

She pivoted on the seat, eyed me up and down. She was wearing a long green dress. Her necklace was strung with tiny brown and white seashells. Her face was brittle too. "Do I know you?"

"No."

"Let me save you the trouble. There's no way."

"I'm not trying to pick you up."

"What, then?"

"Mott."

"What about him?"

"You're his girlfr—his old lady, so I hear."

"So I hear too."

"Maybe he'll come around."

"He usually does." She swept the stirrer through her glass again, took a healthy slug. "Though usually they're a little older than this little twat. What do you need the son of a bitch for?"

"I heard he saw Toby Bonner at some after-hours club a couple weeks ago."

"So?"

"So I'm looking for Toby Bonner."

"Fucking legend." She drained her drink, held it up. "Buy me another?"

"Sure."

I got the second moptop's attention. "The same for the lady."

A man with Art Garfunkel hair and a ZZ Top beard vacated the seat next to Deanna. I slid in. The drink came and I paid for it. She took a taste, nodded, said, "According to Mott, he showed up at Paoletti's one night."

"The Italian restaurant?"

"Upstairs from there."

"And Mott was sure it was him?"

"He was, but he was totally wrecked."

"How long did Toby play?"

"An hour, Mott said. But you know what happens to your time sense when you're smoking dope." She sized me up again. "Or do you?"

"I do. Did they know he was coming?"

"I don't know."

"Did anybody speak to him?"

"I don't know that either."

There was a lot more she didn't know. After a while I got tired of asking her about it. I thanked her and turned to go back to my table.

"Wait," she said.

I looked at her. "You thought of something else?"

She shook her head. "No. But I changed my mind."

"About what?"

"About you. Let's go someplace."

She was trying to look fetching, her eyes hooded, her mouth barely open, her tongue darting about. It might have worked on someone else. It might have worked on me three or four years earlier.

"I meant it before," I said. "I wasn't trying to pick you up. I'm here with someone."

She nodded slowly. "Figures," she said, and swiveled back to her drink.

•

The pseudo-Byrds played another half hour, finishing with "So You Want To Be a Rock and Roll Star," which turned into a psychedelic jam the likes of which I hadn't seen since before I could vote. In a bow to modern technology, they played the trumpet part on a little Casio keyboard. They left the stage, came back when the crowd wouldn't stop clapping, encored with "Mr. Spaceman." After they disappeared for good, ZZ Garfunkel got onstage and said there was no truth to the rumors Arthur Lee was going to be there. He said it with a stupid grin that could have meant he was leading us on and could have meant he was stoned out of his mind.

A couple of burly guys broke down the equipment and three more replaced it. The new setup had bigger amps, a keyboard setup that put Squig's to shame, double bass drums. While they were screwing with cables I gathered everyone's attention, told them about my conversation with Deanna—leaving out the invitation at the end—and asked if anyone knew about the club at Paoletti's.

"I do," Goldie said.

Woz put his arm around her shoulders, said, "My little lady."

She accepted his kiss and turned to me. "What do you want to know?"

"What time it starts, for one thing."

"One, two. Whenever. They don't keep regular hours."

"Every night?"

"They don't keep regular days either."

"Are they liable to be happening tonight?"

"What am I, a fucking psychic?" Some of us got the joke. I leaned over to Gina. "You still want to go?"

"Sure." She came closer, whispered, "You want to invite the rest of these yahoos?"

They were all arguing about whether the guy in Quicksilver Messenger Service was named Dino Valente or Gino Valente. Too bad my friend from the Aerosmith concert wasn't around. He would have known for sure.

Back to Gina. "That's a hell of a way to talk about my bandmates."

"I said it with love. I was just thinking, if you wanted to do intelligence-gathering, it might be easier without Flopsy, Mopsy, and Cottontail."

They'd decided to settle the argument by flipping a coin.

"Let's invite them. If I'm going to be in a band with these guys, I shouldn't be self-conscious about hanging out with them."

ZZ mounted the stage again. He grabbed a mike, it squawked, he said, "Far out." He had better luck on his second try. "Ladies and gents, we're real lucky tonight to have a band which needs no introduction."

"Then get the fuck off the stage," Woz yelled.

"Yeah, yeah, fine," ZZ said. "Okay, folks, here they are ... the Dreidels."

There were five of them, two guitars, keyboards, bass, drums. "Thank you, L.A.," said the bass player, a woman in an op art minidress. The drummer banged his sticks together, counting off, and they broke into their first number.

The song was original. The vibe was thirty-five years old. You'd hear little snippets that would remind you of one band, harmonies that would recall another, a riff that would make you remember a Friday night on the high school football field when you got stoned for the first time. They had a light show too, projected on a screen that dropped down behind the stage, all swirly colors and glimmers of brightness and psychedelic eddies.

I let the music take me away.

Trick of the Light

The guys who cleaned up after the Dreidels left the drum kit and a couple of amps. A buzz went around the room. It mutated into a chant. "Ar-thur, Ar-thur, Ar-thur." This went on until ZZ got up again and said he'd been serious before, that he didn't have any fucking idea where Arthur Lee was. The roadies reappeared and broke down the rest of the equipment. The lights came on. Grumbling ensued. There was foot-stamping, led by Squig and Woz. Then it was just Squig and Woz. Then just Squig. Eventually he got the point and stopped banging his little Beatle boots.

"Guys," I said, "Gina and I are going to check out Paoletti's. Anyone want to come?"

Frampton shook his head. "Not us. I've got to be at work at seven."

"What about the rest of you guys?"

"Not us," Woz said. "We got other things to be doing. Don't we, babe?"

Goldie gave him a pat on the cheek. "Wozzie wants some nookie, hmm?"

"And how."

I turned to Squig. "How about you?"

"I want some nookie too."

"I meant, do you want to go to Paoletti's?"

"Oh. Whaddaya think, Chloe?"

"Sounds okay to me." It was maybe the third thing she'd said all evening.

We gathered our stuff and split. Frampton and June took off in a minivan. Woz and Goldie walked off wrapped around each other like they weren't going to wait until they got home.

I suggested the four of us drive to Paoletti's together. Gina gathered the fabric samples inhabiting the back seat of her Volvo and dumped them in the trunk. We piled in and took off.

Paoletti's was on Melrose, a couple of blocks east of La Brea. We were there in five minutes. I found a spot around the corner and we walked to the entrance. It was closed. The chairs were all up on the tables and the only light was a single fixture over the bar.

"Now what?" Squig said.

I pressed my face against the front window. Nothing. "Maybe there's a secret password."

"And a secret entrance too," Gina said.

We all looked at each other and, without a word, trooped back around the corner and into the alley behind the place. Halfway down was a big metal door with a peephole at eye level.

I marched up and knocked. The peephole opened. There was an eye back there. "Yeah?"

"Is the club open tonight?"

"What club?" The voice was low and rumbly.

"I heard there was an after-hours club upstairs."

"You heard wrong."

The eyehole swung shut. I turned to the others. "That went well."

"Maybe there *is* a secret password," Gina said.

"And that would be …"

"There's the rub."

I rapped on the door again. The eyehole opened. "Yeah?"

"At least tell us this. Is there a secret password?"

"Dumbfuck," he said, and his eye disappeared.

"We are *so* not with it," Gina said.

We meandered away. After a few yards I ran back and banged on the door again. Again I saw the eye. "Hey," the gatekeeper said. "It's the dumbfuck."

"Mott sent us," I said.

"Why didn't you say so?"

The door creaked open. The guard stood there, all six and a half feet and three hundred pounds of him. He had a shaved head and a shaggy beard. It looked like his face was on upside down. He took our money and said, "Hurry on up. Show's about to start." He picked up a *National Geographic* with a mummy on the cover, sat all over a barstool, flipped to his place.

We went up the stairs and into a small dim room with a low ceiling and paneled walls. There was a bar along one side. A dozen or so battered tables were scattered around, two-thirds of them full. A mixed crowd, Gen-X hipsters cheek-to-jowl with combover victims. One table was encircled by half a dozen guys who might have escaped from one of the senior homes down the road.

We took a spot against the wall. Our seats were folding metal chairs. A guy with a bushy white moustache came over with a menu. We ordered a large pepperoni and a round of beers.

There was a tiny stage at the far end, with a curtain behind it. It held a chair, a mic on a stand, and an amp no bigger than mine. A man carrying a guitar case walked from the bar to the stage. He was old and he was black. He opened the case and unveiled an aged Gibson, a fat acoustic-electric with a single cutaway. He plugged it into the amp, sat in the chair, adjusted the mic. "How y'all doing?"

A murmur around the room implied we were all doing well.

"That's good. That's real good," he said, and began to play.

It was a twelve-bar blues—I suspected they were all going to be twelve-bar blueses—about how crappy everything was. His woman had left him. He'd lost his house and home. His dog had run away. It was heartfelt and the guy had a great voice and he played splendid guitar. By the third verse I was bored. I'm not into old blues singers. I know the drill, they've never been given their due, if it weren't for them there wouldn't be any rock and roll, blah blah. I still don't dig it.

When the song ended the crowd roared its approval. Gina and I clapped dutifully. She leaned in. "I hate this shit," she said.

"Philistine."

"You hate it too."

"True. Put up with it for a while. In a little bit I'll do some scouting around."

The applause died down and the singer dived into his next number. It was a lot like the first. Again his woman had left him. This time he'd lost his job too. No word on the dog. I slipped from my chair and made my way downstairs. The gatekeeper stood looking out the peephole. "What?" he said.

Outside, a woman's voice said, "Joe sent us."

I hadn't, but it did the trick. He opened the door and let the new customers in. Two women with wary eyes. They paid the toll and went up the stairs, and I had him to myself.

"What's up?" he said.

"What's the deal with the password?"

A sheepish grin. "You say anyone sent you, you get in. Had a guy last week said Osama Bin Laden sent him. I open the door, the guy's got one of those skullcap things on."

"A *yarmulke*."

"Yeah," he said. "One of those."

I held out a hand. "Joe Portugal."

He put out his own and we shook. "Charley Caine."

"People are saying Toby Bonner showed up here a few weeks ago."

"People are saying that, huh?"

"Did he?"

"Yeah."

"You saw him?"

"Sure did."

"It was him?"

"I saw him a couple of times back in the day. You know how you can't remember if you bought toilet paper, but you can remember the solo on a record you haven't heard since you were seventeen?"

"Yeah."

"It was like that. It was him, all right."

"When exactly was this?"

"Three weeks ago, Wednesday. I had a root canal that day. When Toby was playing I didn't even notice how much it hurt."

"Did you know he was coming?"

"No one did. What happened was, we were supposed to have this Japanese drum guy play that night and—what?"

"Japanese drum guy?"

"Yeah. He was in town to play a show at UCLA. We get all sorts of acts here. A couple of months ago we had that yo-yo guy with the cello. Anyway, this Wednesday night the drum guy gets sick and we're stuck and the opening act's out of songs and we're thinking we ought to just send everyone home. Then suddenly Toby's onstage."

"Suddenly?"

"I didn't see, 'cause I was still down here. I know he sure as hell didn't come in this way. But Marco, that's the manager, he told me later Toby just came in from behind the curtain with his guitar. He plugged it into an amp the openers hadn't taken down yet, and he started playing. I heard and I thought nah, it couldn't be. But I ran upstairs, and there he was."

"And you're sure it was him."

"How many times I got to tell you?"

"How long did he play?"

"An hour or so."

"Anyone talk to him?"

"Don't think so. Everyone was, you know, intimidated."

"What happened when he left?"

"How come you're so interested in this?"

"I was in a band with him back when we were kids. I ran into a couple of the other members. We thought it would be fun to get the whole band together and jam some."

"In a band with Toby? Coo-ool."

Someone else came to the door. Dick Cheney sent her. Charley let her in, and she went up.

"Where was I?" he said. "Oh, yeah. Some asshole was banging on the door, and I went down to let them in, and when I got upstairs he was gone. Marco said he just finished a song and while the clapping was going on he unplugged and went behind the curtain."

"And no one thought to stop him? To talk to him?"

"No. You gotta understand, it was like everyone was tripping from the music. Nobody was thinking very straight. Except me, I guess, maybe 'cause I was down here when he quit. I went in back, but he'd already split."

"How?"

"There's stairs up front, on the street side. He must've gone down them, 'cause there's sure as hell no other way out of there. I went after him, but he was gone. I ran out the door and—"

"The front door? It was open?"

"Sure was," Charley said. "And I sure as shit locked it after they stopped serving down there. Anyway, I ran outside and there was a car burning rubber down Melrose."

"You think he jimmied the door?"

"Sure looked like it. Else how'd he get in?"

"Anyone else here tonight that was here that night?"

"Just the cook, but he's Lithuanian. Don't speak English, outside of food talk."

I thanked Charley and gave him my number in case he thought of anything. We shook hands again. I started up the stairs. I was almost to the top when my brain kicked in. I ran back down. "The car he was driving. Did you see what kind it was?"

"Oh, yeah," he said. "Hard to miss those babies. It was one of those old Triumphs. A TR4, that's what it was."

•

In the latest iteration, the woman had run off and taken the dog, and the singer didn't have a job anymore because the guy she ran off with was his boss.

I started for the table but veered off toward the far end. A sign said the restrooms were behind the curtain. I went through, down a dingy hall lit by a feeble bulb, and found doors sporting male and female stick figures. A bit farther on another door stood slightly ajar. I peeked in and could barely make out stairs leading down.

I opened both restroom doors and flicked on the lights. This threw enough illumination to make out tables and chairs and cardboard cartons filled with paper towels, Christmas lights, candles in Chianti bottles. I don't know what I was looking for, and I didn't find it. I turned off the bathroom lights and made my way back to the table.

Gina leaned in. "Find out anything?"

"Yeah, but wait till we're outside. I don't want to whisper the whole thing."

After a half-dozen more songs the singer thanked us all and finished his set. He packed up his ax and went back to the bar. Someone set up a table onstage. A man with bangs and a wispy beard disappeared behind the curtain and came back with a fancy wood box with an antenna sticking up. He plugged the thing in and began weaving his hands around the antenna. Science-fiction sounds emerged. It was a theremin, the first I'd seen. Not the first I'd ever heard. The wackos next door had one.

We all exchanged grimaces and got up to go. I said I'd meet them downstairs and headed for the john. The men's room door was closed. Light came from the crack at the bottom. Theremin tuning continued.

I waited a minute, checked around, went into the ladies' room. When I came out one of the women who'd said Joe sent them was waiting. I said something inane and headed back to the club room. I was a couple of steps from the curtain when I heard the screams.

Doctor Doctor

The reason people were screaming was Charley the gate-keeper, standing at the top of the stairs in a blood-covered shirt, howling that he needed help downstairs. Along with the screams there was twittering and yammering and some moron yelling "fucking gangbangers" over and over.

Charley didn't seem hurt. It had to be someone else's blood. Someone downstairs.

Gina was downstairs.

I rushed for the stairway. When Charley saw me coming he wheeled and started back down. My jump into action got some other people moving. They followed me down. I blew through the vestibule and burst outside. Two people were on the ground. One had someone leaning over them. The other was Gina, lying facedown.

I dropped to my knees. There was something wet on the ground by her stomach. I thought it was blood. I couldn't be sure in the meager light from the streetlamps.

"Joe?"

"I'm here, babe."

"I think I hurt myself."

"Where?"

"My knee."

She was delirious. We needed help fast. I looked up at the people who'd followed me out. "Has anyone called 911? Or an ambulance? Or any-goddamn-body?"

Somebody said they had. I bent back to Gina. She rolled over onto her back. There was blood all over her sweater and some on the front of her pants. My stomach lurched. I got it under control and began carefully lifting the bottom of her sweater.

"Not now."

I kept at it. It was sticking to her stomach.

"Joe, cut it out. This is no time to be undressing me."

"You're hurt. Badly. I have to see where."

"I told you where. My knee." She sat up in one quick motion, like a vampire coming to unlife, and looked down at herself. She ran a finger across her sweater and inspected what it came away with. For an instant I thought she was going to lick it off. "There's blood all over me. Omigod. Squig." She tried to stand. I pushed her down. "Joe, stop it. We have to help Squig."

"But—"

"This blood's his. He got shot. I'm fine. Go help him."

"But—"

She slapped me across the face. "Go. Help. Squig." She gave my shoulder a weak push. "I mean it."

A dozen people were standing around like dummies. I stood and shoved through them to the other person on the ground. It was Squig, with Chloe all over him, sobbing into his shirt.

I pulled Chloe away, handed her off to somebody, went to my knees. Squig was still breathing. That was it for the good news. I went after his shirt buttons, starting from the bottom. Someone dropped down beside me, said something that included the words *medic* and *Nam* and began on the top ones. Our fingers kept slipping on the blood. Squig's blood. All that blood, on Charley and on Gina, and on Squig and on the ground around him, was his.

When the buttons were all undone the other guy—it was our waiter—peeled Squig's shirt back. There was a lot more blood. In the miserable light I couldn't tell where it was coming from. I fought off another wave of nausea.

I heard a siren, looked up, saw lights bouncing into the end of the alley. The waiter shooed me away. I stumbled up and over to Gina. She was on her feet, brushing off people trying to help her. She saw me and fell into my arms.

•

The paramedics labored to keep yet another person I was more or less close to from dying violently. I felt helpless and pissed-off at the world. Then a gurney appeared and Squig went on it, with Chloe weeping in his wake. More lights and more sirens, retreating into the night.

Then there were police. The cop in charge was a big guy with longish strawberry-blond hair combed straight back. He had thick-rimmed black glasses like Woz's. The cop wore a sport jacket and slacks and one or more of them was blue. His tie was undone. Probably at the end of a shift. All ready to go home and watch Conan O'Brien and all of a sudden there was this to deal with.

Some uniformed officers had pushed everyone who didn't belong there out of the way and thrown up yellow tape. I stood there being protective of Gina. Some more medical types had shown up and checked Charley and her over. They pronounced Charley fit as a fiddle, diagnosed Gina with a scraped knee, bandaged it.

A cop came by. "Sergeant Kalenko wants to see you, ma'am," he said, pointing the way. Gina looked at me, I nodded, she went off with the cop. I started to follow but the cop told me it was just her, sir, we'll get to you in a while if we need you.

I stood around like an idiot, watching Kalenko grill Gina, trying to make out what they were saying. But they were too far away. He quizzed her for fifteen minutes. When she came back she said he wanted to see me.

"You okay?" I said.

"I'm fine."

"Any word on Squig?"

"I didn't think to ask. Sorry."

"You sure you're fine?"

"I'm sure." She plucked at my shirt, where there was blood from when I hugged her. Again she inspected her fingers. A shiver ran through her. "Poor little guy."

The cop came back. "Ma'am, sir, please."

I went over to Kalenko. "You wanted to see me? I really didn't see anything. I was in the john." Like he needed that detail.

"The famous Joe Portugal."

"You know my bug commercials?"

"I know Casillas."

Hector Casillas was another LAPD detective. I'd had two run-ins with him. First, when he was in the Pacific Division, investigating the death of my friend Brenda Belinski. Then a year or so later, after he'd been promoted to the Robbery-Homicide squad. He and I had done much butting of heads, and mine still hurt.

"So you already think I'm an asshole," I said.

He shook his head. "I'll form my own opinion of whether

you're an asshole or not. You turn out to be one, we deal with it. But fact of the matter is, Casillas doesn't think you're one either."

"He doesn't?"

"Nope. He just wishes you'd stay the hell out of police business. Same with me. I want you to answer the questions I ask you, and to cooperate like a good little citizen, and that's all. No interrogating witnesses on your own. No midnight visits to the scene of the crime." Out came a pad and pen. "You say you were in the men's room when the shooting occurred?"

"The women's room, actually."

He gave me a look.

"Someone was hogging the men's."

A fleeting smile. "So you didn't see anything?"

I gestured to some of the others who'd galloped down the stairs. "No more than any of them. You get a report from the hospital yet?"

He one-eyed me, looked around, spotted a lady cop. "Breckenridge."

She trotted over, ready to protect and serve. "Yeah, Sarge?"

"Go find out the how the victim is doing."

"You got it, Sarge." Off she went.

"Okay," Kalenko said. "Tell me about him."

"Squig? I knew him when I was a kid. We hooked up again in the last few weeks."

I told him the rest. He made notes. When I got to the part about the band he asked if we needed a sax player. I hadn't a clue how to answer.

"Just a little joke," he said. "To put you at ease."

"Do I seem uneasy?"

"A little."

"Sorry. It's not every day friends of mine get shot."

"No, just once a year or so."

"You're doing a hell of a job of putting me at ease."

"My specialty. This other old friend, his name would be?"

"Robbie Wozniak. Robert, I guess. Goes by Woz."

"Address?"

"He lives with Squig. On Leland, in Hollywood, he told me."

More notes. "Any idea why anyone would want to shoot Mr. Jones?"

"He's a sweet guy who wouldn't hurt a fly. I can't imagine why anyone would want to take a shot at him. Anyway, wasn't it some kind of random drive-by?"

"Maybe. Maybe not."

Breckenridge came back. "He lost a lot of blood, but the bullet didn't hit anything too vital."

"*Too* vital?" I said.

"They think he's going to pull through."

"They *think?*"

"Yeah. You need me any more, Sarge?"

"Not now," he said, and she retreated.

"Anything else?" I said.

"No. You and Ms. Vela can go."

I stepped away.

"Mr. Portugal."

I looked over my shoulder. "Uh-huh?"

"Remember what I said. No playing detective."

"You got it, Sarge," I said.

•

I drove the Volvo back to Gina's. When we got there she grabbed a plastic garbage bag and took it into the bathroom. She came out in a few seconds, naked, carrying the bag. "Get rid of these, okay?"

"Sure." I took it out to the hall, dumped it down the garbage chute, came back inside. The shower was running. I went in the kitchen, got some decaf going, put up tea water on a low flame. I checked my clothes. Some blood, and generally filthy from crawling around the alley. I put my shirt and pants in another plastic bag, left it by the front door, put on the sweats I kept at her place.

I was sitting on the edge of the bed, staring at the cover of an *Architectural Digest*, when she came out of the shower. She had a ratty robe on and her hair was wrapped in a towel. She sat on the opposite edge of the bed. I watched her over my shoulder. After a bit her shoulders shuddered and I heard sounds I seldom hear from her. I climbed over to her side, put my arm around her, and let her cry.

A while later she asked for a tissue. I got her a couple and she cleaned up. She handed me the wad of soggy paper. I dropped it in the wastebasket and sat beside her again.

"When we saw Brenda dead," she said, "it wasn't that bad. It seemed awful at the moment, but I got over it. Because mostly she just looked asleep. There wasn't any blood. But this was worse, even though nobody was killed. That's right, isn't it? Squig's not going to die, is he?"

"No."

"I mean, the blood. There was so much blood."

"It looked worse than it was."

"But what I saw was how it looked. Not how it was."

Silence, except for rustling trees outside. It would be a blowy night, a clear morning.

"I could use a cup of coffee," she said.

"It should be ready."

"You made?"

"Uh-huh."

"I love you."

"Me too."

I went in the kitchen and poured a cup. I turned off the burner, dropped a teabag in a mug, dumped barely-steaming water over it, and returned to the bedroom. Gina took her cup, sipped, sighed. "I guess I should tell you what happened."

"When you're ready."

"I'm ready." She took a bit more coffee, got up, put the cup on the nightstand. She pulled back the covers and climbed in, leaning against the headboard with a pillow behind her. "They were waiting," she said.

"In what?"

"A Volkswagen. A Beetle."

"Old Beetle or New Beetle?"

"New. Some dark color. When we got outside it started up."

"How many people in it?"

"One. Or two. Maybe more. I don't know."

"How far away was it?"

"I don't know that either. A couple of stores' worth of alley, maybe. Joe?"

"What?"

"It doesn't matter how far. I've seen quite enough blood

for a while. I don't want you playing detective. So the gory details don't matter."

"Okay."

"This is going in one ear and out the other, isn't it?"

"It may be rattling around a little first."

I got a millisecond of smile out of her. "The car started up and drove toward us and pow. And after that everything's blurry. I think one of the bullets hit Squig, and he got turned around and stumbled into me. And I was holding him up, and then I realized what was happening, all the blood and everything. I got lightheaded. I never fainted before, have you?"

"I don't think so."

"And Chloe was screaming. She had her hand over her mouth and she was screaming right into it. Then I saw the man who was guarding the door, he must have come running when he heard the shots. And then I went out. I think the doorman caught Squig when I let go, I don't know, maybe he did and maybe he didn't."

"I think he did. He had blood all over him too."

"I don't think I was out more than a few seconds. I must have fallen on my knee, because when I came to it hurt like a bitch. When I tried to get up I got fainty again, so I just lay there, and then you were there, and I was so glad you weren't hurt."

"I wasn't even there when it happened. I was in the women's room."

A look, much like the one Kalenko gave me when told the same thing.

"The men's was occupied. Look, I'm going to ask something, and I don't think it's anything the average concerned significant other wouldn't ask."

"Go ahead."

"Do you think they were after Squig? I mean, it wasn't a random drive-by?"

"I don't think they were. Why would you think that?"

"I asked Kalenko if it was, and he said maybe, maybe not."

"He didn't want to commit himself. That's how cops are."

"I suppose." I looked down at my untouched tea. Took out the bag, had nowhere to put it, dropped it back in. I took a sip. It was awful. I drank it half down anyway.

"Joe?" Gina said.

"Yeah, babe?"

"You'll be careful, won't you?"

"What do you mean?"

"In your poking around."

"I said I wouldn't, didn't I?"

"No, you never actually said that."

I looked for answers in my tea. Saw only slivers of reflection. "I'm done with that," I said.

"Right."

"I mean it." I put down the mug and took her hand. "I promise, no trying to find who shot Squig. I'll let the cops handle it."

"Good."

Silence, maybe a minute's worth.

"What about your trip?" I said.

"What about it?"

"You still planning on going?"

"It hadn't even crossed my mind." She picked up her coffee cup, took a sip. "I'll have to sleep on it."

"Sounds like a good idea."

"But I'm too hyped to sleep." She looked around the

bedroom like she'd never seen it before. "I wonder what's on TV."

I got up, put down my mug, held out a hand. "Let's go see."

The answer, basically, was nothing. So we watched nothing for an hour and a half, curled up together on her sofa under a blanket, until I heard her snoring softly. I picked her up, carried her into the bedroom, tucked her in. She half-woke, made kissing sounds. I gave her one, smoothed her hair away from her face. She was back asleep before I was out of the room.

I went back in the living room and muted the television. The wind was blowing stronger. Little branches tip-tapped on the dining room window. I returned to the sofa, turned the TV sound on low, clicked the remote until I got to Channel 6. They were running the late replay of their eleven o'clock news. There was another suicide bombing in the Middle East. The idiot blond anchorwoman informed us that it was a very sad thing, and said Channel 6's heart went out to the victims. After that the weather guy babbled about the Catalina eddy and the offshore flow.

I flipped through some more channels and stumbled on another Dana Andrews noir. When justice had been served I turned off the TV and went to bed. The last thing I heard was leaves blowing in the wind.

Sleeping Man

It was a fitful sleep, one that ended at eight-thirty when a leaf-blower started up outside. They'd banned the things in L.A. because of the noise. Too bad Gina lived in West Hollywood.

I left her in bed, got up, threw the sweats on again. I started up the teakettle and turned on the TV. The station I'd left it on, the one with the movie, had an infomercial for something guaranteed to strip the years away. Face cream, herbal Viagra, something like that. I went back to Channel 6. A different weatherman above a map of the L.A. basin. Temperatures were going to be good. Smog was going to be good too, a consequence of the windstorm. Somebody named Louisa was having her ninety-seventh birthday, and the station's best wishes went out to her. Back to you, News Guy Phil.

The top story was a murder-suicide in Hollywood. A couple of senior citizens, husband and wife, discovered by a neighbor who couldn't stand the smell. The police weren't sure yet who did who, but would let us know as soon as they did.

The next piece was on the Middle East. More on the suicide bombing. Shots of bloody people. Reaction from an Arab fanatic and an Israeli one. Balanced journalism.

The third story was ours.

They had a live shot of Terry Takamura, their star reporter, standing in the alley behind Paoletti's. The wind was still up, the palms at the end of the alley were swaying in it, but Terry Takamura's long black hair moved not a whit. Behind her a cop was taking down crime scene tape. In the middle distance someone in an overcoat was pushing a shopping cart laden with bulging garbage bags.

"Police are stumped," Terry Takamura said, "regarding a motive for the shooting of this man." A vague photo of Squig appeared on-screen, banging on an upright piano, with his face bearing a dopey grin. "He is Leonard 'Squig' Jones, forty-nine, of Hollywood. Police were unable to question him last night because of his injuries, but even now are in his room at Cedars-Sinai."

The sound changed subtly, marking a switch to something recorded earlier. "One ironic twist to this story is that victim Jones was in the company of this man."

A photo appeared on the screen. Mine. It was a head shot, not the ancient one Elaine was using but one even older.

"This is Joseph Portugal, also forty-nine, who has twice been instrumental in helping police solve grisly murders."

"They weren't all grisly," I said.

"It's understood that Mr. Portugal is a boyhood friend of victim Jones and is now playing with him in a band. Police are unsure whether the shooting has any connection to this band."

"Of course it doesn't."

Takamura went live again. "We'll have further developments as they break. Back to you, Phil."

The teakettle whistled. I ran in to shut it off. When I got

back they'd gone to commercial, so I jumped to another channel. Then a couple more, but I couldn't find anything more about the shooting. I turned off the TV and poured water over a teabag. The phone went off. After the second ring Gina yelled, "Could you get that? It's probably my mother."

It wasn't her mother. It was my father.

"Joseph?"

"No, Dad, it's six other guys."

"My son, the comedian."

"How'd you know I was here?"

"I tried the house. You weren't there. I thought, where else would he be? You were on the television."

"I know."

"Are you all right?"

"Why shouldn't I be?"

"Again you get mixed up with people with guns."

"I didn't exactly get mixed up. I didn't actually see any guns. Gina saw a gun, but not me."

"You're getting my future daughter-in-law mixed up with the guns now?"

Dream on, father dear. "She got herself mixed. I had nothing to do with it."

"Oh?"

"I was in the bathroom at the time." That ought to help.

"You want protection?"

"What, you're going to get one of the Over-the-Hill Gang to follow me around like the other time?"

"It could be arranged."

"No. I do not want protection. I didn't even have anything to do with it."

"The television said you did."

"Fuck the television. I don't know why they dragged out that old picture, but—"

"You say 'fuck' to your father?"

"You've heard me say it before."

"And what did I do?"

"You washed my mouth out with soap."

"So?"

"So I was six then, Dad. Talking to you is like falling through the looking glass."

"I worry about you."

"I appreciate it."

"Who is this Squiggy guy?"

"Squig. Without the -gy. He's an old friend from when I was a kid. From when you were in prison."

I could see him on the other end, pooching his lower lip out. "You be careful, is all I want to say."

"How many times are we going to have this you-be-careful speech?"

"How many times are you going to get your head almost blown off? All I'm saying is, if you want help from your father, you can have it."

"Thanks. I appreciate it. I've got to go."

We said our good-byes. Gina wandered in, wrapped in the dilapidated robe, a ravishing wreck. "I take it it wasn't my mother."

"My father. He saw a report on last night on TV and he thinks I'm in danger."

"He means well."

"I know. You want me to make coffee? Or breakfast?"

"No. You know me, I get barfy if I fly with food in my stomach."

"Then you're going?"

"Uh-huh. I think I have to. If I don't go I'll just sit around all day dwelling on what happened last night. I go up north and concentrate on business, I'll be better off."

"Sounds reasonable. I suppose your mother's coming to take you to the airport."

"Of course. God forbid I should take off without her praying to the Virgin for me at LAX. She's supposed to be here at a quarter after nine. I better get moving."

"I'm going to head out then."

She came to me, put her arms around me, laid her head on my chest. "You'll be careful?"

"I'll be careful."

"I mean it."

"I know."

She loosened her grip enough to look up at me. "I'll call you."

"I'll be waiting." I kissed her, gathered my bag of dirty clothes, and left.

•

Los Angeles after a windstorm. The smog's as gone as it ever gets. You can see the mountains clearly, and even if you're just looking across the street the air's different, more transparent. The day looks bright and optimism abounds.

There was a gauntlet of fallen palm fronds on Crescent Heights, lying in the gutter like urban driftwood. The car in front of me swerved to avoid one and nearly ran over a Sikh on a bike. The Sikh fell into the street. His turban tumbled off. I pulled over and got out to help him, but by the time I got there he had things together. He thanked me for my concern and cycled off. Somebody yelled for me to get my car the fuck out of their driveway. Optimism bubbled away.

When I got home I threw my two sets of clothes in the hamper, fed the birds, and climbed into the shower. When I got out I looked up and dialed the number for Cedars. Mr. Jones, I was told, was in serious but stable condition. I asked if he could see visitors and was told it was only family until at least the next afternoon. Did he even have any family?

I threw on shorts and a T-shirt and went out back to the greenhouse. One of the echinopsis had aphids all over its buds. I let them be. They never did any real damage, sitting there with their miniscule hindquarters engaged in an insect ballet. Now if only the folks at Olsen's Natural Garden Solutions didn't catch wind of my kindness.

The phone rang. I ran inside to get it. "Hello?"

"Fucking assholes."

"Morning, Woz."

"Bastards."

"I get the point."

"We ought to get them."

"Them? Who, them?"

"The guys who did it."

"You have a clue who that was? Is this about some shady crap you're mixed up in?"

"No. All I'm saying's, they ought to be taken care of. Whoever they are."

"Define 'taken care of.'"

"You know."

"No, Woz, I do not know. Tell me."

"It's an eye for an eye kind of thing. Bastards show up again, we need to be ready."

"Again? You expect them again? You know something about this, you better tell the cops."

"No fucking cops. You in?"

"On what?"

"Whatever happens."

"This conversation is way too theoretical for me."

"Asshole."

"Maybe you should call back when you calm down."

"Maybe you should go fuck yourself." He hung up.

I did too, and sat on the couch. What the hell was Woz talking about? I didn't like this eye for an eye stuff. I didn't know diddly about what the guy had been up to since we were kids. Maybe he was an NRA bigwig. For that matter, I didn't know squat about any of them. Maybe Squig was a drug mule who'd taken a little off the top and gotten caught. Maybe—

No. It wasn't anything as cinematic as that. It was just Woz being pissed because his little buddy had gotten shot by parties unknown. He was making big macho noises because that was the kind of thing guys like Woz did. Can't let the other side, whoever they are, see you're weak. Got to put up a brave front. Like a gorilla pounding his chest.

I went in the bedroom and fooled with my acoustic, but everything came out in a minor key and depressed me. I put the guitar away and farted around the house until I could convince myself it was lunchtime. I drove to Baja Fresh and ate half a burrito. Then on to the Kawamura for a couple of hours repotting cacti. I came home and had another shower, pulled out the guitar again, put it back after ten minutes. I walked to Hollywood Video and found a Jackie Chan I hadn't seen in a while. Watching it wasn't the same without Gina. I was in bed by eight-thirty.

Another Tricky Day

Gina called in the morning, waking me. I don't think I made a whole lot of sense. She asked if I'd been smoking dope again. I assured her I hadn't and asked how the trip was going. She said it was okay, except that she missed me. I said I missed her too. She said she was going to bug out a day early and catch a flight around dinnertime. She'd already arranged for her mother to pick her up. I said to call me when she got back to her place. She said she would. And that she'd bought something, and that I would like it. I asked what it was, but she wouldn't tell me. Said a woman had to have a little mystery. Added that she couldn't believe she'd just said that. Then she said, Love you, and I said, Love you too, and we said good-bye and hung up.

I looked at the clock. Twenty after seven. I'd slept almost eleven hours. I went in the bathroom and waited for my plumbing to get going. When the last trickle was out I crawled back in bed and thought about Gina and me. When we were "just" friends, we'd sometimes say we loved each other. Kind of like the Hollywood love-ya-babe, but with a little more feeling. It didn't indicate anything romantic. But once we started sleeping together again, the words never passed either of our lips. It wasn't a conscious decision, at least on my part. We hadn't used the *L* word in the three years since we'd jumped in the sack together. Until the other night, when I made coffee without being asked and Gina said she loved me and I responded with a chickenshit "me too." And then this morning, when she said it again and I was too bleary to think about things and said, Love you too. Next thing you knew, I'd be saying it with an *I* in front of it. I wondered what it all meant, told myself it probably didn't mean anything, didn't listen to myself.

After I finished my morning routine I stared at the TV for a couple of hours. I thought about eating, but I wasn't hungry. What I was, I decided, was depressed. This explained the eleven hours sleep. And the fact that I hadn't done anything useful in over twenty-four hours. I tried to figure out why I was depressed and remembered there didn't have to be a why.

I called Cedars and found out that Squig could have visitors after two. I took out the SG and played sad songs. I was halfway through "Last Kiss" when the amp cut out. No light, no nothing. The guitar went back in its case. I took out the acoustic, broke a string on the first chord, took it as a sign and put it away too.

I couldn't figure out how to kill the time until I went to the hospital. Finally I broke out the vacuum cleaner. After I finished with it I mopped the kitchen floor. After that it was time to leave. I got a bright idea. I would drop the amp off at Guitar Matrix to get it fixed. I would accomplish one productive thing that afternoon.

Five minutes later I was at the music store. I told my buddy Dex what had happened. He reached in through the back of the amp and jiggled something, then plugged it in. The red light glowed. "Happened to another guy," he said. "One of the connections likes to come off. I gave it a little bend in there that ought to keep it from happening again." I thanked him, stowed the amp in front of the passenger seat, and went off to the hospital.

I parked at Beverly Center because I didn't like the rates at Cedars. I walked down the car ramp, sure that at any second a parking attendant would appear and take me to task for using their valuable real estate for something so unimportant as a hospital visit. But I made it to the sidewalk without incident and walked around the corner to Cedars. They gave me a room number in the north tower. I took the elevator up with a woman holding a flower arrangement so big it threatened to topple her over. She got out the floor before mine. The bouquet brushed against the door frame and a red carnation fell off. When the door closed I picked it up.

Squig had a private room. Later I found that Bonnie had connections at the hospital and set it up. When I went in he was sitting up in bed. He had a pile of crossword puzzle books at his side. One was open to a puzzle that was half filled in, in pen again. He saw me, gave me a strained smile, picked up the book. He looked at the other two people in the room—Chloe and a man about my father's age—and said, "I'll bet Joe knows." To me, "This one has me stumped. Thirty-one down. 'Maple finish.' Eight letters, starting with *BI* and the seventh letter's *Y*."

"Bird's-eye," I said.

"I don't get it."

"Bird's-eye maple. The grain makes patterns that look something like birds' eyes. Gina's coffee table has it."

"See," he told the others, "I knew Joe would know." He started to write it in.

"There's punctuation," I said. "Does that matter?"

"Nope." He finished writing and put down the book. He looked pretty good for someone who'd been shot two days earlier. He was pale and his hair looked more awful than usual. But he didn't seem to be in any pain. A cable from some kind of monitor snaked in under the sheets, and an IV sprouted from his left wrist. There was an empty lunch tray on a rollaway stand and a couple of pots worth of plant life.

I said hi to Chloe and held out a hand to the older guy and told him my name.

His had a good, firm grip. "Herb Wozniak. Robbie's father."

Now that I knew, the resemblance was obvious. The eyes, mostly, that hard look, though in Herb's case it was tempered by the wisdom of years. Like he'd still beat the crap out of you if you did the wrong thing, but his definition of the wrong thing was narrower than Woz's. He had white hair cut fairly long, a matching moustache, a great tan.

I went to the bed and handed the carnation to Squig. "For you."

He took it, didn't seem to know what to do with it, finally dropped it in a paper water cup. "Pretty. A chrysanthemum, right?"

"Carnation."

"I always get those two mixed up."

"Me too. How you feeling?"

"You know."

"Ready to get out of here and jam?"

A distraught look. "I'm not going to be jamming for a while. I'm gonna have to stay in bed."

"How long?"

"A week, two, maybe more. Depends on how I heal up."

I heard footsteps and turned to the door. "Hey, Woz."

"Hey." He stepped into the room and over to Squig. "You're doing too much. Put down the fucking puzzles and lay down."

"When everyone leaves."

Woz pulled over a chair and sat at the side of the bed. He took Squig's hand, enveloped it in both of his own. He glared at Chloe, his father, me, daring us to comment on this touch of tenderness.

We endured half an hour of awkward conversation. It was mostly Herb and me. Chloe was clearly a woman of few words. We talked about when Squig was going to get out, that kind of thing. After a while Herb left. Squig was fading. Woz and I exchanged looks, and Woz told him we were going. Squig thanked us for coming. Woz took away the crossword books and tilted down the head of the bed. I went to Squig, put a hand on his shoulder, told him I'd see him soon. As I moved toward the door Woz bent toward Squig. I thought he was going to kiss him. But he just told him everything would be okay.

I was almost out the door when Squig said, "Guys? Come see me again tonight, okay?"

"Sure, kid," Woz said. "Now get yourself some rest, dig?"

"You too, Joe."

"Will do," I said.

We said good-bye to Chloe, left the room, got on the elevator. The door opened one floor down. The woman I'd gone up with got on. She looked tiny and scared. She glanced at me, squeezed out a smile, stared at the doors. When they opened she practically ran out of the building.

Woz asked where I was parked. I told him. "Me too," he said. "Fucking thieves at this place."

We walked in silence back to San Vicente, waited for the light, crossed. Half a minute later Woz said, "Someone needs to get the guys who did this."

"Is 'get' the same thing as 'take care of'?"

"You know what I mean."

"Please. Don't play vigilante."

"Vigilante. I like that." We walked around the corner, past the Hard Rock, into the shade cast by the monolithic shopping center. When we reached the garage Woz said, "Go for a ride with me."

"I don't like the sound of that."

"Jesus, I'm not going to do anything to you. You're on my fucking side."

"I didn't know I was on anyone's side."

"Just take a ride with me."

When I was in seventh grade, I hung out with a tough kid named Emilio de la Fuente. Emy was my friend, as much as anyone in junior high was my friend, but I was afraid of him. I hung around with him because it carried a certain cachet, but most of the time I was scared shitless he was going to turn on me. He'd say, let's go do X, and I wouldn't want to, and he'd give me a look that said if I didn't do X I was going to get the crap knocked out of me. So I always did what he wanted. Which was usually legally or at least morally reprehensible.

I might as well have been back at junior high. One dirty look from Woz and reason flew out the window. I took a ride with him.

It's a Boy

We got stuck in construction traffic on Pacific Coast Highway. "Jesus H.," Woz said. "I went this way cause they're tearing up the 405 and the Ventura both. Look at this shit."

I asked him for the fifth or sixth time since we'd gotten in the Barracuda where we were headed. For the fifth or sixth time he said, "Wait."

The jam broke at Chautauqua, and soon we were on Topanga Canyon Boulevard, snaking up into the hills. After we passed through the village of Topanga I sat back and watched the scenery. A lot of trees and the occasional open field. After a couple of miles I said, "Where are we going?"

"The Valley."

"I figured that. Where in the Valley?"

"What's the difference? It's all the same."

Debatable, but not worth pursuing. "What's there?"

"A friend."

"What kind of friend?"

"A good friend."

"I should just give up on trying to get you to tell me stuff before you're ready, shouldn't I?"

"Now you're catching on."

An outbreak of mini-malls and office buildings announced our arrival in the San Fernando Valley. A few miles later Woz turned left onto a side street. Two or three more turns put us deep into a residential area crowded with unremarkable houses. The farther we got from the boulevard the lousier the neighborhood got. The lawns got browner, the streets dirtier, the passersby seedier.

Eventually we pulled up in front of a house. It badly needed a paint job and the roof could have used some more shingles. The lawn was half dead and half missing. The only thing not depressing about the place was a monstrous palm tree. Not one of the tall skinny ones like on the TV behind Terry Takamura, thrusting impossibly high into the sky, looking like a good gust would break them in two. This one was no higher than a two-story building. But the trunk must have been five feet across. The fronds stretched the whole width of the lot. Up near the top a whole garden of other plants had taken root among the bases of the fronds.

As we got out of the car a head poked out from behind the palm. It was followed by a body. Both belonged to a boy of about six, dressed in a striped T-shirt and shorts and no shoes. He had a G.I. Joe in one hand and a naked Barbie in the other.

"Whas-*sup?*" the kid said.

"Whas-*sup?*" Woz said.

The boy grinned and ran to Woz, who swept him off the ground, held him in the air, and swirled him around. The kid squealed and giggled and dropped his dolls.

Woz put him down. The kid said, "Did you bring me anything?"

"Sure did. But first say hello to Joe. Joe, meet Billy."

"Hey, Billy."

The kid looked me up and down. "Like G.I. Joe?"

"Yeah, kid," I said. "Like him."

He grinned and said, "Whas-*sup?*"

"Not a whole lot, kid. What's up with you?"

"Not 'what's up.' Whas-*sup*. Dontcha know?" He lost interest in me, swiveled back to Woz. "What'd you bring me?"

"Hang on." Woz opened the car door, reached under the seat, came out with a paper bag and the toy gun he'd scared the shit out of me with in the record store. "Here you go."

Billy grabbed the gun, pointed it at me, kept pulling the trigger. Like father, like son. "You got caps?" he said.

"Sure." Woz reached in the bag, came out with an ancient red, white, and blue box. Billy took it, gathered G.I. Joe and Barbie, ran off behind the tree again.

"You been carrying that thing around all this time?" I said.

"Yeah. What of it?"

"Must not see your kid much."

"I see him enough."

I didn't think so. There was a touch of softness in his face.

"You ready?" he said.

"For what?"

"What do you think?"

"I have no frickin' idea."

"Just come on, you big baby."

He tossed the bag in the gutter. We went to the door and Woz rang the bell. It ding-donged inside, there were footsteps, the door opened.

The woman who stood there was wearing the same outfit

the kid had on. Stripes on the T-shirt, bare feet. She was our age more or less, average height, average weight. She had a tired face and blond hair with the kinds of streaks and highlights you can't get at the beauty parlor. A pair of sunglasses was perched on top of her head. She had a bottle of Bud Light in her right hand. "Hey, hon. Good to see you. Who's your friend?"

"This is Joe. He's in our band."

"Pleased to meet you, Joe. I'm Wanda." She favored me with a smile that was eighty percent genuine. "Come on in."

The décor was no surprise. Beat-up, mismatched furniture. On the walls, dogs playing poker and a Thomas Kinkade. The kitchen featured lots of empties and a refrigerator covered with magnets and crayon drawings.

Wanda drained her beer, tossed it at a plastic garbage bin, swished it. She went to the fridge and jerked on the door. It stuck. She pulled harder. It came open, a magnet flew, a picture fluttered to the once-white linoleum. She ignored it. "Beer?"

"Yeah," Woz said.

"Why not?" I said.

"Light or no?"

"Whatever he's having."

She dipped in, came out with a trio of MGDs, pushed the door shut with her hip, handed us each a beer. She and Woz twisted their caps off and tossed them in the trash with barely a glance. Woz took a swig and belched. I undid my cap, eyed the garbage can, walked over and dropped the top in.

"Let's go out back," Wanda said. We went down a hall

and into a kid's room. Bunk beds, action figures, a poster of Britney Spears. Billy seemed a little young for Britney, but what did I know about kids? A sliding glass door led out to a wooden porch. There were three beach chairs, a chaise, a low metal table with more empties and an ashtray with a cigar butt in it. The webbing on the chairs had seen better days. I couldn't tell about the chaise, since it was hidden by the man lying on it. Well over three hundred pounds, and not a lot of it was fat. Dark features, lots of body hair. He was wearing the uniform: striped T-shirt, shorts, no shoes. When he saw us he broke out in a smile. "Woz."

Woz went over and slapped him five. Then five more. When they got to thirty or so I stopped counting.

"How you doing?" the guy said. The universal greeting of manly men.

"You know," Woz said.

"Yeah. Me too." A chin nod toward me. "Who's this?"

"This is Joe. Joe, say hello to Tiny."

I nodded and walked over. He held out a meaty hand. I didn't know if I was supposed to shake it, slap it, or kiss it. I went with the shake, and things worked out fine.

Woz, Wanda, and I arranged ourselves in the chairs. I eyeballed the yard. About as expected. The lawn matched the one in front. The previous summer's tomato plant skeletons hung off faded bamboo stakes. There were a couple of nondescript trees and a pile of old lumber. A scrawny bougainvillea covered one wall and most of the roof of the garage.

"How's Billy doing in school?" Woz said.

"He's doing good," Tiny said. "Last report card, no problems."

"Cool." Woz slurped up some beer. This prompted Wanda and Tiny to pull on theirs. I didn't want to be left out, so I gulped some of mine down. A couple of us belched.

Woz wiped his mouth on the back of his hand. "Wanda here's my wife. Tiny's her old man."

"Wife, as in current?"

He turned to Wanda and they swapped dopey smiles. "We never got around to the paperwork," Wanda said. "Tiny don't mind, Goldie don't mind. So why bother?"

"No reason I can think of."

We sat for a few minutes, talking about Billy's school mostly. Then Tiny drained his beer, popped it onto the table, and hauled himself off the chaise. "Come on into the garage." He stepped off the porch.

Woz put down his beer, got up, joined him. He looked at me. "Come on."

"What's in the garage?"

"Just come on, okay? Why you need to know everything before it happens?"

"No reason." I added my beer to the collection on the table. It was full except for that one slug I'd had. Woz and Tiny were already headed for the garage. I jogged after them.

The garage door had a big padlock. Tiny undid it with one of a slew of keys on a ring he pulled from his pocket. The saggy door scraped the concrete as he dragged it open.

We went in. A car and a motorcycle were inside. The car was from the forties or early fifties, all rounded fenders and chrome bumpers. There were restoration materials on the roof and on a workbench against the far wall, seating fabric and Bondo and mechanical doohickeys. The motorcycle was a Harley. I only knew this because it said so. It looked a lot newer than the car.

Tiny saw me checking it out. "You ride?"

"Not really. Actually, not at all."

Disappointed in me, shaking his head, he walked to a far corner. Woz followed and I brought up the rear. There was a big metal cabinet back there, four feet wide, three deep, six high. Sturdy looking, almost like a safe. Out came the keys again. Two locks got undone. The door swung open. The cabinet was filled with guns.

We're Not Gonna Take It

I don't know why I was surprised. L.A.'s overrun with guns. Families in my neighborhood had them. Kids in high school, even the "good" ones, had them. Gina had one.

Maybe it was the sheer quantity of the things. There was a rack inside where a dozen shotguns and rifles sat vertically. Below it, two shelves with at least an equal number of handguns, all dark and metallic and lethal-looking. Farther down still, a couple of drawers. God knew what was in them. Ammo or hand grenades or tactical nukes.

Woz and Tiny, wearing matching grins, stood watching me. "Come on over and take a look," Tiny said.

Instead I took a step backward.

"What're you afraid of?" Woz said. "They don't bite." He turned, dipped into the cabinet, came out with one of the handguns. "This one here, you could call it a vigilante special."

"Don't do this," I said.

"Don't do what?"

"Grabbing a bunch of guns and going off after whoever shot Squig. That *is* what this is about, right?"

"Calm down. I'm not going to grab a bunch of guns."

I relaxed a little. "Then—"

"Only two."

"You only have two hands. So two guns might as well be a bunch."

"They're not both for me."

"Who, then?"

The two of them just grinned at me.

Duh.

"No. No way. Are you out of your fucking mind?"

"I need backup."

"What you need is a lobotomy. I'm not getting involved in this."

"We'll see." He returned his attention to Tiny and the gun cabinet. I got the hell out of the garage and stood on the bleak driveway, not sure what to do next.

"Something wrong?" Wanda said.

"Yes. Something's very wrong. Your boyfriend is selling guns to your husband so we can go track down whoever—"

"I don't get involved in the boys' business."

"It doesn't bother you that he's got an arsenal on the premises?"

She glanced toward the garage. "You're going to hang out with Woz, you're gonna have to be a little more broad-minded."

"Maybe I'll have to stop hanging out with Woz."

"Suit yourself." She picked a magazine off the ground. *People.* Britney Spears on the cover. Like mother, like son.

I went up on the porch, through the sliding door, found my way to the front. When I made it to the sidewalk I walked east, toward the boulevard.

I got three blocks before Woz found me. He trolled along behind awhile, then caught up. "Wait."

"I think not."

"I'm sorry. I should've said where we were going."

I kept walking. He rolled down the middle of the narrow street.

"Hey, I said I'm sorry. Just get back in the car, okay?"

I stopped, turned. "No. Not okay."

Across the street, an old woman in a red muumuu stood outside her front door, listening intently. I walked toward the car. Woz slowed to a stop. I stayed far enough away so he couldn't grab me through the window. I dropped my voice. "You can't just go running around like cowboys and Indians after these guys."

"Someone has to."

"You don't even know who they are."

"That's what I need you for. Detective work."

"I've given up detecting, except for finding Toby. Why not just let the cops handle it?"

A baleful stare. "You don't get it, do you?"

"Get what?"

"You take care of your own."

"No. The cops take care of my own."

"Is that what you did a couple years ago when they thought that friend of yours blew someone away?"

"It's not the same thing. I wasn't going around shooting people."

"I thought you'd be man enough to go to bat for your friends."

"The old macho bullshit argument."

"But if you're not, I can live with it. Get in the car. I'll drive you back and that'll be that."

"I doubt it."

I looked up. The old woman was chittering into a cell phone. Something about "suspicious strangers." She edged along her walk, trying to catch Woz's license number.

I ran around the front of the car, got in, slammed the door. "Get out of here."

He was already getting. We reached Topanga Canyon Boulevard and went south, stopping next at a light just before the 101 on-ramp. "Why me?" I said. "Why not Frampton?"

"Frampton's got a family."

"I've got a family."

"Frampton's got kids. So if anything happened … not that anything's going to happen."

"Right. Because after you drop me at Beverly Center, that's the end of it. We weren't going to talk about this anymore, remember?"

"You're the one brought it up."

Halfway back he reached under the seat and pulled out a gun. "This is the one I got for you."

"Very nice. Now put it back."

"It's just a little .22. A girl's gun. Not a lot of firepower, except if you come up and shoot someone in the head with it. Then it jangles around inside and turns their brains to goop." He glanced down at it, then looked at me. "I picked it out for you cause I figured it would be easy for you to handle."

"It'll be real easy to handle if I don't handle it at all. Could you maybe keep your eyes on the road?"

"Shit. Won't even handle a girl's gun."

"Are you done?"

He sighed and regarded me with disgust. "I figured it'd probably be like this."

"I'm glad I didn't disappoint you."

He gave me those eyes of his, and I thought I'd gone too far. That we might see some blood spilled right there in the front seat of the Barracuda. But he just shoved the gun back under the seat.

We reached Beverly Center half an hour later. Before I went to the truck I dropped into California Pizza Kitchen and, ever responsible, used their pay phone to call my machine. There were a bunch of messages from Elaine. A callback for a Sealy Posturepedic spot. She sounded extra pissed. I got hold of her, apologized, rushed to the casting director's office on Beverly. I made it just in time. They watched me lie down for a while and let me go. I got in the truck and started home. When I got there I had company again.

My Generation

I removed my amp and myself from the truck and went up the walk. I stopped just short of the patio and pointed at the faded blue VW microbus out front. "Yours?"

"Yes," Deanna said. "Like it?"

"Uh-huh. Very retro."

Like the first time I saw her, she looked good from a distance. Close up, blowing the old cliché, she looked better in the light of day. The red hair came off as more natural and the lines in her face provided character instead of history. She was sitting in one of the wicker chairs with legs crossed at the ankles and an impenetrable expression. Her big toes were painted, the rest weren't. A multicolored fabric purse dangled from the back of the chair.

"Come sit," she said.

A quick scan showed no orange juice or other sign of illegal entry. I stowed the amp by the door, took the other chair and turned it so I could see her face. "The answer's still no."

"The answer? Oh, you mean about fucking. That's not why I'm here."

"Then why are you?"

"Aren't you interested in how I found you?"

"Standard procedure seems to be looking up my address in the phone book and finding it in the Thomas Guide."

"But I had to get your name first. You didn't tell me that."

"Do I care about this?"

"I got it from Charley at Paoletti's. I was counting on you going over there after I told you about it." She smiled. It was almost attractive. "And here I am."

"Yes. Here you are. Any word from Mott?"

"No."

Giggling came from next door. I looked over, saw Suzy Clement watching a squirrel that twittered at her from their birch tree. Her mom came out, spotted the squirrel, said something about rabies. Nice people, the Clements, but overprotective.

I turned back to Deanna. "You know what? Life's too short, forgive the cliché, and I don't want to sit around playing games. Why are you here?"

She head-gestured in the general direction of the front door. "Nice amp."

"Is it?" Something was wrong with what she'd said. "I didn't think it was anything special."

"Just making conversation."

I had it. Women I knew wouldn't say "amp." They'd say "amplifier," if they had occasion to mention one at all. Like Gina had when she got me the gift certificate. And once I had that …

"Sit there," I said. I got up, unlocked the door, dumped the amp inside, grabbed Toby's first solo album, took it out with me. Looked at the back, at the picture of the band. Then at Deanna. Back and forth, back and forth.

"It's me," she said.

The chick drummer, Dee Knox. It was Deanna.

And so what?

"So you were in a band with him," I said.

"Just like you were."

"Charley told you."

She nodded. "I'm looking for Toby too."

I tried to gauge if she was telling the truth. Tried to decide if I cared. "Why?" I said. "Don't tell me you ran into Spencer Sommers and you're mounting a reunion tour too."

"I haven't seen Spencer in ten years. Why I'm looking for Toby's a little hard to explain. And it doesn't matter right now. What matters is I have an idea where he might be."

"Where?"

"I don't really know where it is. I just know what it is."

"Go away."

"Excuse me?"

"I told you, no games. Get the hell out of here."

"I wasn't trying to pull your chain. I was just saying—"

"I'm going inside."

I slammed the door behind me, tossed the record album on the couch, went into the bathroom to wash my hands. I dried them longer than I had to, staring at the mirror, wondering what someone who hadn't seen me in a long time would think of my face.

I returned to the living room and was only a little surprised when I kept going and flung the front door open. Deanna was still in the chair, sitting peacefully, her head bobbing to some unknown tune. When she saw me she smiled. She didn't wait for an invitation. She just got up and, without a word, squeezed past me into the house and made for the couch.

I sat at the other end. "Talk," I said.

"Mott was there the night Toby was at Paoletti's."

"And you weren't?"

"No. It was supposed to be some drummer from Japan playing that night. Mott loves that kind of stuff. He spent some time in Japan. That's where he got the name. It's really Matt, but it came out Mott there and he took to it. I hate that kind of music, so I stayed home. When he came home afterwards and told me Toby had shown up I felt like killing him."

"He knows you knew Toby?"

"Of course he does."

"Then why didn't he call you?"

"He was stoned, as usual. He said he just didn't think of it." She looked straight at me. "How old are you?"

"Forty-nine. Why?"

"I'm fifty-two. Two-thirds of the way through my life, probably. I've started to think about things."

I didn't have to ask what kind of things.

"Those days as a musician," she said. "They were the best time of my life." She cocked her head, watched me, expecting a comment. When none came she went on. "Toby and I were the best of friends when I was in his band. I was the only girl he wasn't interested in screwing, and the same the other way around. You ever have women friends like that?"

Sure I did. Gina, before things changed. And in my acting days, there were lots of female friends, though deep down I probably wanted to ravage them all. "Yes."

"Then you know what I'm talking about. You don't want to mess things up by letting sex get involved. But one day Toby had a little too much to smoke and he made a move on me. I turned him down. Things were never the same between us after that. And things were never the same for him in general. He started spending more and more time by himself, and getting into heavier drugs."

"You can't think that one little turndown caused his heroin addiction."

"Maybe it contributed. Maybe I should have fucked him, and everything would have been fine, and I could have, I don't know, saved him from himself. Maybe we would have ended up a nice suburban couple with two kids and a dog."

I thought of Frampton. I wondered if he had a dog. I thought of Bonnie, who did have one. How I wished I'd slept with her that night. But it was different. She still would have left Mark and Ginger's, and I still would have lost her for thirty-odd years.

"When I found out Toby was alive—"

"You're sure he is? If Mott was so loaded it could have been Vanilla Ice up there."

"I had the same thought. But Charley said it was Toby too. That's good enough for me."

"Go on."

"When I heard Toby was alive—and remember, I've been in this thoughtful phase, questioning my life, getting misty about the old days, all sorts of crap like that—I suddenly got the idea that I needed to find him. To talk to him."

"What would it accomplish?"

"I don't know. I just feel it's something I have to do. Maybe it won't accomplish anything. Maybe I'll feel my life is complete and I can die happy."

"Why didn't you just tell me you knew him the other night at Da Capo?"

"I thought you might be a narc."

"Not you too."

"Other people do?"

"A couple more in the last week alone."

"You have the look."

"What look?"

"The narc look. But I went to Paoletti's the next day and asked Charley about you and he thought you were legit. Which brings us up to looking you up in the Thomas Guide."

"And to your suspicions about where he is."

"Yes."

"Which would be?"

"Toby had a kind of secret hideaway. It was out in the desert, near Palm Springs. He wouldn't tell anyone exactly where. Wouldn't even mention it to most people."

"He took you there."

That stopped her. "How'd you know that?"

"He took me too."

"That son of a bitch. He told me I was the first. He talked about you all the time, and not once did he mention that. That son of a—"

"Toby talked about me all the time?"

"I got sick of hearing your name."

"What did he say?"

"That he missed you, for one thing, though being a man he had to say it in a roundabout way."

"Did he tell you how he and Bonnie went away and never contacted any of us again?"

"He felt awful about that. But he felt worse that they weren't allowed to take the rest of you with them. He was afraid to face you. Bonnie was too, from what he said. Can we—"

"And after she lost her voice and their group went to hell and he was recording an album with you and Spencer, he still couldn't drop by, send us a letter, even call us on the telephone?"

"He was damaged by then. I'm not saying that's an excuse, but it's a reason."

"Damaged by drugs?"

"By drugs, by the music business … can we get back on the subject?"

"Yeah, sure, whatever."

"You know where his hideaway is? Because that's where I think he is."

"No. All I remember is you get off I-10, head toward the mountains, and it's up there somewhere. That encompasses, what, a jillion square miles? Plus we were smoking the whole way out there."

"Us too. Damn it. I really think that's where he is."

"He shlepped in from there to make a midnight appearance at Paoletti's?"

"I drove seven hundred miles to get to Woodstock."

"That's a lousy analogy."

"It was a lousy objection." She looked like she wanted to say more.

"What?" I said.

"This is going to sound stupid …"

"I've heard a lot that sounded stupid in the last few days."

"I know it sounds like cosmic bullshit, but I feel like there's some fate thing going on here. Why did I run into you that night, when we both wanted to find Toby?"

"You ran into me because I was looking for Mott in a place I knew he hangs out at, and since you're his significant other it stands to reason it's a place you might hang out at too."

"You think that's all it is?"

"Of course that's all it is."

I didn't believe that, not entirely, and that scared me. I don't waste time on things I haven't seen evidence of. Area 51 aliens, energy pyramids, a supreme being, maybe they exist and maybe they don't. If someone shows me proof I'll believe it, and until then, I don't really give a rat's ass.

So what was scary was that I was giving at least a little credence to what Deanna was saying. That fate threw the two of us together. That there was something beyond sheer chance going on.

But I wasn't ready to admit it.

"Let's play what-if," I said.

"Go ahead."

"What if I said, fine, the gods have made our paths cross and we're destined to find Toby—leaving aside, for the moment, the question of what we do if we do find him—then how would we begin?"

"We'd put our heads together and see what we remember about the place. Maybe we could get some synergy going and together we might be able to remember how to get there. So you're in?"

"When did I say that?"

"You didn't say you were out."

The *Jeopardy!* theme played in my head. I had thirty seconds to come up with an answer. I knew that wasn't right, that I had as much time as I needed. But the answer I came up with in thirty minutes, thirty hours, thirty years wasn't going to be any better than the one I chose after thirty seconds.

I didn't know why I was on the fence. What she'd said was right. That synergy business. Two heads are better than one. In unity there is strength. There were probably other proverbs I was missing.

Maybe I was just suspicious of this other person dropping into my lap, trying to accomplish the same thing I was. It was too cosmic for me.

When I opened my mouth I wasn't sure what was going to come out. Once I heard it, I was satisfied it was the right thing. "I'm in," I said.

Boris the Spider

"I thought you were going catatonic on me," Deanna said.

"I'll save that for later, when we're out in the desert dying of thirst. So what do we do now?"

"We talk about our trips with Toby. One of us says something, it sparks something in the other—"

"And after a few minutes one of us goes, 'Holy shit! I remember where it is. Not only that, but I have an auto club map in my closet with the route laid out in blue highlighter."

She laughed. "Why blue?"

"You don't like blue? It can be yellow, if you want. Or pink. I think those are the main highlighter colors."

"Let's get started."

"Right now?" I said.

"'There's no time like the right time—'"

"'—and baby, the right time is now.' Blues Project, '66."

"'67, I think."

"Whichever it is," I said, "now is not the right time."

"Why not?"

"I've got to see a friend in the hospital." Not for another hour or two, but I needed time to digest.

She opened her purse, took out a Bic and a wrinkled

credit card receipt, wrote on the back. "Here's my number. Call me when you're ready. Don't make it too long, okay? And if that asshole Mott answers the phone, don't leave a message with him. I'll never get it."

"You expect him back?"

"I never know what to expect with him."

She dropped the slip of paper on the coffee table, shut her purse, headed for the door. I followed to let her out. She suddenly turned, pressed against me, tried to kiss me. No. Did kiss me. I pressed back. I may have kissed back. The feel of a different woman after three years confused the hell out of me.

Good thing my mind's had a lifetime of experience in getting in the way of what my body wants to do. It was just taken by surprise. Once it figured out that what was going on was a really bad idea, I pushed away. As soon as I did she stepped back. She looked into my eyes and put on a smile dipped in regret. "I just had to be sure," she said. Then she opened the door and slipped out. I closed the door behind her and stood there until I heard the microbus fire up and drive away.

•

I put on Buffalo Springfield and lay on my back on the couch. A spider on the ceiling caught my attention. Near the corner, one of those long-legged ones like Woz had watched outside. Everyone calls them daddy long-legs, but some nitwit at the cactus club told me they're really something else. I could never figure out why they chose to build their ill-formed webs up there, where there wasn't anything to eat.

I went to the kitchen and got a glass. Pulled a chair into

the corner, stood on it, and scooped the spider in. I took it outside and dumped it off the patio, under the bushes. It skittered away and was lost to sight.

Next door, little Suzy was playing daredevil with the squirrel again. I sat down on one of the wicker chairs and watched her. The sun played peekaboo behind the evergreen across the street. Suzy's mom called her inside for dinner. I kept watching the squirrel until it ran up the big ficus in front of the Clement house.

I went inside and picked up the charge slip with Deanna's phone number. She'd written her name too. It was still Knox. That was what I was looking for. I looked up Alberta Burns's phone number and dialed it.

Burns was a homicide detective. She'd been Hector Casillas's partner before he got bumped upstairs to Robbery-Homicide. I got to know her when my friend Brenda got herself killed. Then Burns helped me out the second time I got mixed up with murder. We'd gotten friendly and went out for coffee now and then.

I got her on her cell. "Burns."

"Hi, Burns."

"Portugal? That you?"

"Uh-huh."

"How you doing?"

"Okay. You?"

"Not so good."

"What's the matter?"

"I got shot."

"What? Where?"

"Oakwood."

"No, I meant—"

"I knew what you meant. My leg."

"You okay? I mean, any lasting damage?"

"They say I'll be good as new after a while."

"That's good."

"Meanwhile, I get to sit home and watch the soaps."

"So what happened?"

"A gangbanger on a roof."

"Wow. They catch him?"

"My partner took him down."

"Killed him, you mean?"

"Uh-huh. He was fourteen."

"God."

"Yeah. God. So what's up with you? Been playing detective lately?"

"As a matter of fact, I have."

"And you haven't called me for information? I'm hurt."

"I am now."

"It'll cost you."

"How much?"

"Bagels at that place in the Marina."

"I can handle that."

"What do you need?"

"Whatever you have on three people."

"Three? That might be worth dinner."

"I can handle that too."

"Let me grab a pencil. Okay, go ahead."

"First one's name's Robbie Wozniak. He goes by Woz."

"Anything more to go on?"

"Date of birth, somewhere near mine, which would put it around '52."

"That'll help. Next?"

"Deanna Knox. At some point also known as Dee."

"DOB?"

"Let's see. She's fifty-two. So '50 or so."

"The last one?"

"Toby Bonner. He's probably a year older than me."

"Got it."

"You might have a file on him."

"Why?"

"He was, or is, a musician. A three-hit wonder back in the sixties."

"I work for LAPD, not ASCAP."

"He disappeared sometime around 1980."

"You suspect foul play?"

"I don't know what I suspect."

"This may be worth dinner at a real restaurant. The cloth-napkin type."

"You're a hard woman, Burns."

"Got to be in my line of work. Okay. I'll see what I can find out."

"Thanks a lot."

"In the meantime, don't get yourself killed."

"I'll try not to."

"At least," she said, "until I collect on my dinner. Good-bye, Portugal."

Amazing Journey

I didn't want to go see Squig again. I thought I'd get to the hospital around eight-thirty. Visiting hours couldn't go much beyond that. In the meantime I had time to kill. I sat on the couch and turned on the TV. I stopped at Animal Planet. It reminded me of Marlin Perkins and how he was always sending Jim to wrestle the anaconda while he stayed safe on the bank with W.K. the chimp. *That* was a nature show. Not this *Crocodile Hunter* shit.

You're turning into your father.

It wasn't the first time I'd had the thought. Nor the second nor the third nor the hundredth. That pining for the stuff of one's youth. Next thing you knew I'd be missing Tricky Dick.

At six I switched to the Channel 6 news. There weren't any high-speed chases, so they led off with the Middle East. There were two more suicide bombings. Arafat's headquarters under attack by the Israelis. Recriminations all around.

They gave that three or four minutes and moved onto the usual assortment of dumb local stories. They had an update on the murder-suicide in Hollywood. The husband had whacked the wife with an ax, cut off his own hand, and bled to death. There was a shot of an irregular circle of dried blood on a carpet. It could have been from the house where it had happened and it could have been stock footage. One bloody carpet looks pretty much like the next.

More local tragedies, a preview of the sports, a story about a kid who got his head stuck between the bars of a fence. They showed his mother, extolling the virtues of the firefighters who got him out, equating what they'd done with September 11 heroics. The graphic showed her name and, beneath it, MOTHER, like that was the sum total of her existence.

A commercial came on, and I went to pee. I was doing it a lot lately. My doctor had fingered my prostate and drawn blood for a PSA test and assured me everything was normal. That as men grew older their urinary systems grew weirder. "A natural consequence of aging," she told me, like that would make me feel better.

After the last drop dribbled out I washed my hands and went in the bedroom. I plugged in, strummed a few chords, did a little picking. The D string was out of tune. I fiddled with it until I realized it didn't want to get fixed. Sometimes it's like that. It's flat, you move it up, it gets sharp. You move it back down, you go too far. You try to hone in on the right note and it just won't happen. I wondered what Toby Bonner —if he happened to be alive—did in a situation like that.

I put the guitar away, eyed the Epiphone, remembered the broken string, went out to the backyard. Into the greenhouse and right back out. I needed to be doing something but I didn't know what it was.

"Hey!"

It was Theta, one of the spaced oddities next door. She

had a lot of red hair and a Southern accent and a laugh like a doped-up hyena. She was standing on something and watching me over the fence. She'd do this "Hey!" thing every once in a while, scaring the crap out of me more often than not. Twice she caught me naked, drying off after a shower. After the second time I introduced myself. I always like women who've seen my penis to know my name.

"Hey," I said.

"Been meaning to tell you. You rock."

"Huh? Oh, you mean the guitar."

"Of course I mean the guitar. It's hot. Makes me want to boogie."

"It's not too loud?"

She gave me a you-dumbshit look worthy of Woz. "Rock and roll's supposed to be loud. Besides, with the racket we make over here, you think I'd have the balls to complain?"

"I guess not. And thanks. For what you said."

"Bring your gear over sometime. We'll break out the theremin."

"Sometime."

"Right on," she said, and dropped from sight like Punxsutawney Phil on a sunny February 2.

•

The parking attendant at Beverly Center gave me the eye. She knew I wasn't going shopping.

Paranoia strikes deep.

I retraced my steps from earlier in the day. This time I shared the elevator with a man with a goiter. I tried not looking at it. Ever try not staring at a goiter?

The door to Squig's room was partway shut. I knocked. A voice told me to come in. It didn't sound like Squig's.

It wasn't. There was a fat guy in the bed. He had an overgrown goatee, deepset eyes, and tiny ears. "You the proctologist?" he said.

Squig's been abducted, I thought. Whoever shot him came and got him, and that left the room open for this ass patient.

Into your life it will creep.

I looked at the number on the door. I was one room short of where I needed to be. "Sorry. Wrong room."

"You sure you're not the proctologist?"

"I'm sure. But I've seen my share of assholes."

His laugh echoed down the corridor as I walked away. Glad to brighten his day, I moved down a door and knocked. This time the voice was familiar. It was Woz's. I walked in. "Hi, guys, Chloe."

"Five letters," Squig said, "Was Dahomey, whatever that is. Starts with a *B*."

"Benin," I said.

"Spell it."

I did.

"It fits. How do you know shit like that?"

"I have a plant from there."

"Fuckin' A."

I turned to Woz. "What's happening?"

"Nothing much. You?"

"The same."

Squig was consumed with his puzzle. Chloe was consumed with Squig. Woz went to the door and head-gestured. "Come on out." In the corridor he said, "That shit this afternoon. I shouldn't've done that."

I waved a dismissive hand. "Water over the dam."

He held out a meaty one. "Bygones be bygones?"

I put mine in his. Got it pretty much crushed. We went back in and watched Squig work on his crossword. Woz surprised me by coming up with a couple of answers. Chloe said maybe four words.

After a while I went out and called Gina. She'd just gotten in and was trying to get rid of her mother. I told her I'd be over after I finished at the hospital. We exchanged love-yous and I went back to the room.

A teenage volunteer came in at nine and told us visiting hours were over. Woz and I said good-bye and started out. The volunteer said to Chloe, "You too, ma'am." Chloe gave her a Woz-quality glare. The volunteer fled in terror.

•

Woz was parked at Beverly Center too. We walked over together and went to our cars. I paid up, left the garage, and headed north on La Cienega. A little past Beverly, Woz pulled even on my left. We exchanged waves like a couple of suburban dads leaving their kids' soccer game. He moved ahead and made the right onto Melrose ahead of me. I lost sight of him.

I wanted to get Gina some welcome-home flowers at Moe's, so I stayed on Melrose to Crescent Heights and got in the left turn lane. There were several cars ahead of me, two of them already in the intersection, Woz's Barracuda and a BMW. When the light turned red they finished the turn. The Mustang behind them went through too. It wasn't legal, but it wasn't unusual.

Then another car went through, way after the light changed. A New Beetle, black or navy. He barely missed the first couple of cars starting south on the green.

Once more, paranoia struck deep. I could hear Gina the night Squig was shot. *A Volkswagen. A Beetle.*

And after that: *New. Some dark color.*

There was still one car, a Kia, in front of me in the left turn lane. I pulled around to the left of it. This put me in the oncoming lane. There was a lineup of vehicles headed south. One of them was a big SUV. He was going a little slower than the guy in front of him. Slow enough that I thought I could make it across.

I stomped on the gas. The SUV bore down on me. I barely made it through and hung a left. This put me in the northbound lane, which, I'd conveniently forgotten, also had cars in it. A guy driving a big sedan stomped on his brakes when I jerked in ahead of him. He leaned on the horn and probably called me a fucking asshole. That's what I would have done.

I drove way too fast up Crescent Heights. I ran another light at Santa Monica, saw the VW turn right on Fountain, and followed. A block later I spotted the Barracuda. The Beetle dropped in two cars behind it. I dropped in two cars behind the Beetle. One too many, as it turned out.

We crossed Fairfax, crossed La Brea, approached Highland. Woz went through on the yellow. The Volkswagen ran another red. The guy in front of me stopped. I did too, an instant too late. My bumper kissed his.

He was out of his crappy old Civic wagon and inspecting his bumper in about four seconds. Then he was yelling at me, a sweathog in an undershirt and shorts, questioning my driving ability and my lineage. The VW's taillights receded on the other side of Highland.

I leaned out the window. "Police. Undercover. Following a suspect. Get the fuck out of my way."

I lucked out. This guy wanted nothing to do with the cops. "Sorry, officer," he said. He dived into the driver's seat and squealed right onto Highland.

A lot of good my impersonation did me. I still couldn't get through the light until it changed. There were too many cars for a daredevil routine. This gave me a chance to think. I decided I was probably out of my mind. Whoever was in the VW wasn't following Woz. There were thousands of dark New Beetles in L.A.

The light took its sweet time. When it finally changed I sped across. I reached Vine without seeing a Beetle or a Barracuda. I turned right, pulled to the curb, dug under the seat for the Thomas Guide. It was hard to read under the street lights. My dome bulb was long gone and so was the flashlight that once lived under the seat. I went through half a dozen Lelands before I found a Leland Way that was supposedly in the vicinity. I searched the coordinates it was supposed to be at. I couldn't find it. I threw the Thomas Guide aside and tried to choke the steering wheel. Squig had said he and Woz lived off something. What was it?

For once, the hundreds of sixties song lyrics taking up valuable real estate in my head came in handy. Paul Revere and the Raiders, no less.

Cherokee people … Cherokee tribe.

I drove around the block and west on Fountain to Cherokee Avenue. Left or right? Right, probably, to the north. If it was south of Fountain, Woz would have taken Santa Monica. Assuming he was headed home, and that he wasn't toking up in the car and taking the long way around to dig on the lights.

I made the right and drove slowly north, through a neighborhood that might have been nice once. I crossed De Longpre. The lights and traffic on Sunset rose up ahead.

I almost missed it. A narrow street, off to the right, dead-ending at Cherokee. Leland Way. I made the turn. The VW was parked on the right side two houses down from Cherokee. I tried to look in, but it was too dark to see anything except someone moving around in there. If they lived on the block, they would have had plenty of time to go into their house while I was touring Hollywood.

I kept my cool enough to maintain my speed. Woz's Barracuda was parked halfway down the block. He wasn't in it. I kept going and made a right at the next corner. Then another. And another. One more and I'd be driving past the VW again.

I constructed a plan. A lousy one, but it was all I had.

I made the last right turn.

Let's See Action

Again I passed the VW, and continued down the block, past the rundown bungalows and the boxy pastel apartment buildings. Parking was tight, but I found a spot two behind the Barracuda, and got out of the truck.

I stood there trying to guess which house was Squig's and Woz's. This was the extent of my plan. Figure out where they lived and warn Woz some guys might be following him around. Like I said, lousy.

An elderly woman watched me from under a streetlight across the way. She resembled the one in the Valley after my visit to Tiny's armory, draped in a muumuu, cell phone in hand. Maybe they were running a package deal. Buy a phone, get a muumuu free. Or the other way around.

Then I heard the music. "Summertime Blues." Not the Eddie Cochran original, nor the version on *The Who Live at Leeds*. It was the travesty by Blue Cheer.

I tracked it to a house two up on the other side of the street. Once I got there the sound was earsplitting. Either the neighbors were used to it, they were deaf, or Woz kept them all well-stocked with ganja.

I rang the bell. No answer. I knocked. I knocked again. Nothing.

I went around the side of the house and found a window that was open a few inches. Inside, there were hundreds of records and tapes, a few CDs. The enormous Hendrix poster on the wall was coming loose at one corner. The lighting included a lava lamp, a blacklight, and a floor lamp with a Tiffany shade and a troll doll sitting on top. Woz sat on a venerable blue couch with his back to me, head moving to and fro sort of in time to the music. He looked like he was davening.

"Woz."

No answer. Not surprising.

"Woz!"

Still nothing.

"*Woz!*"

He sat up straight, craning his head like a hungry baby bird.

"Over here!"

He heard me. I don't know how. Maybe he'd just gotten bitten by a radioactive spider and it heightened his senses. He turned and saw me. He said something—I'm nearly certain it was "what the fuck?"—and a hash pipe fell from his mouth.

"Let me in."

"Huh?"

"Let me in, goddamn it." I pointed at the front of the house. He got it and wobbled toward the door. I ran around and he opened up. The hashish smell wasn't strong. It didn't have to be to take me back a couple dozen years.

I went to the stereo and berthed the tone arm. Woz stared at one of the speakers like it would tell him what happened. Then he discovered the hash pipe wasn't in his mouth. He felt around a bit to be sure and said his favorite line. "What the fuck?"

"It's on the floor, but forget that now. The guys who shot Squig may be out there."

"Out where?"

"Outside."

He went to the front window, looked out, turned his head first right, then left. "I don't see anyone."

"That's because it's dark out. Trust me, they're out there."

"Who?"

"Jesus, Woz, come in for a landing. Two guys. In a dark VW. The guys who shot Squig were in a dark VW."

"Oh." He spotted his pipe, picked it up, looked at it like he'd never seen it before. Then at me with the same expression. "How'd you—"

"They followed you from Beverly Center. There's no time to stand around gabbing. We have to do something."

"Oh."

He stared out the window for at least a minute. When he turned to face me he looked like a whole different person. The one I was used to. He said, "Let's get the fuckers."

"No. Let's call the cops."

"No cops. We take care of our own."

"What are you going to do, run down the street with guns blazing?"

"Nope."

"What, then?"

"Gonna sneak up on 'em. Come on."

"I'm calling the cops." I went to the phone and picked it up. Woz stomped over, grabbed it from my hand, slapped it down. "Forget it."

"I followed them here so I could warn you and you could avoid whatever the hell they're planning to do to you. Not so you could play Indian scout."

"Come on."

"No."

"You are *such* a pussy."

He headed toward the back of the house. Before he got there he detoured into another room, and when he came out he had a gun in his hand. A man's gun, from the size of it. He tossed off a glare and went out the back door.

I stood there. Only for a few seconds. Then I went after him.

•

Maybe I had a contact high. Maybe a little bit of that take-care-of-your-own philosophy had sunk in. Maybe I just couldn't give up on trying to convince him not to do it.

When I got outside he was out of sight, but the side door to the garage was open. I ran in. The overhead door was open too. Woz saw me. He said, "Maybe you're not such a pussy," and headed left down the weed-infested alley.

I followed, a house or two behind. When he got to the end of the alley he stood under the streetlight, looking left, right, straight, trying to figure out his next clever move. That was where I caught up with him. He had the gun tucked into the front of his pants, and he'd buttoned his shirt over it, but the shirt wasn't that long and the gun wasn't that hidden. "What do you think?" he said.

"I think we should go up to Sunset and find a pay phone and call the cops."

"Not gonna happen. Okay. Here's the choices. We could go left and have to cross Leland where they might see us. Or we could go on up Cherokee to Sunset—"

"And call the cops."

"—and go around the block, only it'd have to be two blocks 'cause otherwise we'd end up on Leland again." He pointed vaguely south. "And then come back this way and then this way ..." More nebulous hand motions. "And then we'll end up at the corner there and they won't see us."

"You lost me."

"Fuck it. Let's take the bull by the balls. Cover me." His hand dived in his pocket and came out with the other gun. The girl's gun. "Take it."

"Hell I will. I never shot a gun in my life. Even if I took it, there's no way I'd shoot it, and if I did I'd be just as likely to shoot you as them."

He grabbed my hand, rammed the gun into it, and closed my fingers around the thing. "There. It's easy. You point it and you pull the trigger." A quizzical look. "You know what the trigger is, right?"

I looked down at the deadly hunk of metal in my hand. "Uh, yeah. Where's the safety?"

"It's a revolver. It doesn't have a safety." He left the alley, crossed Cherokee, started slinking south along the sidewalk.

I wanted to throw the gun in the weeds. But if I did that, sure as shit, some four-year-old would find it there and shoot his baby sister to death. I looked it over. I'd seen enough spaghetti Westerns to know you could make the cylindrical part with the bullets flip out to dump them. I couldn't see how. If I tried to figure it out I'd probably shoot myself.

So I stuffed the gun in my pocket and watched what Woz was up to. There was a big magnolia just south of where

Leland dead-ended. Woz, God help him, was hiding behind it and peering out like a cartoon character. I half-expected his eyes to bug out on stalks.

I crept a little way toward the intersection, keeping my back hard against the tall eugenia hedge that stretched the length of the corner house. No one else was around. They knew there was going to be a showdown and had gathered their womenfolk and children, hustled them inside, and barred the door.

Woz slunk back across Cherokee to our side. There was no magnolia there. Just a skinny ficus. He hid behind it anyway.

I heard a noise back toward the alley. I turned just in time to see someone duck back in. The bastard must have come to the house, not found us, figured out where we went, and followed. I pushed my back harder into the hedge and peered over my right shoulder. The hedge was sparse there at the corner of the property. There were gaps where I could see into the alley without exposing myself to whoever might be in there.

I had no idea what I was doing.

I was scared shitless.

Sometimes you come to a point in life where there's no right path. There's a bad way to go, and there's a worse one. You can argue with yourself about what to do for hours, and it really doesn't matter because either way you're screwed.

Choice One: Get the hell out of there. Just run away as fast as I could, hope I didn't get shot in the back, get to a major street, and find a pay phone or a passerby with a cell and call 911, or Detective Kalenko, or Alberta Burns, or some-fucking-body better equipped to handle the situation than I was. This would make Woz very mad at me. Assuming he survived.

Choice Two: Take care of my own. Calling Woz my own was stretching things, but could I just desert him? Maybe I'd gotten him into this situation. Maybe if I hadn't come to his door he would have spotted the bad guy when he showed up and dealt with the whole thing right then. Unlikely, given Woz's condition when I appeared, but I couldn't be sure.

I went back and forth for what seemed like an hour. I was stuck. So maybe it was a good thing that my decision was made for me.

LOOKIN' FOR ADVENTURE

A Legal Matter

I kept expecting to hear gunfire from around the corner. A *ka-pow* or two, or three or four or nine, and maybe a groan or a scream. Shattering glass, exploding Beetles, that kind of thing.

But there was nothing.

I looked through the gaps in the hedge. Didn't see anyone.

No. Wait. Movement.

A girl, about twelve. She was coming from the direction of Woz's house, walking slowly. I opened my mouth to yell at her to get the hell out of there. Before I could there was a sharp noise and something came flying through the eugenia inches from my head. A branch cracked and bits of vegetation showered my face.

I checked the kid. Still alive, still standing, but it was deer in the headlights time. I sprang from my hiding spot. The plan was to grab the kid and whisk her away around the corner of the garage.

It was my night for crappy plans. When I got near her she snapped out of her freeze, sidestepped, and zigged away. The wrong way, back toward Woz's place. She must have thought I was the one doing the shooting.

Another shot. Bits of stucco burst from a wall. The kid froze in place again. This time I did too. We looked at each other. We came to the same conclusion. Get out of there immediately. We'd both taken a step toward the street when there was another shot and the girl screamed.

I looked down at her. There was blood on her arm. I was moving too fast to be sure how much. I grabbed her under the arms and rushed for the end of the alley. A fourth shot. Others, barely noticed, coming from back where Woz was.

The girl shrieked, louder this time. I tensed against the searing pain of a bullet ripping into my back.

It didn't come. I stumbled out of the alley with the kid in my arms, tripped, fell on top of her. She was still yelling her head off, only now there was crying too. I picked us both up and ran north along Cherokee.

A man came the other way. He could have been a bad guy. Or just one of Woz's deaf neighbors out for his evening constitutional. I didn't stick around to find out. The front door of the apartment building across the street was ajar. I ran for it. I went through the building and out the back door and emerged into another alley.

The kid was squirming and saying things twelve-year-olds never said in an adult's presence when I was a kid. I didn't want her running off in the wrong direction, so I hung onto her. I jogged a block before I felt safe enough to slow down. This took us to De Longpre. I crossed it, went a block west, and stopped in front of a sagging apartment building. There were palm trees in front of it, and under them a little patch of lawn with a lamp on a post hovering over it. I lay the kid down on the grass. She'd stopped crying, but tears sparkled on her cheeks and snot bubbled from her nose.

"Fuck you," she said.

I almost returned the compliment but managed to hold back. I looked her over. She was one of those impossibly beautiful children with Aztec or Inca or Mayan in their background. Long black hair, stunning features. She was wearing a T-shirt, shorts that were too big for her, and Nikes. "Kid," I said, "it's screwed enough that you've got a mouth like a longshoreman. But you might want to consider that I just rescued you from someone who was shooting at us." I knelt beside her. "Let me look at that arm."

As soon as I touched it she snatched it away. As she did she laid eyes on the blood. She stared at it and turned to me and erupted into more tears.

"It's okay," I said. The general purpose balm when you have nothing more comforting to say. "Come on, let me look at it. It's probably not so bad."

I heard the first siren. It could have been a fire engine or an ambulance, but I was fairly sure it was the first of many police cars that were going to be appearing on Leland Way.

I had a denim shirt on, unbuttoned, over a T-shirt. I took off the overshirt and used part of it to wipe the blood off her arm. She was lucky. It didn't look serious. Just a flesh wound. I tore at the shirt, trying to rip off a piece to use as a bandage. I got nowhere. I wrapped the whole thing around her arm.

"Where do you live?" I said.

"Nowhere."

"What's that supposed to mean?"

"I live somewhere for a while, and then I live somewhere else for a while."

"You mean like foster homes?"

"No."

"Then what?"

"You know. Wherever."

A street kid? Were there really such things, beyond the essays in the Sunday *Times* magazine? "Where are your parents?"

"They're dead."

"Other relatives?"

She shook her head.

I wanted to push it, but it wasn't the time. "Got to get you to the emergency room."

"No way."

"Kid, you're still bleeding. That shirt isn't going to sop it up for very long. You lucked out a minute ago, but that arm still needs attending to."

She watched my face. She clearly didn't trust me. I heard another siren, from a different direction. And the first one was louder.

"Well?" I said.

"Okay. You can take me somewhere and fix my arm."

For the first time since the alley I thought of Woz. I wondered if he was bleeding too. But standing there wondering wasn't doing us any good. I considered my next move. If the two of us went back for the truck, the cops—who were, judging from the sirens, seconds away from the site of the shootout—might spot the kid's bloody arm, and we'd never get away. I supposed I could leave her, get the truck, come back for her. But the muumuu lady or some other civic-minded neighbor who'd seen me through the window would probably bust me. Even if they didn't, the kid would likely be gone when I got back. And I felt responsible for her. Go figure.

"What's your name?" I said.

"Aricela."

"That's a pretty name."

"It's okay. What's your name?"

"Joe."

"That's a pretty name." Mimicking me.

I smiled. "It's okay."

She wanted to smile back, I was sure of it. "Where're you taking me, mister?"

"Joe, not mister. There's a hospital over towards Silver Lake. I'll find a phone and call a cab."

"Uh-uh." She shook her pretty little head. "No hospital."

"But—"

"Mister ... Joe ... you know I could get away from you if I really wanted to."

"You could?"

"Sure I could. Want to see?"

"Not particularly."

"So I'll hang out with you for a while, because I think you're probably okay, but no hospital."

"We've got to get your arm fixed up."

"So take me to your place."

"That's probably not a good idea."

"Why not?"

The real answer was, I was worried if I brought her some meddling do-gooder would find out and accuse me of child molestation or something. Unlikely? I'd read enough about the wrongfully accused, like that McMartin Preschool business a while back. It was a stupid reaction, but it was the first one I had. "It's too far away. I don't have enough money for a cab all that way and I don't know which buses to take."

"I know about the buses."

"I'll bet you do." I watched her. She was growing on me. "Anyway, I've got a better place to take you."

"Where?"

"A friend."

"What friend?"

"My girlfriend."

"Will I like her?"

"I do. That good enough for you?"

"I guess."

"Then let's go find us a phone booth."

•

Gina took the kid in stride. She merely tossed off a quizzical look. I responded with my all-will-be-explained one. She used a fabric sample to wrap Aricela's arm better, and we were off. Halfway to her place I remembered I still had the gun in my pocket. "Shit."

Aricela took enough time out from playing with the power windows to say, "You've got a mouth like a long-shoreman."

"Smartass kid," Gina said.

We stopped at a light. Gina looked at me and mouthed, "What's wrong?"

I leaned over and whispered, "I've got a gun in my pocket."

"Hey," Aricela said. "No secrets."

"And I thought you were just happy to see me," Gina said.

Our little vaudeville troupe made it back to her place

without further incident. The second we were in the condo Aricela said, "I gotta pee." After she closed the bathroom door I gave Gina the super-condensed version of my evening. Aricela came out; Gina hustled her back in to take care of her arm. I turned on the TV. Channel 6 had cut into its evening movie. They had a graphic that said BREAKING NEWS over a helicopter shot of a residential neighborhood.

They switched to their man on the ground, the male Hispanic version of Terry Takamura. "Behind me," he said, "and I can't get any closer because it's a crime scene, you see the bullet-riddled—"

Corpse of local resident Robbie Wozniak ...

"—Volkswagen that seems to be at the center of this event. You'll remember that two evenings ago, there was another shooting not far from here which also involved a dark VW. Police are mum as to whether the two events are related."

"Of course they're related, moron," I said.

"However, unlike the other night, there don't seem to be any casualties from tonight's events."

"Casualties?" I said. "What is this, frickin' Afghanistan?"

"At least, none have been found. But local residents say they saw a man with a shaven head running by holding a gun."

They went to tape. On the bottom of the screen it said NEIGHBORS. A guy with hair like Clarabelle the Clown said, "Yeah, there was this black guy came flying by with this big machine gun or something in his hand. Like this." He held his hands apart to show the hugeness of the gun.

A skinny blond with a nose ring said, "No, it was a white guy."

"Is it possible that there were two shaven-headed men?" said the reporter's disembodied voice. "One white and one black?" Cunning investigative reporting.

Clarabelle and his friend exchanged stupid looks. "Yeah, I guess so," said the guy.

Then they were back live, and the reporter said, "The shattering of the night by gunfire this evening came as a surprise to those and other Angelenos in this area. Though formerly a crime- and drug-ridden district, recent community efforts have resulted in a lessening of violence."

Tape again, and another NEIGHBOR giving his opinion. He was standing in the street, right in front of my truck. "Yeah, it's weird. I mean, we used to hear shots all the time around here, but not lately."

The NEIGHBOR was Woz.

"What about drugs?" said the invisible reporter.

"Oh, you know," Woz said. "A little pot around, is all. But you got that stuff everywhere in the city. Even Beverly Hills, you got your people who want to smoke a little dope."

They went live yet again, and the reporter kept babbling, and I tuned out. Somehow Woz—after, I assumed, pumping a bunch of rounds into the Volkswagen—had managed to escape the firefight and make it back to his house and stash his gun before the cops arrived. Then he'd moseyed outside to play innocent bystander. Of course, sooner or later somebody was going to put together that Squig, the other night's victim, lived on that very same street. But for the moment things were cool.

Meanwhile, the one or two baldies and any other miscreants had fled the scene, leaving behind their mortally wounded Beetle, a large piece of evidence if I ever saw one.

And speaking of stashing guns …

I went into Gina's bedroom, opened her closet, and took down the heavy Ferragamo shoebox at the back of the top shelf. I laid it carefully on her nightstand and took off the top. Nestled inside were Gina's gun and an ammunition clip. I made room for the pistol in my pocket, took it out, carefully placed it in.

But there was a kid in the place. She probably wouldn't be there long, but any length of time with a loaded gun and a child in the house is too long. I picked up the .22 again, pointed it away from me, managed to flip out the cylinder. I laid one of the ever-present fabric samples on the bed, and dumped the bullets.

"What're you doing?"

I jammed the gun in my pocket and snapped around. Aricela, newly cleaned up and with a wad of gauze taped to her arm, stood in the doorway to the bedroom. Gina's Frankie Goes to Hollywood T-shirt reached past her knees.

"I'm just emptying my pockets," I said. Without taking my eyes off her I reached down with my free hand, wrapped the sample around the bullets, shoved the package in other pocket.

"Looks like you're putting stuff *in* them."

"Looks can be deceiving, kid."

"How come you're acting all guilty?"

"Gina doesn't like me to empty my pockets on the bed."

"That's dumb."

I gave her my most dazzling grin. "I agree."

"I'm gonna tell Gina what you said."

"Go right ahead, kiddo." Kiddo?

"Are you coming to watch TV?"

"In a minute. Go ahead without me."

She went away. I closed the door and put "my" gun in with Gina's. I almost added the bullets, but decided it was a bad idea. From what I'd seen of Aricela, loading a revolver was well within the range of her talents. Though if she was capable of that she could probably shove a clip in the bottom of Gina's gun. Gina could deal with that.

I put the top on the box, replaced the box on the shelf, and left the bullets in my pocket. I wasn't totally comfortable with that—somehow, I thought, they might blow up in there—but it had to do for the time being.

I washed my face and went into the living room. Aricela was surfing channels. She came to a *Three's Company* on one of the nostalgia channels. Mr. Roper was trying to sneak a peek at one of the girls undressing. Aricela put down the clicker.

I went in the kitchen with Gina. She'd put on coffee and water for tea and dug out the makings of peanut butter and jelly sandwiches, as well as a box of assorted Pepperidge Farm cookies. She put everything together and took a sandwich and cookies and a glass of milk in to Aricela. She came back in and we shared a sandwich. In a low voice I expanded on what had gone on since I left Beverly Center. I concluded with how I stashed the "girl's gun" in her closet and told her my fears about her ammo. She said she'd take care of it. She went in the living room, saw the cookies were gone, replenished the supply. When she returned she said, "Now what?"

"I suppose I get hold of Woz and—what?"

She was shaking her head. "I mean about the kid."

"I don't know."

"We ought to call Family Services."

"We ought to," I said.

"It would be the right thing to do."

"I suppose. Though I guess we could do it in the morning."

"You mean, have her stay here tonight? She's probably got parents looking for her. We could cause them pain and anguish."

"She says her parents are dead."

"And you believe her?"

"Not totally." I craned my head around to check on Aricela. She'd moved on to *The Dick Van Dyke Show*, the one with the closet full of walnuts. "What if the Family Services people see her bullet wound? How're we going to explain that?"

"How can they tell it's a bullet wound? They're social workers, not forensics experts."

"They have ways." I took another look at the kid. She was two feet from the screen. Morey Amsterdam was on one side of her head and Rose Marie on the other. "I guess I just don't want to pour her into the system quite yet."

"The system."

"The bowels of bureaucracy."

"I think you've been hanging out with your hippie friends too much."

"Maybe."

She thought about it. "Okay. She stays here tonight. But in the morning we have to do something about her."

"Sounds like a plan."

"What about you?"

"What about me what?"

"Are you staying here tonight?"

"I hadn't thought about it. But, yeah, I think I will. I've missed sleeping with you. In the literal sense."

"Only in the literal sense?"

"Well, the other too, but right now the literal sense is what I need."

"You're sure we won't set little Aricela a bad example? I mean, two unmarried people sharing a bed?"

I shook my head. "I doubt it. I think little Aricela has seen a lot worse behavior than anything we could come up with."

Turned out I was on the money. She'd seen worse, all right. Way worse.

Did You Steal My Money?

Gina set to work convincing Aricela she ought to go to bed. I went in the bedroom, called information for Squig and Woz's number, turned down their offer to connect me for forty-five cents, dialed it myself.

"Yeah?"

"It's Joe."

"Hey, Joe. Whaddaya know?"

"I know you and your friends shot up the whole neighborhood a little while ago. I know you managed to avoid being killed or fingered and posed as an innocent bystander."

"Then you know as much as I do."

"Want to tell me what happened?"

"It wasn't much. I was sneaking up on the Vee-Dub when I heard the shots from over where you were. The guy in the Vee-Dub hears 'em too, and he jumps out with his gun out, and he sees me standing there, so he takes a shot. Only the gun jams. He throws it at me and takes off down the block. I run after him, I take a couple of shots."

"Hit him?"

"Don't think so. He kept running."

"Recognize him?"

"Uh-uh. Too dark. He had his head shaved, is all I could tell."

"You the one shot up the VW?"

"Yeah."

"What for?"

"Had to shoot something, know what I mean?"

No, psycho, not really. "Then what?"

"Then the cops came, and the TV people, and I was standing around like a good citizen, and guess what. The TV people interviewed me, and I was on TV."

"I know."

"You saw?"

"Of course I did. That's how I knew you posed as an innocent bystander."

"Oh. Right."

"So what about the other guy? The one who came after me?"

"I dunno. Never saw him. I figured you scared him away."

"Didn't happen that way. He started shooting, I got my ass out of there."

"Pussy."

"Better to be a live pussy than a dead duck." Reserve my place in the Stupid Remarks Hall of Fame. "You got any idea what those characters want?"

"Uh-uh."

"No drug deal gone sour, no screwing someone else's wife?"

"Nothing I can think of."

A couple of seconds went by. I wandered into the hall with the cordless.

"Where you now?" he said.

"Gina's."

"She's hot."

I looked into the living room. Gina and Aricela were deep in conversation. *En español*. Usually the only Spanish Gina uses is profanity.

"Good fuck?" Woz said.

I beat it back to the bedroom. "You know, this part of the conversation really isn't necessary."

"I bet she is. Most of those Latin chicks are."

"Can we get back to the subject?"

"What subject?"

"Guns and stuff like that."

"Yeah, sure."

"What do you plan to do next?"

"Fuck, Joe, I don't know. Lay low for a while, I guess. Maybe I'll go over to Goldie's and hang with her awhile."

"Good idea. Because sooner or later the cops are going to figure out that the guy who was shot the other night by someone in a dark VW lives on the same street as all the shit tonight went down on, and they'll come knocking. You're sure your stuff is hidden in a good place?"

"Yeah."

"Give me Goldie's phone number."

"What for?"

"What, you think I want to move in on her? So I can get hold of you if I need to."

We swapped old ladies' numbers, I told him to be careful, he told me he could take care of any assholes who tried anything, we hung up. I felt someone watching me. I turned toward the doorway. Aricela was standing there.

"What?" I said.

"I'm supposed to say good night."

"Supposed to?"

"Gina said I should."

"Then I guess you should."

"Can I stay here?"

"You can tonight."

"Cool beans. What about after?"

"You'll have to take that up with Gina."

"You're the man. What you say goes."

I went and knelt in front of her, gently put my hands on her shoulders. I spotted Gina a few feet away, in the hall, standing quietly with her arms crossed. "It doesn't always work that way anymore, kid."

"It doesn't?"

"Nope."

She thought about it a moment. "Okay. Good night."

"Night, kiddo. Sleep tight. Don't let the bedbugs bite."

"Ewww."

"It's an expression. There aren't any bedbugs."

She smiled. A big, broad one, the first I'd seen. "I knew that. I was just fooling." She turned to Gina. "You can show me my room now," she said.

•

Gina put Aricela to bed in the guest room and sat with her until the kid fell asleep, not more than five minutes. We got ready for bed and climbed in. She jumped right out, went to her dresser, pulled a white plastic bag from a drawer. "Here's what I bought you."

From the shape, it had to be a record. I pulled it out. Splinter. *The Place I Love.*

"A while back you said you were looking for this, and I saw a place called Amoeba Music, biggest record store I ever saw, and I went in and there it was."

"Wow," I said. "Thanks."

"You don't like it."

"I love it."

"It's the wrong one."

"It's the right one."

"Then what's wrong?"

"I already found it. The day I ran into Squig and Woz. Up in North Hollywood. Didn't I tell you?"

"Fuck."

"Actually, I found it twice. The second time at the Amoeba down here."

"Double fuck."

"It's the thought that counts."

"Screw that. I fucked up."

"How could you know?"

"That's not the point."

"Of course it's the point." I pulled the record out of the sleeve and did my inspection thing. "And as a matter of fact, the other copies are both scratched. I only bought the first one because it was better than nothing. And I bought the second because it was a little better than the first." I tilted it five or ten degrees. "This one's perfect."

"You can tell that by looking at it?"

"Sure I can."

"Bullshit."

"Okay, I can't. But can I tell you how much you getting this for me means?"

"I don't know, can you?"

"A whole hell of a lot. I love you."

And there it was. I'd said all three words, in the proper order, unprompted, spontaneously.

"I love you too," she said. "Jesus, are we sappy or what?"

"I vote for 'or what.'"

She got back in bed. We held each other for a while, then rolled over on our backs. We lay there, hips touching, with only the lamp on my nightstand on, each finding something of intense interest on the ceiling.

Finally I said, "What?"

I felt her shrug. "Nothing."

"What kind of nothing?"

"I was just thinking. It's kind of … different having a kid in the house."

"Different."

"You know. Familial."

"And you're a very familial person, with how you get along with your mother and everything."

"This is different."

I leaned on my elbow and propped my chin on my hand. "How is it different?"

She tilted her head and looked up at me. "I'm not sure."

"Gi, you've always said having kids was the last thing in the world you wanted to do."

"Giving birth to them. Raising them through diapers and kindergarten and tons of snot. But that child in the other room is readymade."

"You make her sound like a set of drapes."

"The interior designer talking." She waited for a response. I didn't have one. "Someone else has done all the grunt work. That's what I mean. I guess I'm thinking, wouldn't it be nice someday to have a grown child?"

"No."

"Maybe it would."

"If that's what you're after, the one in the other room still has a way to go. Not to mention that she's probably got parents looking for her."

"You think so?"

"Seems likely. I don't think a twelve-year-old—"

"Thirteen. She's thirteen. She told me that."

"Small for her age."

"So am I."

I kissed her forehead. "Thirteen, then. I don't think a thirteen-year-old could have been living on the street for very long like she says she has."

"She's pretty smart."

"The city's pretty nasty."

She chewed on that. I lay back down and studied the ceiling some more. After a while her breathing became slow and regular. I turned off the light and went to sleep.

•

Somebody was shaking me. I opened my eyes. Daylight. And Gina.

"What?"

"She's gone."

"Who?"

"Aricela."

"Who?

"Aricela. The kid. Remember?"

Consciousness returned. I sat up. "She's gone? Where?"

"I don't *know*, Portugal, you dumbass."

I threw off the covers, got up, went into the other bedroom. Sure enough, no Aricela. Just a slept-in bed. "Well, that takes care of that," I said.

"What are you talking about?"

"She's moved on. Had enough of us already."

"We have to find her."

"Why?"

"We're responsible for her."

"We are? After one night?"

"You're being a dick, Portugal, you know that?"

I went to the front door. The doorknob lock was on, the deadbolt off. I shot it into place. "At least she didn't climb out a window."

Gina glared, seemed about to say something, then dashed off into the kitchen. She opened the junk drawer, shuffled crap around, slammed it shut. "She took the money."

"What money?"

"The money I keep in here so if I spend everything in my purse I have some for pizza deliveries and stuff like that."

"How much?"

"I don't know, twenty-five, thirty dollars, something like that."

"How the hell did she guess where it was?"

"She knows people keep money in junk drawers. She's probably pulled this scam on dozens of people."

"You mean the one where she gets shot and goes to their houses to get bandaged up?"

"Now that you put it that way …"

"The kid needs it more than you do."

"You're obnoxious, you know that?" She pushed past me and into her bedroom. I followed. She grabbed some clothes, shed her nightgown, started dressing.

"What are you doing?" I said.

"Going to look for her. She couldn't have gotten far."

I grabbed her by the shoulders. "Stop."

She struggled to get loose. But only for a moment. Then she went limp.

Then she was crying.

Twice in four days. Definitely a record.

She collapsed against me. I let her let the tears out, stroking her hair, mumbling soothing words. We stood like that however long, until she asked for a tissue. I disentangled and got her one. She used it up, grabbed some more, wiped her eyes, blew her nose, dabbed her eyes some more. She threw them in the general direction of the wastebasket. One went in. She took half a step toward the basket, said, "Fuck it," looked at me and said, "What's *happening* to me?"

"I can hazard a guess."

"Go ahead and hazard."

"You're getting in touch with your mortality."

"Please."

"No, I mean it. A few nights ago you were nearly shot. That kind of thing happens, you start to think, another few inches and I could have died."

She frowned. "I have to admit, I had a few of those thoughts while I was up north, in the hotel room, all by myself."

I waited for more.

"I started to think, if I died now, who would care? God, this sounds so feeble. Like a fucking midlife crisis or something."

"Makes sense. You're in midlife."

"No, I'm not."

"Unless you're planning on living past ninety-five, you are."

"You know who I came up with? Who would care about me? Two people. You and my mother."

"Gi, there's lots of—"

"My mother would say I died because I didn't pray to the Virgin enough. She'd probably love it. She could be a martyr. So that leaves you."

"I would care a lot if something happened to you. When I saw you on the ground with the blood, I—"

"Don't say it. You don't need to say it. But you're just one person."

She sat on the bed, picked at a thread coming loose from the spread. "The kid just showed up when I was vulnerable. That's all. I was caught up in the meaning of life and there she was and some hormone turned on. I'm pre-menopausal, probably. I'll get over it. I'm almost over it already."

"Are you?"

"You're right. She's not our responsibility. We did our—what does your dad call it?"

"A *mitzvah*."

"Right. We did our *mitzvah* by rescuing her from the bad guys and feeding her and giving her a place to sleep for a night."

"Not to mention the thirty bucks."

"That too." She sighed, looked around the bedroom, stood up. "I'll get cleaned up and make us some breakfast." She came over, gave me a kiss, headed for the bathroom. I heard water running.

The doorbell rang. Gina yelled, "That's probably Rosa." Her cleaning woman. "Could you get it?"

"Sure."

I pulled my pants on, went to the door, opened it. It wasn't Rosa. It was Aricela, carrying a brown paper bag, which she held up to me. "I got bagels," she said.

I Can't Reach You

Noah's was the closest bagel place, just a block up and one over on Santa Monica Boulevard. But what they call bagels are puffy lumps of dough. Aricela, showing her street smarts, found the Brooklyn Bagel another block west. She got us a baker's dozen with a tub of cream cheese. I unloaded the bag while Gina proved that she wasn't over it after all. You would have thought the kid was hers, the way she reacted when she saw her.

When Aricela managed to break loose she went to the junk drawer, pulled it open, and solemnly put several bills and some change in. She slid it shut, looked at us, opened it again. Took out two dollars and put it in her pocket. "Delivery charge," she said.

I cut up a few bagels, put aside a couple to take home, plastic-bagged some and put them in the freezer. Gina set out plates and utensils, and we sat around eating breakfast like a nice little family. Rosa showed up and got to work. When we were done she and Aricela argued over who would clear the table. Aricela won. Rosa retreated into the bathroom.

When Aricela finished in the kitchen she looked at us like she was expecting praise, so we gave her some. She went into the living room, turned on the TV, and sat down to watch Channel 6's morning show, where "entertainment reporter" Timmy Gold was filling us in on Russell Crowe's latest debacle.

Gina and I went into the bedroom. I told her it was time to call Family Services. She said, just another day, okay? I said if it were her kid, would she want whoever had her to hold onto her an extra day before calling? She said, no, she guessed not.

I got out the phone book and found the number for L.A. County's Children and Family Services Department. I called and got the voice mail system. I pressed a bunch of numbers and pound signs and stars, sat through two for-better-service-we-may-be-monitoring-this-call   messages, took a side trip along Español Boulevard, finally got to All Representatives Are Busy Land. Where I sat. And sat. And sat some more. Then there was a click. I thought someone was coming on. Instead I got a dial tone.

I tried again. Different route, same results. I put down the phone and said, "I hate voice mail."

"Couldn't get through?"

"Not to a human being. Maybe we should take her down there."

"Where are they?"

"Near downtown."

"Pretty far."

"Yeah. Maybe we should try again in a little while."

"Yeah," she said. "In a little while."

I killed a few minutes looking at the *Times*, while Gina went in the living room and watched TV with Aricela. Nine o'clock came and went. They switched to Regis and Kelly.

Dennis Quaid was on, talking about his new movie, about some guy who always wanted to be a major league pitcher and became one at thirty-five. Kelly said something about following your dreams. She was an improvement on Kathie Lee. Talk about damning with faint praise.

I tossed the paper aside and joined them in the living room. "I'm going to head out." I said.

"Where you going?" Aricela said.

"Home."

"Can I go with you?"

Gina and I said "uh" several times each. Then she said, "It's probably better if you stay with me."

"Why?" Aricela said.

"Because."

"Why because?"

"Just because."

"That's what they always say."

"Who?" I said. "Your parents?"

"I *told* you. My parents are dead. It's what adults always say when they want me to do something but don't have a reason. It's okay, Gina. I'll stay with you."

"Good," Gina said. She looked at me, smiled, said, "How are you getting to your truck?"

Right. It was still over at Squig and Woz's. "I'll take the bus."

"Dumb. We'll drive you."

Twenty minutes later we pulled up next to my truck. I got out and checked it over. No bullet holes that I could see. Woz's house was quiet. The VW's corpse was gone.

I squatted by Gina's door. "Don't forget that call."

"I won't." She craned her neck to kiss me. "Now get going. Us girls have stuff to do."

I stood up straight and the Volvo drove away. I eyed Woz's house again. Decided nothing good could come of knocking on his door. I fired up the truck and drove home.

•

There was a note on the door from Theta, attached by a little sticker with a picture of a flower. She'd accepted a UPS package for me. I plucked the note off and went inside. I took the fabric sample full of bullets from my pocket and shoved it under a pile of socks in my dresser. I was still half-convinced they could blow up at any time.

I checked the machine. No calls from Elaine or anyone else. I fed the canaries and talked to them awhile. I don't know why I habitually did this. They never talked back. It just seemed healthier than talking to myself.

I took a shower and went out back to air-dry. I got an idea. I'd turn the tables on Theta. I went in and threw on some shorts, assembled a few cinder blocks, climbed up on them to say, "Hey!"

She was sunbathing. Nude. It seemed fair. She'd seen me that way. But I was one up on the other woman soaking up rays, an early-twenties blond who looked like a *Playboy* centerfold, right down to the dark pubic hair.

Theta spotted me. "Hey, neighbor."

"Hey."

The other one shrieked and grabbed a towel to cover up. "Theta! You said no one would see."

"Guess I was wrong. Life in the big city. Joe, this is my cousin Ronnie. From Arkansas. Ronnie, Joe."

"Hey," I said.

Ronnie wrapped the towel tighter and wiggled a couple of fingers. "Hey."

I looked at Theta but didn't say anything.

"What's the matter?" she said.

"Um …"

"Oh, I get it." She casually picked up a towel and draped it over her chest and crotch. "Better?"

"Yeah. Thanks. You have a package for me?"

"Sure do." She and her towel got up and went into the house. Ronnie and her towel followed. Theta came back out with a brown cardboard box a foot square and a couple of inches thick.

I took it, thanked her, and said, "Tell the kid not to worry about it."

"Shit, no. I'm gonna give her a hard time. Teach her to go around naked." I stepped down. I stood there a minute with lust in my heart, then went inside and looked over my package. It was from someone named Frank de Vinci in New Jersey. I hesitated. Residual anthrax anxiety. Then I got the box cutter from my junk drawer and slit the packing tape. Inside, nestled among a bunch of biodegradable noodles, was something a little bigger than one of my eight-by-tens, half an inch thick, wrapped in the *New York Post*. The headline screamed IT'S CHANDRA. They'd discovered the unfortunate Ms. Levy's body a week or so back.

I removed my prize, laid it on the dining room table, went back outside and dumped the noodles on the lawn, so next time I watered they'd melt into the ground. I was sustaining the suspense. When I'd sustained it all I could I went in and ripped off the newspaper.

It was an autographed eight-by-ten of Pete Townshend, in a dime-store frame. From the early seventies by the look of it, windmilling a guitar to death. Incredibly cool.

There was a sheet of paper taped to the back. I scanned it.

Somebody'd bought the photo on eBay—the price was cut off—and gave my house for the shipping address. Somebody whose ID was WHDesigner. WH for West Hollywood. Scrawled at the bottom was a note from Frank da Vinci himself. "Lady who bought this said to tell you it's for inspiration. Hope you like it. Rock on."

What Kind of People
Are They?

I took Frank da Vinci's advice. I was in the bedroom beating "Pinball Wizard" to a pulp when the phone rang. "Hello?"

"Hey, Portugal. Burns here."

"Hi, Burns. How's the leg?"

"Better. I'm curious. You there last night?"

"There, where?"

"The big shootout in Hollywood."

"Oh, that. I heard about it on TV this morning."

She heard the hitch in my voice. "You were, weren't you?"

"What makes you think that?"

"Come on, Joe, don't play games."

It was only the second time she'd called me by my first name. "Yeah. I was there. Sort of got caught in the crossfire."

"But you got away before my esteemed colleagues got there."

"Yeah. Why'd you think I was there?"

"I saw this Wozniak character on the news last night."

"Oh."

"Standing in front of your truck. The shot-up Volkswagen …I don't suppose you know who put the holes in it."

"I didn't see it happen."

"I see." She waited long enough for me to create a whole future where I told her Woz did it, he went to prison on firearms charges, and however many years later got out, tracked me down, and cut my balls off.

I didn't get a chance to squeal. "I got your info," Burns said.

"Great."

"First this Deanna Knox woman. One minor pot bust in '76. Got probation. Been clean since."

"That's it?"

"Did you think there'd be more?"

"I don't know what I thought. What about Woz?"

"Let me save him for last. First the missing Mr. Bonner."

"What have you got?"

"Not much there either."

"This dinner I'm buying you's starting to sound like a ripoff."

"Some drug stuff for him too, back in the early seventies. Heroin. But he cleaned up his act and was a good little boy after that."

"What about his disappearance?"

"There's nothing."

"There must be."

"Portugal, it's not like he was living with a wife and seven kids and went out for a pack of cigarettes and never came back."

"I suppose not."

"No one's ever asked the department to look for him."

"What if I asked now?"

"Don't push it."

"Yeah, okay. What about Woz?"

"Small stuff. Pot, disturbing the peace. Oh, and a DUI. Never spent more than a night in jail. A model citizen."

"That it?"

"Why shouldn't it be?"

"No reason."

"There is one thing more."

"What?"

"His father has a record."

"So does mine. It doesn't make him a bad person."

"Him, the father, or him, your friend?"

"Either one."

"His father knew your father."

"He did? How'd you find that out?"

"One of the guys I work with goes way back."

"How'd they know each other?"

"Seems they did some jobs together back then. Wozniak Senior, full name Herbert no middle name Wozniak, was into the same small-time stuff as your father. Truck hijackings, things like that."

"Was he there the night my father got arrested?"

"If he was, he got away before the police arrived."

"Has he been in prison?"

"Yes. Not long after your father, he got busted for breaking and entering. Went to San Quentin."

"Same place my father was."

"Uh-huh."

"Do you think they—"

"Portugal."

"What?"

"Go to the source."

"The source doesn't like to talk about that stuff."

"Okay, then. That's all I have. I'll be going now."

"You think I should ask him."

"Up to you."

"But if it were you, you would."

"Yes."

"Though what it would have to do with anything, I couldn't guess. I mean, his father, my father. It doesn't really have any bearing on anything that's going on now."

"Some detective you are."

"What do you mean?"

"I mean, don't you think it's an awfully big coincidence you and your friend ending up at the same runaway rescue operation, given that your fathers worked together?

"That's in the files?"

"Enough of it was."

"That's probably all it is. A coincidence."

"I don't think so, and neither do you."

"I don't?"

"Talk to your father. You might find out something useful. Look, I've got to go. My sister's coming to take me to the doctor."

"Okay. Thanks. For all of it."

"You're welcome. When I get back home I'm getting out my Zagat Guide. Find us a nice expensive place. See you." She was gone.

I put the phone down. It rang again. "Hello?"

"You pussy."

"Enough with the pussy already. What's up?"

"We got to talk."

"What about?"

"All this shit that's going down."

"Fine. Let's talk."

"Not on the phone."

"You getting paranoid?"

"Café of 1000 Dances. At six."

"That place on Melrose?"

"Yeah. Later, man."

Five minutes later the phone went off yet again. "Grand Central Station."

"Joe?"

"That's me."

"It's Deanna."

"Hi."

"Let's get started."

"I suppose we ought to."

"Can we get together tonight? We can figure out a plan."

"I'm not sure. My social calendar's filling up. Let me check." I took a beat. "Your place or mine?"

"I've been over there. Your turn. Eight?"

"Sure."

"Got a pencil?"

"Yeah."

She gave me an address on Yucca in Hollywood. A lousy part of town.

"One more thing," she said. "Mott's back."

"Congratulations, I guess."

"Gee, thanks." *Click.*

•

I dialed the phone before someone else had a chance to call me.

"Hello?"

"Catherine?"

"Yes?"

"Joe."

"Long time, no see."

Catherine was one of my father's housemates. In her sixties, a widow who resembled my mother more than a little, and a nice Catholic girl to balance out my father and their other roomie Leonard.

"I've been kind of busy," I said.

"You and my daughter."

"Your daughter lives in Alaska. Kind of tough for her to drop by."

"They have airports up there. Hang on, I'll get your father on the phone."

Half a minute went by. Somebody started up a jackhammer next door at Theta's. The noise stopped, replaced by a howl of pain.

"Joseph?"

"No, Dad, it's five other guys."

"Last time it was six."

"One of them joined the Marines. How you doing?"

"I'm doing good. I got a hot date tonight."

"That's fantastic. Who with?"

"A girl from the senior center. A *shikse*."

"What's her name?"

"Mary Elizabeth."

"A good *shikse* name. Think you'll get lucky?"

"I should be so lucky as to get lucky. What's up?"

"I need to ask you about something."

"So ask."

"I want to ask in person."

"You're going to make time to visit your father?"

"Dad, I'm sorry, I've been—"

"Yes, yes, busy, I know. Joseph, it's all right. You have your life."

"You doing anything this afternoon? Say around four?"

"That would be good. Come then. We'll have a nice man-to-man talk."

"Great. I'll see you then. Thanks, Dad."

"What are you thanking me for?"

"For … I don't know. For making the time for me, I guess."

"You don't need to thank me for that. Four o'clock. Don't be late. I'll need time after to get ready for my *shikse*."

"I'll be on the dot."

"Good. Good-bye, son."

"Good-bye, father."

I put down the phone, called Gina, got the machine. Decided not to try the cell. If she was in the middle of dropping Aricela off with the authorities, I wanted nothing to do with it.

So Sad About Us

I had some time to kill before I was due at my father's. I drove up to Amoeba, found a spot down the street, and fed the meter some change. I was about to go in when my eyes fell on a sign on one of the office buildings across Sunset. There was something I had to do. It was as good a time as any.

Somebody probably thought the lobby looked classy, but mostly what it was was overdesigned. Something was wrong with the fake waterfall, unless a puny dribble was part of the design. There were a couple of swoopy metal sculptures lying around.

A guard accosted me and asked who I wanted to see. I told her. She said that without an appointment I wasn't liable to get in. I gave her my name and said to call up. She did, looked surprised, had me sign a book, and gave me a pass. I took an elevator up to seventeen. The lobby it dumped me into had lots of wood and leather and gold records on the walls. I went to the desk. A pretty young man dressed all in black sat there. He had one of those tiny ear-phone-microphones on. He held up a finger, told whoever was on the other end not to get their panties in a twist, mashed a button on the phone, and looked up at me.

"Joe Portugal," I said. "To see Ms. Chapman."

"She's expecting you."

He pressed another button and announced my arrival. He nodded, clicked off, told me she'd be out in a few minutes. I sat on a leather loveseat and leafed through a copy of *Billboard*. I found the charts and counted how many of the top hundred albums were by artists whose work I was familiar with. I came up with eight, and two of those were dead.

Bonnie came out, dressed in dark green and looking fabulous. We exchanged air kisses and she led me to her office. It was bigger than anyone needs. A window stretched the width of the far wall, unveiling the spread of Los Angeles below. I walked to it and took in the view. I probably could have seen Leland Way if I knew where to look.

There were more gold records, along with photos of people I'd heard of and people I hadn't. A couple of framed certificates, a picture of Darren and his band, another of Bonnie kneeling by Papa Cass or another basset hound and rubbing its ears.

I pointed at Darren's band shot. "What were they called?"

"Changing Its Spots." She turned toward the bar. "Can I get you something to drink?"

I had a bottle of Pellegrino from the minifridge. We sat on the leather sofa and chitchatted. I asked about Darren's band again.

"Why are you so interested?" she said.

I shrugged. "Just making conversation."

"No, you're not."

"I guess you're right." I sipped my pricey water. "It's just that, out of all the weirdness since we all got reacquainted, I think you having a grown son is the hardest to accept."

"I see." She got up and went to a dark wood entertainment unit. She pulled out a drawer at the bottom, grabbed a CD, brought it back. "Here."

I took a look. The cover showed a photo of a giraffe with its legs spread wide apart, drinking from a water hole. I pried the case open, took out the booklet, leafed through. Four guys, four haircuts. One shaved head, one longhair, a black guy in dreads, and a fairly shaggy Darren.

"Take it home, give it a listen," she said.

"I will. Is Doldrum Records a branch of Hysteria?"

"It's not a branch of anything. They made the CD themselves and thought it would be more impressive if it looked like it came from a real company."

"Why isn't he on your label?"

"Two reasons. First, the old bit about wanting to get where you get by your own efforts. First time I came to see them he told me he didn't want any favors."

"Worked out well."

"What do you mean?"

"I'm guessing the second reason is they weren't good enough for you to want to record them."

"How'd you know?"

"Your reaction the other night, when I asked how good he was."

She watched my eyes. "You didn't come here to talk about Darren."

"No. I got distracted. Or I was stalling."

"So why did you?"

"I need to tell you something."

"I thought so."

Why was I so damned nervous? I caught her scent. That didn't help. "Do you know how many times I've kicked myself for turning you down?"

"How many?"

"Hundreds. Thousands, maybe."

"That's very sweet, Joe."

"It's the truth."

"What am I supposed to say?"

"That you've regretted it too."

"I've regretted it too."

"Now *that* sounds sincere."

"It is." She smiled, touched a hand to my face. "It is. Trust me."

I looked away. Her fingers slipped off. I turned back to her and took her hand. "This is the part where, in the movies, someone always says, 'It's not too late.'"

"This isn't the movies."

"No," I said. "And I'm with Gina."

"Lucky girl." She glanced down at our hands, decided they were okay where they were. "That's why you came here today? To tell me that?"

"It had to be said, if we're going to work together. I just felt the need."

"I'm glad you told me."

"Me too," I said.

A Quick One, While He's Away

I rang my father's doorbell at twenty seconds to four. Rang it again at ten seconds after. I heard someone opening the little brass door that covered the peephole, saw Leonard looking out. I don't know why he bothered. He was legally blind.

"Joseph?"

"It's me."

Now I knew two people named Leonard. This one and Squig, formerly Lenny, Jones. I filed this piece of useless information away with the rest of the dross.

He let me in, we told each other we were fine, and he said my father was out back. I stopped in the kitchen to give Catherine's cheek a kiss. She said I looked well and asked about Gina. I said she was fine. She asked when we were getting married. I said it wouldn't be anytime soon. She smiled like she knew better and went back to her chicken breasts.

I stuck my head out the back door. "Dad?"

He was over in the corner, on his knees, pulling weeds from a patch of his beloved posies. They were really impatiens, but he called anything that flowered and died the same year a posy. He looked up at me, glanced at his watch, said, "You're late."

"I rang the doorbell before four."

"I heard. I was just breaking your balls."

"I need to make a couple of quick phone calls before we talk."

"Go. Just remember I don't have a lot of time."

"Your hot date."

"You got it, kid."

I checked my machine first. Nothing but a guy who just happened to be in my neighborhood and was dying to install Dish Network at my house. I erased him, hung up, called Gina. She picked up on the first ring. "Yes?" I heard the TV in the background.

"Is that any way to answer the phone?"

"Oh, it's you. I've had three telemarketers in the half hour we've been home. Two long distances and a satellite system."

"The satellite one just happened to be in your neighborhood, right?"

"Right."

"You said 'we've.'"

"I did?"

"So how's our little girl?"

The TV noise faded as she took the portable into another room. "She's fine."

"Did you call the Family Services people?"

"Yes."

"And?"

"You know how I hate voice mail systems."

"I'm the technophobe here, not you."

"Oh. Right."

"You didn't try very hard, did you?"

"No."

"Gi. We can't just hold onto this kid like she's a lost kitten or something."

"I know."

"So what's the problem?"

"I asked her about her parents again. She swore they were dead."

"Someone must be guardianing her."

"One more night."

"No."

"Come on. It's after four now. Even if I got through, they wouldn't be able to do anything until tomorrow."

"I don't think these people stick to nine-to-five."

"One more night."

"I just don't—"

"Joseph!" It was my father, standing just inside the back door, with his lower lip puffed out. I held up a finger. He went back out.

"I've got to go," I said. "We'll talk about this some more."

"Yes, Daddy."

"Very funny. Bye."

"Bye."

When I went out my father was sitting at the table. A fancy wood thing Gina'd picked up for a song. I took a chair and moved closer to him.

"Something going on with your girlfriend?" he said.

"You could say that."

"What?"

"Long story, Dad. And since you don't have a lot of time, one I'm not going to tell now."

"Whatever you say. So. What do you want from me?"

"It's about the old days."

"Which old days?"

"The old days before you went to prison. And while you were there."

"You know I don't like to talk about those days."

"Yes."

"Then why are you asking?"

"Because it's important."

He looked at the back of his hand. He used a fingernail on the other one to remove the soil from under a nail on the first. Now the dirt was under the new nail. He made a face and looked up at me.

"This girl," he said. "The one I have the date with."

"I'd love to hear about her, Dad, but does it have anything to do with—"

He held up a hand—the one that now had the dirty fingernail—and I shut up.

"I've been seeing her for a while."

"Define 'a while.'"

"Two months. More, maybe."

"I had no idea."

He tilted his head toward the house. "Those two know. You can't hide anything from them. But I haven't said anything to anyone else."

"You didn't want to have to explain if things went wrong."

He looked astounded that I was capable of such insight. "You got it."

"And this is leading where?"

He leaned forward, put a hand on mine, said, "I told her."

"Told her what?"

"About jail and everything."

"And?"

"She said it doesn't mean anything. Water under the dam."

"Over the dam."

"Over, under, what's the difference?"

"How much did you tell her?"

"Everything. I didn't just tell her about being a hoodlum and going to jail. I *discussed* it."

"I'm not getting you."

"I talked like I would talk to you about going to *shul* last Saturday. Like it's something in my life that happened just like anything else in my life that happened."

"That's good, Dad."

"I haven't said anything to anyone about this for all these years because I thought it wasn't fit conversation. Even with my son."

"And now you do."

"Yes."

"You've had an epiphany."

"A what?"

"A moment of enlightenment."

"Now you're a Hindu."

He still had his hand on mine. He saw it there, reclaimed it, leaned back in his chair. "So what do you want to talk about?"

"Herb Wozniak."

A smile grew. He nodded slowly, said, "Herb. I haven't seen him since—"

"Jail?"

"I was going to say, since January."

"You still know him?"

"I don't see him much. But I saw him in January. At the dry cleaners. I was picking up, he was bringing in." He turned and looked in the house through a window. There was a cuckoo clock in there. "Getting later," he said.

"Remember your epiphany. Talk to me."

He looked at me again, smiled, said, "This has to do with all the shooting."

"What shooting?"

"Don't fuck around with your father."

It shut me up. He didn't use the word often.

"I saw it on the television," he said.

"I know. We discussed this. The story about Squig getting shot."

"And the other. This business with the Volkswagen."

"What makes you think I was—"

"I saw your truck. I saw Robbie Wozniak."

He pulled a half-smoked cigar and a disposable lighter from his shirt pocket. He flicked on the flame and held it to the cigar, which he effortlessly rolled between his fingers to get an even burn. When I was a kid, I loved to watch that. It was such a grown-up-man thing. I knew when I was able to do that, I'd have made it out of childhood. But the only time I ever tried a cigar, I ended up puking my guts out.

He got the stogie lit, took it out of his mouth, regarded the end with approval. "Herb Wozniak and me," he said, "we didn't travel in the same circles a lot. He had his guys and I had mine. But once in a while we got together for something. A big job, needed more men. He was a hell of a guy. You could count on him. And strong like a bull."

"Was he with you the night you got busted?"

"No. He was up in Fresno. There was a truckload of girdles."

"Girdles."

"There was big money in girdles those days. Herb wanted me to go, but I already had the thing with my regular crew." He drew on the cigar and blew a smoke ring. Another man thing I loved when I was a kid. "Sometimes I wish I would have gone with him that night. Everything would have been different."

"Water under the dam."

He looked at me, frowned, went on. "Anyway, I got sent up for killing that guy—"

"Which I'm still not convinced you did, by the way—"

He dismissed me with a wave of the hand. "I was up there six months, and Herb showed up. He picked the wrong truck too. We started palling around together up there, him and me, a lot closer than we were on the outside. We talked about a lot of things."

"What kinds of things?"

"Some of the old guys, the real gangsters from the thirties and the forties. And what we were going to do when we got out. And our families." A toke on the cigar. "How much we missed them, and how *meshugga* we were for getting in a line of work that put us away from them for so long." He stared at the cigar, stubbed it out, put it back in his pocket. He never smoked them for long. "One thing we talked about was our boys."

"I had no idea."

"There are a lot of things you have no idea about. Your mother, may she rest in peace, and Herb's wife Selma, we would hear about you from them. In letters mostly, because it was hard for them to visit." He shook his head. "I thought it was bad with you, all the trouble you were getting in, but then I heard the kinds of things Robbie did. I was getting off lucky. One day he broke the camel's back and that was that."

I knew about the camel. Robbie and some biker friends had a party one day when his mother was at work. One of the bikers ODed.

"For three months," my father said, "Herb couldn't think about anything but Robbie. Wondering where he was, and blaming himself for what happened. He was like a lunatic. Then Selma came one visiting day. She said she found Robbie. He was in a place up in the Hills, a place for problem kids like him. Selma was crazy happy because the boy was getting straightened out. Mostly I think she was happy to know he was all right and that she wasn't the one who had to deal with him."

"Is this leading where I think it's leading?"

He looked in at the clock again. Then back to me. "I can be a little late. She's a good woman."

"I'll have to meet her."

"Soon. We'll go on a double date. Where was I?"

"Selma telling Herb about Robbie getting his act together at Mark and Ginger's. I assume it's Mark and Ginger's we're talking about."

He neither confirmed nor denied it. "Herb still had some friends around here, a couple of cops included, and they checked the place out and found out it was legit. So we made arrangements."

"What kind of arrangements?"

"You're a smart boy. You figure it out."

"You're saying you're responsible for me ending up at Mark and Ginger's."

He did the poochy-lip thing, and I thought I'd totally misjudged where this was going and he was about to chastise me for being such an idiot. Then he said, "Not just me. Your mother too."

"Mom? I don't get it."

"She talked to your friends. She found out where you liked to go."

"My friends? My friends told my mother about me?"

"They were worried about you too."

"You're saying it wasn't an accident that Mark found me at Ben Frank's that day."

He nodded. "Your mother came home, found you took your things, she knew what to do. Called the number we got from Herb and Selma. We were lucky. We got to this Mark right away. He looked at his list. Ben Frank's was at the top." He flashed a smile. "I used to like Ben Frank's a hell of a lot too. It's gone now, did you know that?"

"Uh-huh."

"You're not saying anything."

"I'm a little stunned."

"Why should you be stunned?"

"I've gone around all this time being so proud of myself for running away from home and not ending up dead or worse. And after all these years I find out my parents arranged the whole thing. Why didn't you ever tell me?"

"It never came up. Plus, you know, like we talked about a little while ago. I wasn't comfortable."

"Do you know I've also spent all these years thinking Mom dying so young was at least partially my fault?"

"I suspected."

"You *suspected?*"

"I'm not the only one who hasn't told the other a lot about his life. And besides, when I got out, you were mostly over it. Or hiding it."

He was right. The guilt was overwhelming when I first moved home. Then time did its thing, and the guilt diminished until I could bury it under a mental rock. Always there, not often considered.

"Did Elaine know any of this?"

He shook his head, then checked the cuckoo clock one more time. "Now I really got to get going. Look at these fingernails. You think I ought to shave? I shaved this morning, but you know my beard. Like steel wool. Yes. I should shave. I want a smooth face for Mary Elizabeth, you know what I mean?"

Was my father leering? This was a bit disconcerting. "Just a couple more questions, Dad. Did—"

He held up a hand. "Not now. Another time, we'll talk more. We'll talk a lot more now, won't we?"

"I guess we will."

"I got to say, I'm happy about that."

"Me too."

"Good. Now get your *tuchis* out of here and let me make myself handsome."

•

Café of 1000 Dances was five minutes from my father's place, on the strip of Melrose that used to be the West Coast headquarters of hip. I didn't have change for a meter and everything for a block on either side of Melrose was permit parking. I left the truck on Clinton and hiked back. The breeze was up and the jacarandas were shedding. Spent lavender blossoms lay everywhere. I could smell an orange tree somewhere around.

Outside the café two young women in black gave me the once over. They saw I wasn't worth their valuable time and went back to their conversation. An old man in a gray beret sat with a sketchpad, drawing what was on the next table over, a collection of salt and pepper shakers set up like bowling pins. The headpin was a bottle of Tabasco sauce.

There was a juke box just inside the entrance, playing the Searchers' "Needles and Pins." I scanned the offerings. The Zombies and Charlie Pride, the Sex Pistols and Barry Manilow, No Doubt and Vic Damone. There were framed 45s all over the walls. The nearest was "I Got Caught in the Washing Machine" by someone named Johnny Shur. "Hey Jude" was next over.

They had a row of purple vinyl booths, some Formica tables, a long counter. The young woman behind the counter wore a tight T-shirt advertising the place. She had a pencil behind her ear and hair piled up on top of her head like waitresses since time immemorial. "Anywhere," she said.

I slid into a booth. Another snug-shirted babe, this one blond, came by with a menu. I sent her off for an iced tea and checked my watch. A little after five. I was way early. I spotted a pile of *New Times* and got up to get one. Knee-jerk liberal stuff, but not as bad as the *Weekly*, and it didn't come off on your fingers. The waitress came back with my tea and asked if I was ready to order. I told her I was waiting for someone and she went away. I tasted the tea. It wasn't bad for that mango stuff.

I sat back and watched what was going on. I'd expected a

crowd of self-conscious fake hipsters. There were some of those, but there were some real hipsters too. The couple at the next table, deconstructing the latest art-house movie: fake. The buzz-cut woman at the counter, reading Kierkegaard: real. I can't explain the difference. I just know them when I see them.

I read my rag and got caught up on the latest municipal scandal. After twenty minutes I ordered a piece of blueberry pie. That kept me going until Woz showed up at six. On the way to the booth he stopped to say hi to the woman behind the counter. She asked how he was doing and he said, You know. He said, You? and she said Red had gone back to Portland. He told her that was too bad, she said, Thanks, he said she'd find someone else. She smiled like she didn't think it was true and Woz finished his trip to the table.

"Poor kid," he said as he sat opposite me. "Don't know how to pick 'em."

"Like you said, the right guy will come along."

"Who said anything about guys? Chick's a lesbo."

"Then the right girl will come along."

"You got anything against lesbos?"

"No, Woz, I don't have anything against lesbos."

"Some of my best friends are lesbos."

"Mine too. Can we stop with the lesbos?"

He picked up a menu and immediately tossed it aside. "They got great grilled cheese." He turned, caught our waitress's eye. "Hey, Rhonda. Get us a couple of grilled cheeses over here, and some O-rings. And coffee and a root beer."

He faced me again, looked me over. "You okay?"

"Yeah, I think so. I just found out something I really didn't expect."

"What's that?"

I told him about my conversation with my father. His root beer and coffee came and he alternated between them as he listened. Our sandwiches showed up. Woz was right. The best grilled cheese in memory, even better than Bonnie's.

I finished the story, and we killed our sandwiches. Woz leaned back, stifled a belch, said, "Your old man and mine. Who would've known?"

"You didn't?"

"No idea. What was yours up for?" Something I'd left out.

"Does it matter?"

"What, it was murder or something? The look on your face. It was."

"I don't think he did it."

He nodded like he was humoring me, wiped his mouth on the back of his hand, said, "Want to know what I found out?"

"Yeah."

"Nothing."

"Heavy, man."

"Yeah, I asked around, everyone I knew. Then I had everyone I knew ask everyone they knew. Nothing. No one knows why these guys are shooting up half the band."

Duh.

"Hey," Woz said. "'Smoke on the Water.' I never get tired of that one. Why you looking at me like that?"

"What you just said. About shooting up the band."

"What about it?"

"I've been assuming all the shooting is about you and Squig. What if it actually has to do with the band?"

"Why would someone want to fuck up our band?"

"I don't know. But don't you think it's worth pursuing?"

"Like how?"

"Like—" Good question. Which of my celebrated investigatory techniques was I going to put into play? "I don't know. Maybe we should talk to Bonnie, see if she has any ideas. Someone who wouldn't want her to record again, though if that were the case I would think they'd go after her instead. Because you can always get new musicians."

"Hey, thanks a lot."

"And here's another thought. Maybe we should warn some people."

"Like Frampton, you mean."

"And Gina and Goldie and anyone else whose place someone might think we were at."

"You're a little crazy here."

"Maybe. But it doesn't hurt to be careful. You got Frampton's number?"

He pulled out his wallet. "Son of a bitch has business cards. Fucking weird." He found the card and tossed it across the table.

I slid out of the booth and found the pay phone in the back by the restrooms. I dialed Gina's number. A girlish voice said, "Vela residence."

It took me a second. "Aricela?"

"Is that Joe? Hi, Joe. When are you coming home?"

It was home already. How nice. "I'm not sure. Put Gina on, would you?"

"Okay. But come soon."

I heard her yell, "Gina," and a few seconds later a couple of words back and forth. Then Gina came on. "Hi."

"Do me a favor. Stay there."

"What do you mean?"

"There. In the condo. And make sure the door is locked. And the windows."

"I live on the third floor. You really think I need to lock the windows to prevent whoever it is you're warning me about from coming in through them? And who *are* you warning me about?"

"We think all this shooting might have something to do with the band."

"Why would that be? And who's 'we'?"

"Woz and me. I'm just being cautious. But I'd feel more comfortable if you didn't go out."

"But we were going to go see *Ice Age*. "

"Put it off. Find a movie on cable. Or have those Kozmo.com people deliver one."

"Kozmo went under months ago."

"Cable, then. Just do it, okay? And I'll be over later."

"Aricela will be disappointed."

"Life in the big city. And tomorrow we *really* have to do something about her."

"I know." Her tone told me she didn't know, not at all.

"Okay," I said. "I'll be over as soon as I can. Love you, babe."

"Love you too."

That word again. It was tripping off our tongues like we'd been saying it for years.

I dialed the home number that was handwritten on the back of Frampton's card.

"Yeah."

"Frampton?"

"Who's this?"

"Joe."

"Oh, hey. Look, I can't talk, we got a situation here."

"What kind of situation?"

"Someone on the block called the cops about a car parked in front of their house. Cops showed up, the car took off, the cops went after it. Look, I can't—"

"What kind of car?" I said.

"It was a Beetle," Frampton said. "A silver Beetle."

Had Enough

I hung up and told Woz what was happening.

"Let's go," he said.

"So you can shoot up Frampton's neighborhood too?"

"If I have to." He threw some money on the table on the way out. Fifteen seconds later we were at the Barracuda. It was right there on Stanley. Permit parking didn't concern Woz.

We ran several stop signs on the way, used the shoulder to skirt a tie-up on the 405, hit eighty-five on the Marina Freeway. Nineteen minutes after we left, Woz pulled to the curb on a residential street off Alla. A cop car was double-parked at the end of the block. Woz turned off the engine and told me to get out.

"What for?"

"So you can go see what's going on."

"Why don't you go see what's going on?"

"Look at me. Look at you. Who's gonna get the cops' attention?"

I got out, crossed the street, and meandered a few houses down, until I could see all the cars near the end of the block. Frampton and two county cops stood on his front walk, with a few neighbors hanging around to view the excitement.

I went back and made my report.

"Good job," Woz said.

"Thank you, Fearless Leader. Now what?"

"Now we wait."

"For what?"

"For the cops to leave."

I climbed back in. Woz started up an Iron Butterfly cassette. We were deep into the interminable drum solo in "In-A-Gadda-Da-Vida" when the cop car passed by. Woz popped the cassette. We got out and walked down the block. Frampton was still out front, wearing droopy shorts and a tank top, filling the neighbors in. He saw us coming, looked surprised, recovered quickly. When we reached his house he hustled us inside. He did have a dog, a little white yappy thing.

As soon as the door closed Woz said, "What happened?"

"What happened?" Frampton said. "I'll tell you what happened. We had a goddamned high-speed chase right here in our neighborhood. Jesus, guys."

"Any shooting?" I said.

"No, thank God. There's lots of kids around here. I guess the guys in the Beetle saw the cops coming. They pulled out into the street and almost ran over a kid on a bike. Then they went squealing around the corner. The cops went after them. Sirens, the whole works. He turned on Woz. "This is your fault."

"What're you talking about?"

"This is a nice neighborhood."

"So what?"

"So you and your hood friends are fucking things up."

"What do you mean? I didn't have nothing to do with this."

"Bullshit."

"Look, I been trying to find out who these guys are and why they'd be after me and Squig. And I can't find out. And I know people, and they can't find out either. And then these characters showing up here means to me that something Joe thought could be right. That this is about the band. Which means it ain't my fault."

"Doesn't make any difference."

"What do you mean?"

"I'm out. Take your rock and roll revival and stick it up your ass."

"Frampton. Calm down, man."

"I am calm. You hear me yelling?"

"We're gonna take care of this."

"Get out."

"Hey, Frampton—"

"Didn't you hear me? Get your sorry ass out of here. And take actor boy here with you."

"Frampton," I said. "Look, I know you're upset, but—"

"Joe," he said.

"Uh-huh?"

"Shut up."

"But—"

"Just shut up and get the fuck out."

"But—"

"You don't have children, do you?"

"No, but—"

"If you had kids you'd understand. Now get out."

I followed orders. So, surprisingly, did Woz. "He'll come around," he said. We walked back to the Barracuda. Woz sat there, flexing his hands on the wheel. "Guess I ought to get you back."

"You're serious, aren't you."

"What about?"

"You really think he'll come around. He'll forget this whole thing, thugs parked in front of his house with a street full of kids all around. You really think that."

"Uh-huh."

"How can you think that? You know, he's not the only one ready to quit."

"What the fuck you mean?"

"I mean I'm about done with it too."

"No, you're not."

"I'm not? What, you're going to beat me up to make me stick around? Go ahead. Beat me up. I don't care. I've got a girlfriend to think of. One who nearly got shot the other night. And a family."

"What family? You ain't even married."

"I've got a father and a surrogate aunt and uncle and a cousin with a husband and kids of their own." Come to think of it, it wasn't much of a family. "Who knows who these assholes will go after next?"

"Yeah, sure. Whatever you say."

He fired up the car, and we headed back to West Hollywood. Neither of us said a word until we were a couple of blocks from Café of 1000 Dances and Woz asked where my truck was. I told him, and he pulled in at the curb behind it. I undid my seatbelt before we got there, had the door open before we'd stopped.

"Wait," Woz said.

"Wait for what?"

"You're not gonna do this."

"Why not?"

" 'Cause you got rock and roll in your blood."

What do you say to a statement like that? Just what I said. Nothing.

He shrugged. "Don't believe me. You'll find out. You're not gonna throw this band away. Not you, and not Frampton neither."

"You just go on thinking that." I completed my exit and walked to the truck. The Barracuda thundered to life. It pulled from the curb and even with me. Woz leaned over the passenger seat. "Give it a little time. You'll see." He sat up and roared away.

"Yeah, Woz, keep on believing that."

I got in the truck, turned over the engine, and sat there. Poor deluded Woz. Not believing I'd had enough of the Platypuses. Not believing that I was going to drop the whole thing, the nostalgia, the music, the dreams of concert-hall glory. Not believing I thought it more important to protect my loved ones. Boy, was he mistaken.

But if he was so wrong, why was I still planning on keeping my appointment with Deanna?

•

I caught Bonnie at the office and told her about the creeps showing up at Frampton's. I said I thought we could all be in danger.

"I've got security people here who I can press into service," she said. "Don't worry about me. I'll be safe."

"Have them keep an eye on Darren too, if they can."

"Sure."

"By the way, Frampton quit."

"He can't."

"He did."

"I'll talk to him."

"Figured you'd say that. Maybe you ought to talk to me too."

"Not you too."

"I'm thinking about it."

"Don't do anything right now. Not until we work through this shooting business."

"All right, I guess."

"Promise me."

"I promise."

I don't think she believed me, but she was kind enough not to mention it.

Cobwebs and Strange

Deanna lived in a three-story apartment building on the outskirts of the seediest part of Yucca. I parked a block away and tried to ignore the shapes looming in the shadows. I pressed the button next to the nameplate that said Festerling and Knox. A couple seconds later Deanna came on and buzzed me in.

I took the stairs to the second floor. She was standing outside her door, dressed in a skimpy yellow tank top and jeans. Sounds of battle blasted into the hall. When I went in I confirmed that they came from the TV. Men running around, explosions, blood. It could have been any of hundreds of movies. The noise erupting from the stereo speakers was as loud as I imagined real warfare to be.

The apartment had white walls and cottage cheese ceilings and one-step-up-from-the-cheapest carpet. It smelled of cigarettes and disinfectant and old marijuana. The furniture was dull and aged, Herculon upholstery and fake wood tables. There were a couple of travel posters on the walls, along with cheesy reproductions of modern art and the same Hendrix poster Woz had, coming loose at the same corner.

The most interesting adornment was sprawled on the sofa. He had long frizzy hair. A beer was in his hand and a cigarette in his mouth. Bare feet, jeans, naked torso featuring a nice round potbelly with a few curly black hairs.

Deanna picked up the clicker and muted the TV. "Joe, this is Mott. Mott, Joe."

He managed to raise a hand. "Hey, man."

"Hey." I took the hand. Hard yet limp. Like he had a good grip but it was too much trouble to use it. "Want a beer?" he said.

"No, thanks. What's the movie?"

"*Dirty Dancing.*"

"You mean *Dirty Dozen*, don't you?"

"Yeah, that. Lee Marvin, Charlie Bronson, all those guys. Ernie Borgnine. You watch *McHale's Navy*?"

"Once in a while."

"Far out." His attention returned to the screen. He didn't seem to care that there was no sound.

I resisted the urge to say "far *fucking* out" and looked to Deanna for guidance.

"Let's go in the bedroom," she said. "Sooner or later he's going to realize the sound's off, and he'll turn it back on. It's the only place we'll be able to hear ourselves think."

I followed her in. If you'd seen the living room you knew what the bedroom would look like. "Hey," Mott yelled. "If you're gonna ball her, close the door. She makes a lot of noise." The explosions returned.

She looked at me, smiled, said, "He's right, you know." Then she closed the door and directed me toward a small desk along the wall. A photo album sat atop it. She pulled a wooden chair out from the desk and told me to sit down. Then she opened the album and stood behind my right shoulder.

It was a scrapbook. Scenes from a middle-class childhood. Photos of children standing stiffly at amusement parks, birthday party invitations, report cards. Deanna pointed at one of the kids in one of the photos. "Me. And my brother Damon and my sister Daphne."

I turned a couple of pages. The kids got older. There was a shot of Damon with a toy rocket, one of Daphne in a big-girl dress. More pages, more nostalgia. Her parents, I assumed, on a cruise ship. Deanna looking very small behind a drum kit. Then, a ticket stub. The Beatles at Hollywood Bowl, August 29, 1965. "You went?"

"Yes. Both times, but I lost the ticket from the first one. I cried for days."

"You didn't."

"Okay, not days. Hours, maybe."

"Woodstock and the Beatles at the Bowl. Lucky you."

"That wasn't all." She bent and reached for a photo in a cheap frame sitting at the far left corner of the desk. This put her left breast six inches from my face. The tank top fell away, revealing all. It might have been deliberate and it might not have. She stood straight again and handed me the photo. The girl facing the camera was her, with long straight sixties hair, wearing a miniskirt. The other person was a man with his back to the camera.

"This must be someone significant," I said.

"Keith Moon."

"Wow." I looked again. I couldn't tell if it was the Who's drummer or not. "Who took the picture?"

"My dad. He had an in at Capitol Records. That was how I managed to get into both Bowl concerts."

"The Who was on Decca."

"You know your rock trivia. His in at Capitol had an in at Decca."

I put the picture down on the desk and returned to the scrapbook. There were more photos of Deanna and her drums. One of them showed two longish-haired boys on guitar and a black kid with a rudimentary Afro on bass.

"My first group. The Dalmatians."

"Black and white."

"We thought we were so clever."

"Must have been weird to be a girl drummer in those days."

"Very. Honey Lantree was my idol."

"Who's that?"

"The chick in the Honeycombs."

"One-hit wonders."

"Over here. They had another in England. Honey sang lead."

"Didn't the Velvet Underground have a chick drummer?"

"They did. She ended up working in a Wal-Mart."

"You know your rock trivia."

It raised a laugh. I kept going. Deanna and her siblings got older. Her groups looked more professional. The backgrounds changed from family rooms to clubs. Another ticket stub, from Blues Palace in Ventura. "My first paid gig. Twenty dollars. A group called the Ridgebacks."

"Carrying on the canine theme."

I turned a couple more pages and came face-to-face with Toby Bonner. He was standing in a studio with his Les Paul around his neck and a bottle of Coke in one hand. Then there were more, lots more, some with Toby and Deanna, some of Toby playing, a couple of the two of them at an amusement park. A tiny newspaper ad for Toby Bonner, with a tinier picture of Toby and itty-bitty ones of Deanna and Spencer Sommers. A review from a rock and roll mag I'd never heard of. An unpasted copy of the label from Side 1 of their record. And a stub from a royalty check for six dollars and seventy-seven cents.

After that, nothing. Almost half the book was blank pages. "What happened?"

"I lost interest."

"How come?"

"It started to seem stupid. Pointless. I nearly tossed the thing half a dozen times. I'm glad I didn't."

"You've been looking at it a lot lately."

"How'd you know?"

I turned my chair around to face the room. "That midlife crisis stuff we talked about."

She nodded and moved toward the bed. She slipped off her sandals, swung her feet up, scooted back until she was leaning against the pillows stacked against the wall. Early in these maneuvers the right strap on her top worked its way loose, and as she shimmied back I got to view the previously unseen breast. It looked a lot like the other one. Once she was settled back there, she "discovered" the strap, touched it, left it where it was.

"Mrs. Robinson," I said. "You're trying to seduce me, aren't you?"

"Is it working?"

"Deanna, you have a fine set of breasts, but I really don't want to see any more of them." Okay, the last part wasn't exactly true. "I told you, I'm spoken for. I thought we were past this."

"I guess not."

"And if I wasn't attached, I don't know that I'd be up for

screwing with your boyfriend watching Charles Bronson in the other room. Or being on sheets he's been on, for that matter."

"He wouldn't mind. He really wouldn't. And I have other sheets."

"The scary thing is that I believe you."

"About the sheets?"

"Stop it. You know what I meant. Let's keep this strictly business, okay?"

"He's not very good in bed. Especially when he's high, which is most of the time."

"He runs off with teenyboppers, he's lousy in the sack, and he doesn't care if you have sex with other men. So why do you stay with him?"

"He has really good dope."

"That's a crummy reason."

She put the strap back into place, glanced at me, wouldn't meet my eyes. "I guess it's lame to say that I love him."

"Not if you really do."

"I really do. Loser that he is, I really do." Now she looked right at me. "I'm one of those women you read about, who keep picking the worst possible men."

"I'm not the one to talk to about it. I've had my share of worst possibles in my life."

"But now you're with someone good."

"So you see? There's always hope. Can we—"

What I was going to say was, Can we get back on track here? But I stopped, because I didn't want to get back on track. What I wanted was to be somewhere else.

So what I said was, "Can we do this another time?"

"What's wrong?"

"Too much on my mind."

"That sounds like a bullshit excuse."

"No, I ... you're right. It's bullshit. I just don't want to talk about finding Toby now. I'm not sure if I want to talk about finding Toby ever."

I thought she was going to try to change my mind. But she just got up, went to the closet, and got a denim shirt that she pulled on over the tank. "Call me if you change your mind," she said.

"I will." I got up, opened the door, and walked out, into the living room. Things were still blowing up on TV. Things were also status quo on the couch. I went to the front door, looked back at Deanna. She was watching Mott watch TV. She glanced over at me, waved a tiny good-bye, and went to sit on the arm of the couch. I let myself out.

The Kids Are Alright

Half an hour later I was seated at Gina's dining room table. The TV droned on, with the volume down. I'd briefed Gina on the latest.

We were eating ice cream, the three of us. I had a bowlful. They each had a pint of Häagen-Dazs, vanilla Swiss almond for Gina, chocolate chocolate chip for Aricela. I looked from one to the other and back again. There was definitely a resemblance. Around the eyes. Maybe around the mouth. Definitely around the attitude.

My latest fantasy: Aricela was Gina's daughter. She'd given her up for adoption back when the kid was born, just before Gina and I re-entered each other's lives. Fate had conspired to bring Aricela into our world again.

You'd think they'd known each other for years. Looking at each other and bursting out into giggles. Finishing each other's sentences. I didn't like it, not one bit. This was going to turn out badly, when we figured out who the kid belonged to and she went home. Because I was sure her story was just that. The more I saw her, the more I was convinced she wasn't an urchin who'd spent the last several years, at least, depending on the kindness of strangers. She had some street smarts, yes. But she didn't fool me.

Somewhere there was someone who cared about her. In the morning we would start finding out who that was.

Except … that part about not liking it one bit, this familiarity between the two of them. It wasn't quite true. Because Gina was clearly loving every minute of it, and was happier than I'd seen her in a long time. That was the bit I liked. Maybe the business about her mortality, about the bloody episode the other night opening her up to all sorts of new things, maybe that was true. Or maybe she'd felt this way all along and, knowing I didn't want kids, hid it. But that didn't make sense. Because all the years we were best buddies, she said the same sorts of things. And why would she have hidden her true feelings about children from me then?

•

At ten I went in the living room, sat on the sofa, boosted the volume on the TV. It was set to Channel 6 and I left it there. On the left side of the screen were scrunched-up sitcom credits. On the right the anchor tandem was telling us what exciting stories they had in store for us. "More bloodshed in the Middle East. A high-speed chase ends in a spectacular crash near LAX. And a heartwarming story about a boy, a ferret, and a school lunch worker. Stay with us."

High-speed chase. Spectacular crash.

LAX. Not terribly far from Frampton's neighborhood.

"Hey, Gi. Come see this."

She shared a final chuckle with Aricela and, ice cream container in hand, sat beside me. The kid got up too, capped her pint and put it in the freezer, came and squeezed in between us.

"What are we going to see?" Gina said.

"Just watch."

Two commercials, a promo, FX shots of L.A. over theme music. Then: "Good evening, I'm Jim Abernathy."

"And I'm Lilah Pike. A high-speed chase ended badly today when a car carrying two suspects went off an overpass. Terry Takamura has the report."

There was Takamura again, her hair rigid as ever, standing straight and tall in a dark street with a couple of cop cars in the background. "Yes, Lilah, I'm standing near Los Angeles International Airport, just a few feet from where a car carrying two suspects went off an overpass this evening, a spectacular ending to a high-speed chase."

"Kind of what the other chick just covered," Gina said.

"Ssh."

They switched to an aerial shot, taped earlier. Even from above, I could tell it was a Beetle. I couldn't make out the color, but it could well have been silver. It was zooming down the freeway, cutting in and out of traffic, followed by a brace of police cruisers. Terry Takamura's voiceover: "It started in a quiet residential neighborhood near Marina del Rey. Police responded to a 911 call of suspicious characters lurking in front of a house."

"'Lurking'?" Gina said. "Did she really say 'lurking'?"

"When police responded to the call, the suspects fled. They drove onto the Marina Freeway, then south on the San Diego Freeway, in the waning stages of rush hour. Our Chopper 6 beamed back these exclusive images."

Back to the live shot of Takamura. "The vehicle, driving on the shoulder with police in hot pursuit—"

"Did she say 'hot pursuit'?" Gina said.

"—tried to go around a van that was stopped for a tire change at the side of the road. The driver lost control and—"

She pointed, and the camera followed her finger to a shot of the freeway, crossing over a surface street, with a broken guard rail. Below were more cop cars and a wrecker.

"—smashed right through this guard rail and onto Arbor Vitae Street below. Miraculously, none of the cars on Arbor Vitae were struck, though vehicles avoiding the falling car caused a multi-car pileup. Fortunately, only minor injuries resulted. The driver and passenger of the Volkswagen, apparently not seriously hurt, bystanders reported, fled the scene into the underbrush."

The camera swung back to Takamura. "Police are mum on the possibility that the two men were involved in a series of gunfire incidents over the past week. You may remember the shooting of forty-eight-year-old Leonard 'Squig' Jones on earlier this week. The gunmen in that incident were also driving a vehicle similar to the one that crashed here. Then, just last night, a shootout in Hollywood, where a bullet-riddled vehicle similar to this one was left behind."

Tape of a police spokesman. Cop-speak, the gist of which was, we don't know anything, or if we do we're not telling. Then one of the people who was traveling on Arbor Vitae: "It came down like a bat out of hell."

Takamura, in her wrapping-up voice, said, "Police have reported that the car that crashed was stolen, as was the one shot in the previous incident. Investigators will work on into the night, looking for clues. This is Terry Takamura, reporting from near LAX. Back to you, Lilah and Jim."

"Thank you, Terry," said Jim. "In other news, seventeen people died today as a suicide bomber struck a fast food restaurant in Jerusalem."

I muted the TV. "Were those the men who were shooting at us?" Aricela said.

"I think so, honey." Honey?

"Too bad they didn't die."

I almost said something parental. Something like, "We shouldn't ever wish anyone to be dead, no matter how bad a person they were."

But fact of the matter was, I wouldn't have shed a tear. If they were dead, whoever they were, they wouldn't be popping up in any of the Platypuses' neighborhoods anymore. We could get back to the serious business of making rock and roll music. Frampton would get over his mad and return to lay that backbeat down. I'd find Toby Bonner, and Bonnie and the boys would make a record and everything would be cool.

Yeah, right. And the suicide bombings would stop too. And every little boy and every ferret would have a kindly school lunch worker to get them out of every predicament they ever got into.

Like Aerosmith said … "Dream on … dream on … dream on …"

•

An hour later. Aricela, after protesting that she wasn't tired, had fallen asleep as soon as we put her to bed. Gina and I had climbed into the sack too. "Hey," I said.

"Uh-huh?"

"I got a package from New Jersey today."

"Oh?"

"An autographed photo of Pete Townsend."

"Really? I wonder who could have sent you that."

"One of my legions of female admirers."

"You'll have to thank her properly sometime."

"Yes," I said. "I will."

We lay there for a few moments. Gina said, "So."

"So. You know what we have to do tomorrow."

"Yes."

"Do you want help?"

"I don't think so. I'll take her down there myself."

"You're sure?"

"Yeah."

A couple of minutes later: "Gi?"

"Yeah?"

"You want to talk about it?"

"Talk about what?"

"The kid."

"She's not an it. And she has a name."

"Sorry."

"What is there to discuss?"

"For starters, how come you have these sudden maternal feelings?"

"What maternal feelings?"

"Come on. You're treating her like she's your daughter."

"Bullshit."

"Oh. Excuse me. I was mistaken."

She let it go a few seconds, then said, "Not like my daughter. More like my niece."

"The difference being?"

"A niece goes home at the end of the day. You're not responsible for her. A daughter, you're responsible for."

"So what you're saying is, you like having a kid around, but you don't want the responsibility that goes with it."

"Uh-huh."

"Yet you're not wanting her to go home at the end of the day."

"Not yet. It's kind of like she came to visit for the weekend. I'm having fun with her, damn it. I'm as surprised as you are."

"I see."

I had more to say. While I was figuring out which part of it to bring up next, Gina fell asleep. I kissed her cheek, adjusted her pillow, and rolled over.

Several times I thought sleep was imminent. Errant thoughts kept snatching me back. After an hour I slipped out of bed, went into the living room, and sat on the couch. I turned the TV on, way down low, and looked for a movie. I found something noirish called *Murder, My Sweet* and settled in to watch. There was a character called Moose Malloy in it. Any movie with a character named Moose is okay by me. I watched it through. Moose got killed at the end. It made me sad. I kind of liked the big lug.

Let My Love
Open the Door

When I went to bed again I had no trouble sleeping. I dreamed about a guy named Moose. Then he turned into a talking moose. He and Captain Kangaroo were talking about Volkswagens. The talking moose liked the new ones and the Captain preferred the old.

When I woke up the shower was going, and I was alone in bed. I checked the clock. Ten to eight. I fell asleep again, woke up again. Nine-thirty. Gina was gone. So was Aricela.

I got up, got dressed, let myself out, drove home. When I got there, Theta's cousin Ronnie was standing on the lawn next door, almost dressed in a bikini top and snug chartreuse capris. She was talking to a guy with green hair and an orange dab under his bottom lip. She saw me, waved, and ran over. "Hey, neighbor."

My eyes—sometimes they have a mind of their own—went to her cleavage. It was quite a cleavage. Some might call it spectacular. "Hey," I managed.

"How you doing?"

"Fine. You?"

"Just peachy." She dropped her voice. "That's my cousin Raoul. He has the hots for me. I told him it was gross to think about your cousin that way. He still looks at me like … well, you can guess."

An admission: When I was sharing a house with Elaine, I thought of her that way once or twice, after I accidentally saw her naked one day. I was sixteen. I had no control over my hormones.

"Anyway," Ronnie said, "I hear you're an actor."

"You might say that."

"I'm an actress."

Sure, kid, you and every other pair of tits in town. "Really."

"Think you could give me some pointers?"

"I don't know. I—"

"Just some real basic stuff, like where I get pictures and how I get to try out for movies and things like that."

"Why don't we talk about this later?" I said.

"Okay. If you want, come over later. I'll make us some lemonade."

"Sounds good," I said, and escaped inside.

•

Elaine had called with an audition that afternoon for AT&T Broadband, whatever that was. I looked at the time and planned my day. Any way I cut it, I had more time than things to fill it with. I did some straightening-up and watched a program about Vietnam. I wondered what I would have done if I'd been called.

Around two I called Gina.

"Hello?"

"Me," I said. "You took her in?"

"Uh-huh."

"How'd it go?"

"Okay."

"Want to talk about it?"

"What's to talk about? I explained where we got her from

and they took her and said they'd try to find where she belonged."

"It's for the best, Gi."

"Then I suffered through the look she gave me as they took her away."

"I'm sorry. I should have gone with you."

"Come over, okay?"

"What's going on?"

"Just get your ass over here."

"Give me half an hour."

•

Without a word, she took my hand and led me to the bedroom. She pushed me down on the bed and went after my shirt buttons. A minute later she was riding me and in another we were both done. She lay atop me for a long time, then rolled off and climbed under the blankets. After a few seconds I joined her.

"What was that all about?" I said.

"It has to be about something?"

"You haven't been like that ... I can't think of any time you've been like that."

"I don't know what's happening to me. I cry, I get all gaga over some kid, I come almost as soon as you're in me."

"The last one is a bad thing?"

"It wasn't today. I wouldn't want it as a steady diet."

After a while I said, "I'm sorry about Aricela. That I let you give her back by yourself. I should have been with you."

"If I'd wanted you there I would have woken you up." She sat up, reached behind, and arranged the pillows into a sort of throne. She looked down at herself, then at me, and said, "I'm in pretty good shape for someone my age, aren't I?"

"You're in great shape for someone any age. I love your shape."

"My boobs are starting to sag."

"I hadn't noticed."

"You're sweet." She nestled a hand under one, gently bounced it up and down. "Good thing I didn't have any kids. They'd be dragging on the floor by now." She switched to the other breast, gave it a quick taste of the same treatment. "You know when this started?"

"When you started bouncing your boobs around?"

"No, idiot. Getting uncomfortable about my life."

"When?"

"When you started playing your guitar again. There you were, almost fifty and trying to do what you never did while you were a kid, and what was I doing? Looking through fabric books for people I can't stand."

"You can stand some of them."

"This is my breakdown. Give me some leeway."

"Sorry."

"Then I almost got shot, and I saw Squig almost die, and it's like, whoops, that could happen to me tomorrow. And then I had to go off to San Francisco, so I didn't even have you around, and I lay there in that hotel bed and got all weird." She looked me in the eye. "Don't say it."

"What?"

"'More weird than normally?'"

"I won't say it."

"Then I come home and there's this kid on my doorstep, and she's a neat kid and she's beyond the diapers-and-doo-doo stage, and I'm having a good time with her. And I'm thinking, whoa, maybe I've been wrong all along, maybe kids would be a good thing, and now that I'm forty-seven it's not likely that I'm going to have any, and then I have to take her to that *place*."

"Where they'll find her parents, and there'll be a happy reunion."

"Maybe it's menopause."

"The other night you thought you were pre-menopausal, and now you're already there?"

"Did I say that?"

"Uh-huh. Do they even have early onset menopause?"

"I'll have to get on the Net and check it out." A big sigh led to a small smile. "I need to make a confession."

"Always what a guy likes to hear."

"It's about your guitar renaissance."

"What of it?"

"I had a hand in it."

"I know you did. You took me to the Aerosmith concert, screwed my brains out till my guard was down, and connived me into playing again. Why are you grinning like that?"

"I didn't buy the Aerosmith tickets."

"No? Who did?"

"No one."

"A gift from God. Your mother should be pleased."

"Someone in the biz got them for me."

"Who?"

"Think about it."

It took me two seconds. "Oh. My. God."

She kept smiling while it finished sinking in.

"Bonnie put you up to it?" I said.

"She figured, thirty years, you might not care about being in a band, so she thought she'd check things out before she got hold of you. She'd seen the bug commercials, so she called SAG to find out who your agent was, got hold of Elaine, explained what she was up to."

"Elaine was in on this too?"

"Uh-huh. She sicced Bonnie on me. I told her I thought it would be good for you to be in a band, what with your mood lately. I mentioned how you always talked about picking up your electric guitar. We decided I'd go to work on you. Aerosmith was a good place to start, and with her connections it was easy to get us tickets."

"So she knew all along I had a girlfriend."

"Why? Did she put the moves on you?"

"Of course not. It's just that she acted like she didn't."

"Makes sense. She couldn't admit she knew about me, could she? By the way, she did the same thing with Frampton."

"That schemer. She had me believing it was some cosmic force at work, me playing my SG again."

"It was, sort of."

"And you just went along with this?"

"For free Aerosmith tickets? Of course I did."

•

We lay there like a couple of slugs until I had to get cleaned up for my audition. I drove to the casting office on Highland. The casting director had me sit in front of an imaginary computer and complain about how much time I was wasting because of my narrowband Internet connection. Then my pet parrot told me about AT&T Broadband. One of the assistants read the parrot's lines, and not all that well. I was in and out in ten minutes.

I called Gina when I was done, and we each drove to my

place. We had an early dinner plan with our friends Sybil and Eugene. Then Gina had to drive back because her great-aunt Consuela was in from Santa Maria and she'd promised her mother to sit and listen to Auntie C. bitch about everything. I was invited but begged off. I'd gotten roped into tagging along the last time the old witch was in town. Once was enough.

We got to Culver City a little after five. My new buddy Ronnie got up off the porch next door and sauntered over. She'd changed into short shorts and a tight T-shirt. Welcome to Nipple City.

"Hey, neighbor," she said.

"Hey." I made introductions. "Ronnie's from Arkansas."

"Really?" Gina said. "Where in Arkansas?" Like she'd know one part from another.

"Little town called Bonesaw," Ronnie said.

"I don't believe I've heard of it. What brings you to L.A.?"

"I'm an actress."

"Really?" Gina gave me an evil look. "Did you know Joe here is an actor?"

"I sure did. I was hoping he could show me the ropes. He hasn't decided yet."

The evil look morphed into an equally devilish grin. "Go ahead, Joe. Show the girl some ropes."

"Umm ..."

"Come on, make some time for her. You remember how tough it was when *you* were first starting out."

It wasn't tough at all. Having a cousin who was an agent helped a lot. Not giving a shit whether I got acting jobs or not helped more.

"Sure," I said. "I'll tell you some stuff. In a couple of days, okay?"

"You mean it?" Ronnie said.

"Definitely."

"Wow. I got to tell everyone." She jiggled back to her place. "Theta! Raoul! Wait'll you hear this!"

Gina waltzed to my front door and waited for me to let her in. When we were inside I said, "Thanks a lot."

"You're welcome. Give her some help, you might get to show her your rope."

"I've seen her naked, you know."

"In your dreams."

"I stumbled on her sunbathing. Theta too."

"Does she look as good naked as she does with clothes sort of on?"

"Theta?"

"Arkansas Barbie."

"Don't tell me you're going bi again."

"I've never stopped. I'd do her in a minute if I wasn't with you."

"Can I watch?"

"Girl on girl. Every man's dream."

Sybil and Eugene showed up at five-thirty. We went to East Wind, got caught up, and were back at my place by seven-thirty. Ten minutes later I was alone. I turned on the television, found nothing worthwhile, watched anyway. A little after nine the phone rang.

It was Deanna. "Toby did another drop-in," she said.

Rough Boys

"Where?" I said.

"A biker bar near Ojai."

"How'd you find that out?"

"Used to go out with a biker."

"You do know how to pick 'em, don't you."

"I'm headed up there while the trail's still hot. Want to go?"

"Now?"

"That a problem?"

"How biker-y is this place?"

"Don't tell me you're scared."

Not enough to admit it. "Of course not."

"Cool, dude. You come up here, I'll drive to Ojai. Deal?"

"Deal."

•

Deanna and I passed the time relating our life stories. She'd lost interest in drumming in the early seventies and gone to court reporting school. Did that for a couple of years, liked the money but not the work, was thinking about quitting when she got busted for pot. I didn't tell her I already knew about that. That I'd been checking her out with the police.

The bust settled the court reporting question, and she drifted through a series of pointless jobs. One day she woke up and found she was forty and decided it was time to have a real career. She went for vocational counseling. They put her through a battery of tests and suggested court reporting. She took this as a sign and found an old guy who wanted to support her in exchange for occasional sex. This lasted six or seven years, until she found Jesus and dumped the old man. A couple of months later she found Mott and dumped Jesus. Between her temp work and his dope dealing, ends met. He did his running-off thing once or twice a year. She would retaliate by finding someone of her own to screw around with. When Mott came back this time more quickly than usual—the teenybopper went back to Bakersfield— Deanna decided she was still entitled to an extracurricular fuck or two, which was why she was still coming on to me the night before.

"You still looking to even the score?" I said.

"No."

"Because you decided not to, or because you got some?"

"I'm not saying. A girl has to have a little mystery, you know." Same thing Gina'd said the morning before.

We passed Oxnard and Ventura and picked up Highway 33. Half an hour later we pulled into the lot of a place called Muskie's. There were half a dozen pickups there, several souped-up Mustangs, a Trans Am or two. Plus about two dozen motorcycles, in two neat lines, one parallel to the road and one perpendicular.

Deanna found a spot at the back of the lot, under a big evergreen. A man who resembled a Viking, tall and broad and blond-bearded, was relieving himself on the other side of the tree. He said, Hey, and I said, How's it going? and he said, You know.

Deanna dragged me away by the arm, and we walked

toward the entrance. Music blasted into the chill air. A million points of light winked down at us.

The entrance was in front, off a porch a couple of wooden steps up from ground level. The area was poorly lit and smelled like old beer. A bug-zapper at the far end was doing landmark business. There were a couple more Norsemen on the stairs, laughing hysterically, blocking the way. One was holding a bottle of Corona. The other was holding two of them. Deanna walked up behind Two-beer and said, "Hey. Lardass. Out of my way."

The laugh cut off like someone flicked a switch. The other guy tossed off one more guffaw, which trickled off into a manly giggle. The first one turned around and looked straight out, then, like a cartoon character, ratcheted his gaze downward. He peered at Deanna and frowned. I tried to remember if my affairs were in order.

A huge, missing-toothed smile appeared in the middle of the behemoth's beard. He clodhopped down the stairs and wrapped Deanna in a bear hug. The beers smashed together alarmingly behind her back. After a while she told him to let go. When he didn't she gave him a shot to the kidneys that did the trick.

He handed her one of his beers. "Dee. Ain't seen you in months."

"I ain't seen you neither, Hoss." She tossed me a look that said, What can you do?

"Where you been?"

"Down in the city." She threw back the remains of the beer.

"What're you doing there? You still with that motherfucker Mott?"

"Still with the motherfucker."

"Whyn't you bring him up?"

"He didn't want to come. I brought Joe here instead."

The shaggy head creaked in my direction. He looked me up and down. I'd worn jeans and a denim jacket and some weird old fur-lined boots, but I still looked as out of place as a pig at the opera.

"Hello, Joe," Hoss said. "Just got back from a rodeo show."

I hadn't heard that one since junior high. Emy de la Fuente used to say it. "Hey, Hoss. Good to meet you." He shoved the other beer in my direction. I took it in self-defense. He held out a hand. I did the same. Ten seconds later I took it back. The damage wasn't too bad. I could get some ice from the kitchen to pack it in on the ride back.

"Look at us. Hoss and Little Joe. Like on *Bonanza*. How do you know Dee here?"

"We like the same music."

"Very fine, very fine." He turned to the other leviathan. "Hey, Buck. Meet Joe."

I avoided further digital damage by shooting him a salute.

"Hey, everybody," Hoss said. "Dee's here. And some guy named Joe."

My new biker friends came down to greet us. They all made a lot of noise. They were all drunk. When the ceremonies were over Deanna grabbed my hand and squeezed us through the crowd and into the place.

There were half a dozen neon signs advertising as many brands of beer, a pool table, a couple of pinball machines. A big racetrack-shaped bar in the middle, staffed by two skinny guys with handlebar moustaches and two skinny women with cleavage. They were handing out beers as fast as they could pull them from under the bar or squirt them from the tap. More people than the fire department wanted to know about were squashed against the bar or standing around watching the band. The crowd was about half bikers. There were roughly three men to every two women. Cigarette smoke grayed the air. In L.A. no one smoked indoors anymore. There were laws. There were probably laws here too.

We pushed toward the bar and deposited our bottles. Deanna yelled, "Hey, Pam!"

One of the female bartenders turned her head, spotted Deanna, grew a big smile. She marched over, leaned over the bar, gave Deanna a big kiss on the lips. "How you doing, girl?"

"I'm good. This is Joe."

"Hey, Joe."

"Hey," I said. I was getting good at it.

"We got to go talk," Deanna said. "About Toby Bonner."

"Give me ten minutes. I got a break coming. 'Kay?"

" 'Kay."

Pam went back to dishing out suds. Deanna pushed me toward the four-inch platform that served as a bandstand. There was a miniscule dance floor in front of it, jammed with people. There wasn't room for them to do any more than squirm. Deanna took my hand and pulled me into the press. We wriggled along with everyone else. I butted asses with someone. It was Buck. He shouted, "Hey, Little Joe. How's things back on the Ponderosa?" Then he leaned his head back and brayed like a donkey.

The song ended and the crowd hooted. The singer announced they were going to do one by Lynyrd Skynyrd and broke into "Free Bird." Partway through Pam joined our dance crew. She was carrying a six-pack of Tecate. When the song was over she took Deanna's hand and Deanna took mine yet again and we slipped back through the masses. We headed toward a door in the far wall. Somewhere along the line Hoss joined us. Pam unlocked the door, we went through, she closed it behind us.

We were outside. Down a couple of steps, past a rusted-out tireless pickup, into the woods. The path traveled downhill. The night under the new moon was dark as Osama's heart. We kept going until the music diminished to a dull roar. Hoss tripped over a rock and fell flat on his face. He thought this was the funniest thing in the world.

A few more steps and we were in a tiny clearing. I heard crickets or frogs or some other peeping thing. My eyes had gotten used to the darkness, and I could make out a picnic table. We stumbled forward and got ourselves seated around it, Hoss and me on one side, the women on the other. Pam deposited the six-pack on the table, pulled out bottles, undid caps. We each took one and sampled it. Hoss belched. "'Scuse me."

"While I kiss the sky," I said.

A lighter flared by Hoss's face. He lit a joint and pulled in a roomful of air. Then the jay was in front of my nose.

This is how the whole thing started, I thought. A joint in my face. There were reasons I should've just passed it along. Probably a whole host of them.

I took the jay, took a hit, held my breath in as I gave it to Pam. The end of the joint glowed. I couldn't take my eyes off it. They followed it as Pam gave it to Deanna and Deanna passed it back to Hoss. Someone giggled, maybe me. Somewhere in the dim recesses I remembered how much stronger twenty-first-century dope was than the stuff back in the sixties. I took another hit and kept the joint moving. When it got to Deanna again I said, "Okay, people. Spill."

"It was a fucking miracle," Pam said.

"A fucking miracle," Hoss said.

"Tell us what happened," Deanna said.

The joint materialized in front of my face. "I'll pass," I said. The old barn-door-and-stolen-horse thing.

"It was a Monday night," Pam said. "You know how slow it is on Monday nights. This one was extra slow."

"King Cobra was playing," Hoss said.

"Who're they?" I said.

"Local band. Mighty good." Another belch. This time he didn't bother to excuse himself. "They been playing around here for ten, fifteen years. Got a guy blows harp like—"

"Hoss," Deanna said. "Shut up."

Hoss shut up. Pam said, "So they play until twelve thirty, quarter to one. And a couple of them leave and the rest are sitting around having a beer, and there's maybe a dozen people in the place, and all of a sudden there he is."

"Toby Bonner," I said.

"Well, yeah, Toby Bonner. Isn't that who we're talking about? "

"Uh-huh."

"He comes in right through that door we just came out of."

"You're sure it was him?"

"Well, I didn't know who he was—I mean, I'd heard of him, but I wouldn't've known what he looked like—but one of the guys from the band says, Holy shit, and I say Holy shit, what? and he says who it is up there. And I say, No fucking way, and he says, Yes fucking way, and then another guy says, No fucking way, and—"

I was going to have to introduce this chick to Squig. They could talk all night and not say a thing. "I get it. People didn't believe it. What happened then?"

"The band guys who're left, they're just watching the stage like it's Eric Clapton. Then he takes his guitar from the case, plugs into an amplifier the guys hadn't got around to taking down yet, and he pulls over a mic, and then he starts playing. And everything stops."

"It was like being in church, man," Hoss said.

"How long did he play?" I said.

"How long, Pammie, about an hour?"

"About right," Pam said.

"Anyone talk to him?" I said.

"A couple of the band guys tried to, when he was done. They were, like, in awe. But he just unconnected and went out the back again. A couple of us went out after him, but he was already on the move."

"In what?"

"An old Triumph," Hoss said.

"And no one knew he was coming?" Deanna said.

"Nope. Total surprise."

Deanna and I plumbed these depths for all they were worth. When Pam said she had to get back, I got up to go too.

"Holy shitting mother of God," Hoss said.

I sat back down.

"I just remembered something," he said. "Don't you remember, Pammie?"

"You tell me what I ought to remember," she said, "I could tell you if I remember it."

"That thing about the beach."

"What beach?"

"In the song."

"What song?"

"The one about the beach."

"Hoss, sweetie?" Deanna said.

"Yeah?"

"It doesn't matter if she remembers or not. Why don't you tell us what *you* remember."

"Right on. The beach. There was a song about a beach."

"I must've been in the ladies' room," Pam said.

"What was the name of it again? Shit. Something with a P."

"*Playa?*" I said.

"Hey! Right on the money."

"It just means beach in Spanish."

"Not just playa. It was *playa de la* something-or-other."

"That's a big help."

"*De la* something with a *P*."

"Now we're getting somewhere."

"I got it! Playa de la Playa."

"Beach of the beach? That's just stupid." As was calling a guy built like The Rock stupid.

"Something like that. Playa de la Paya. Playa de la Palala. Playa de la Pala! That's it!"

"Beach of the shovel," Deanna said. "Or shovel beach."

"Sure as shit," Hoss said, "that's it, I swear on my mother's grave."

"Your mother's still alive," Pam said.

"My grandmother's, then. Playa de la Pala. The whole

song was about it, how he would go down there and there'd be the sun and the waves and music and shit. Pammie, you gotta remember that."

"I told you, I was in the bathroom."

"For a whole fucking song?"

"I couldn't find a Tampax, okay?"

"Gang?" I said.

"What?" they both said.

"It doesn't matter if Pam heard it or not. What matters is, does anyone know where this Playa de la Pala is?"

"Nope," Pam said.

"Never heard of it," Hoss said.

"Deanna?"

"Me, neither," she said.

"Maybe he made it up," I said. "Just a fake beach in a song."

"I really got to get back," Pam said.

We trooped up the path. Right outside the door Hoss said, "Shit. Whyn't I think of this? Buck'll know where it is. He knows all kinds of stuff like that."

We went inside and tracked down Buck.

"Playa de la Pala?" he said. "Sure I know it. It's a little south of where 33 hits 101. I'll draw you a map." He snatched a napkin from the bar and a pen from the bartender and drew a bunch of squiggles. He and Deanna and I went over it until we had every hieroglyphic down. Then we bade our friends a fond farewell and headed back to the coast.

What Are We Doing Here?

Last time I was in a microbus I was on the way home from a Cat Stevens concert, way back before he became a Muslim. Everyone, including the driver, was flying high on mescaline. He still drove better than Deanna was. She kept wandering over the center line, overcompensating, stirring up the shoulder. Funny how I'd never drive with someone who was drunk, but rationalized putting my life in the hands of someone high on pot. A remnant of the old days. Booze = bad. Pot = good.

"Buck knows a lot about the area," I said.

"He ought to. He teaches history at the high school."

"He what?"

"Yeah, and Hoss teaches science."

"Science."

"Uh-huh."

"These are your biker friends?"

"You got a problem with that?"

"I guess I feel cheated. Here I thought I was buddying up to some dangerous characters, and all they were was a bunch of high school teachers."

"You've got plenty of dangerous characters around already. You don't need any more."

"I suppose. How come you know Spanish?"

"I don't."

"You knew about *pala*."

"And not much more. When I had my sugar daddy I got tired of the gardener and me never understanding each other. So I learned as much Spanish as I had to, which included the words for shovel and trowel and hoe and crap like that."

We reached the freeway, turned south, went a few miles, and exited toward the ocean. A couple of turns later we went over a small rise and the road ended at a *T*. Deanna stopped the bus. I caught my first whiff of sea air. I flicked on the flashlight I'd dug up behind the seat and consulted the napkin. "Left."

She made the turn, and we motored along. The road got narrower as we meandered down toward the water. The ocean smell got stronger. After a mile or two the road petered out, ending in a parking area. Deanna drove in a circle, passing the headlights around the periphery of the lot. It was surrounded by a chain-link fence, eight or nine feet high. There was a gate with a big padlock. Beyond it a path led dimly downward.

She kept the engine running and the headlights pointing at the gate as we got out and inspected it. A sign was mounted halfway up. PLAYA DE LA PALA. CLOSED UNTIL FURTHER NOTICE. We could hear waves breaking, though how far away I couldn't tell. There were ship lights straight out in the distance and off to their right what I guessed was an oil platform.

The sea air was starting to break up the marijuana haze. "Dee," I said.

"Don't call me that. I hate it."

"Sorry."

"What were you going to say?"

"This is dumb. Why don't we come back in the daylight?"

"Because if he's living here he's sure to be here now. In the day he may be at the store or something."

"What if he's gone somewhere for another drop-in?"

"A little longer. What could it hurt to look?"

"We could fall off a cliff and break our necks."

"We'll be careful."

"And here's a thought. If by some insane chance Toby's living on the beach wouldn't someone have discovered him by now? This isn't *that* isolated."

"Who knows?"

"Besides, with the beach gated, how would he go back and forth?"

"He might know another way."

"I suppose."

"Or he could climb the fence."

"That's a possibility too."

"Let's try it."

"Not a chance. You're talking to mister uncoordinated here. Last time I climbed a fence I ended up with blood pouring out of my scalp."

"When was that?" Deanna said.

"When I was a kid. Some juvenile delinquents were chasing me."

"Time to get over it." She walked toward the van.

"What are you doing?"

"The electrical system in the bus. You leave it idling too long, it starts to discharge."

"Another reason to come back in the daylight."

She opened the door. The headlights blinked off. The smaller beam of the flashlight flicked on. Gravel crunched as she came back.

"When was the last time *you* climbed a fence," I said.

"I don't remember. Come on, point that thing at the top."

There was no stopping her. I aimed the beam at the upper part of the fence. She started up. "It's not hard," she said, moving through the light and swinging onto the other side. I tried to show the way with the flash. She reached the ground unscathed. "Give me the light." I passed it through a gap under the gate. "Now you."

I wasn't going to let a mere girl show me up. I grabbed the fence, gave it a tug, tried to get one of my clumsy boots into one of the diamond-shaped openings. It lodged in place, more or less. I hoisted myself up, fought to find a hold for my other boot. I might have been clearing up mentally, but physically I was still zonked. Deanna led me higher with the flashlight. Finally I made it to the top. I threw one leg over, straddled the thing, eased myself over to the other side, made my way down.

"See," she said. "You did fine. Let's go."

We inched downward, with Deanna and the flash in the lead and me following a couple of careful steps behind. The path was lined with dry vegetation on both sides. It wasn't very steep, but the bottoms of my boots were long since worn slick.

I thought I heard another car somewhere up above. I grabbed Deanna's arm, told her to hold still, listened. Nothing but the waves. I was clearly spooked. The effects of the dope were moving to another phase. Paranoia, striking deep.

I whispered for Deanna to go ahead. We crept forward and down. Suddenly there was sand under my boots. Deanna shot the beam around. The hill came right down to the water, marking one end of the beach. The other end could have been fifty yards away, or five miles. Too bad we hadn't asked Buck.

"He's not here," I said. "It was just a song. Let's go back."

"We came this far. Might as well keep going."

The beach was narrow, not more than fifteen yards, and Deanna swept the light back and forth at irregular intervals, turning up nothing but seaweed, driftwood, and a mannequin's head. We slogged for fifteen or twenty minutes, until another hill met the sea. "The end," I said.

"Was worth a shot."

We turned around and started back. Somewhere along the way a bolt of reason came through. It said that we were insane to imagine Toby might be there, that Deanna was a loser who'd pissed away her life, that I was in danger of becoming one too. Toby was probably dead, and the person who'd been showing up at clubs was a clever impersonator. And if he was alive, we weren't going to find him unless he wanted to be found. The best thing I could do now would be to go back to the bus, let Deanna drive me back to the city, and call Bonnie in the morning and say I'd failed miserably.

We reached the foot of the path and started up. Just as we spotted the fence, the flashlight went out. Deanna banged on it with her hand. There was one brief flicker, enough to get our hopes up. Then nothing. "No big deal," she said. "We can climb it in the dark, can't we?"

"I hope so. I don't want to spend the night here."

We covered the remaining distance by shuffling along, holding hands, with our free ones out in front of us. We made course corrections each time one of us hit the bushes. We were almost on top of the fence before we saw its outline, a darker shadow against a black sky. Deanna shoved the dead flash under the gate and scurried over as if it were broad daylight. A regular squirrel, that one.

I started up, managed to make my way to the top, took a deep breath, threw a leg over, then the other. I was about to start down when someone began shooting at me.

Magic Bus

There were two bullets at first. One zinged off the fence not far from my leg. Somewhere out in the wilderness I saw or imagined a flash. I heard another shot, and something ripped through my jacket, not necessarily in that order. I let go of the fence.

One leg crumpled under me when I hit. I fell, cracked an elbow, yelled in pain, cut it off. No noise, I thought. It would help them find me. Though if they came that close in that kind of blackness, they had to have high-tech equipment. They didn't need me making a racket to know where I was.

The fourth gunshot snapped me out of it. I looked around for cover, a tough task in absolute darkness. I ran for where I guessed the microbus was, nearly smashing into it before I realized it was there. I felt along the sheet metal, trying to put the vehicle between the shooter and me. I found a wheel well and hunkered down by a tire.

Yet another shot echoed, this one a lot closer than the others. The guy had scampered down the hill, and he and his night vision would find me in a minute. Or he had a partner, one who'd been down where we were all along, waiting for the first one to flush us out. I felt around on the ground for a rock. It would be better than nothing if the guy came—

More gunfire, very near. I clawed at the wheel, trying to pull off a hubcap. I could throw it at the guy, like Oddjob in *Goldfinger*. Or use it as a very small shield.

"Joe!"

Deanna's stage whisper came from close by. She was too near where the guy with the gun was. He'd see her and—

The next gunshot came from so close by that I could make out the shooter's face in the flash. It was Deanna. "You okay?" she said.

"Uh-huh. Where'd you get the gun?"

"From under the seat."

"In the first place."

"Mott brought it home. Said I should keep it around for protection. Shitty neighborhood, you know? I think someone traded it to him for dope."

"Do you know how to use it?"

"I took it out in the hills once."

A shot hit something nearby. Deanna fired off one of her own. Another came back in reply.

"How many bullets in that thing?" I said.

"Seven, I think. Or was it nine? Mott told me. I don't remember. Maybe it was fifteen."

"How many have you shot off?"

"Three, four, maybe."

One of our windows bit the dust. Deanna fired back twice.

"Make that five or six," she said.

"So you might just have one left."

"I might. Or three. Or … shit, I suck at math. I'm not

doing a whole lot of good with this thing. You want to give it a try?"

"I can't even climb a goddamn fence. I'm not going to be much good with a gun."

"That's logical."

"Coordination, that's all I mean. I don't have any."

Another window got destroyed. Deanna fired right back. "I can see the flash," she said. "I'm kind of shooting at that."

"You may have just kind of used your last bullet."

"Oh."

"Can't you knock the clip out and count them?"

"I told you, I don't know how to work this thing. I'd probably drop them all on the ground."

Two more shots smacked the microbus. "Here's a question," I said.

"Uh-huh?"

"He knows we're behind the bus. It's doing a pretty good job of protecting us. So why is he still shooting? Why doesn't he come down closer so he can go after us at close range?"

"I don't know, why?"

"I think he's trying to get you to use up your bullets."

"I hadn't thought of that."

"Because you keep shooting back at him. He's just sitting up there, taking potshots at the van, knowing each time he does you use at least one of your own."

"Fuck," she said. "So what do we do now?"

"Don't shoot back. Make him think we've used up our bullets."

"And then what?"

"Then he comes down here."

"That sounds promising."

"And then you nail him."

"I don't know if I could do that."

"What do you mean? These bastards are trying to kill us. We've got to defend ourselves."

"That's not what I meant. I meant, even if the guy was five feet away I don't know if I could hit him."

"Sure you could."

"I don't think so. Maybe you should take the gun."

A couple more thumps into the other side of the bus. Deanna fired one of her own back. "Damn it," she said.

"I thought we were going to—"

"I know, I know. It was instinct. At least we know I didn't use up all the bullets before."

"But we don't know whether you used them up just now."

"I don't think so. I'm pretty sure there was an odd number."

"How sure are you of how many you've shot off?"

"I'm pretty sure it's eight now."

"So we have two pretty sures. We multiply them and get one maybe. God, that stuff stinks. The gunpowder."

"I think you're right about letting them come down here."

"Maybe you *should* give me the gun."

"Really, I'll be all right. I can get my itchy trigger finger under control."

"You'd better."

We sat there a couple of minutes. No shots from up above. "Maybe *he's* out of ammo," Deanna said.

"I have the feeling this guy would've brought more with him."

Two more bullets splashed into the VW. One hit metal. The other went through one of the empty windows and continued through the other side, the one we were hiding behind, way too close to my head.

I threw myself on my stomach and shoved myself under the chassis. "Get on the ground," I said.

"Why?"

"Because—"

I heard the shot and the scream at the same time. The shot came from above, the scream from Deanna. It tore through the darkness, loud and sharp. She fell to the ground, hard.

"Dee!"

The voice was a whisper. "I told you not to call me that."

"What the hell?"

"Ssh. I'm playing possum."

I racked down my volume. "Why?"

"Because our other plan sucked. Him coming down here and us jumping out from behind the bus and shooting him? I don't think so."

"So how is this better?"

"A couple of ways. If he thinks he's gotten us both, we have the element of surprise. Or maybe he just leaves."

"Don't they usually come down to pump a couple of bullets into their victims' heads to be sure?"

"I don't know."

"And what's this 'gotten us both' stuff?"

"You're supposed to be an actor. Here's the role of a lifetime."

"Next time he shoots I scream and make falling-down noises?"

"Uh-huh. Got a better idea?"

"At the moment, no."

"So get ready for your cue."

I took a deep breath and blew it out. Another. A third. "I guess this is our best chance. Assuming you still have bullets in the gun."

"Maybe it *was* eight."

"We're dead."

"Are you ready?"

"I suppose."

I lay there scrunched against the bottom of the VW. It was going to be tough to make falling-down noises when I was already flat on my stomach, but that was a bridge I could blow up later. I took one more deep breath and waited for a shot.

It came. I missed it.

"Joe!" Still whispering, but she got her point across.

"Sorry. I guess my mind was wandering. I'll do better next time."

"How could you let your mind wander at a time like this?"

"Blame your friend Hoss."

"What's he got to do with it?"

"I'm still feeling the dope. I keep thinking I'm fine, and then I drift away."

"Try mooring yourself to the dock."

"Nice simile. Metaphor. Whatever. Okay, I'm concentrating now."

A minute passed. Two. Three.

Pow!

"Aaaiiiiieeeeeee!"

I slid out and got to my knees and slammed my body into the side of the van. I made scrabbling noises with my fingernails, then plotzed back on my stomach. The big finale was a mournful, lingering moan.

"How was that?" I whispered.

"Not bad, except for the moan."

"What was wrong with the moan?"

"Makes him think he didn't kill you."

"I didn't think of that. Maybe I should draw another shot."

"Just keep quiet, and he'll figure you lasted a minute before you died."

We lay there. And lay there. Five minutes. Ten. Twenty. I tried to slide back under the bus but my jacket got hung up on some metal protrusion that refused to let go. My squirming dislodged a rock that sounded thunderous but didn't bring a response. "Maybe he left," I said.

"We would have heard the car. Now please shut up."

Another ten or fifteen minutes.

We heard the car.

It was coming closer.

It stopped. A car door opened and closed again. He didn't slam it, but he wasn't trying to be quiet with it either.

A minute or two later: footsteps. Crunch, crunch, crunch on the dirt and gravel. They came closer. Closer. Closer still.

When the footsteps reached the other side of the microbus, I did the atheists-in-foxholes thing.

The steps moved around the back of the vehicle. Crunch, crunch. He'd get a chance to shoot me before Deanna took him out. Or before he took her out.

He came around from the back. He walked along the side of the bus. His feet stopped less than a foot from my head.

Who Are You

I knew about the feet because of the flashlight that flicked on. It was the gunman's. Ours was back at the fence, not that it would have done anyone any good except as a small club. His was shining down at the ground, but it still dazzled me.

"Son of a bitch," the guy said. I twisted my neck up to see what was what, and I saw the gun. It was like a bigger version of the one Woz had bought for me. A revolver, reeking of gunpowder. Like something you'd see on *Bonanza*. Where there were characters named Hoss and Little Joe. The actors were both dead, and soon I would be too.

I tried to wedge myself tighter but my jacket was still caught. Lots of my torso was exposed, with all sorts of vulnerable organs inside.

The guy crouched down. He shined the light in my face. I couldn't see anything but that damned light. But I knew he was selecting a target. Maybe it would be my head. That would hurt the least, wouldn't it? The brain would shut down immediately, and I would go off to the next world in a relatively painless fashion. It wasn't a little gun that would turn my brains to goop. It was a big gun that would kill me cleanly.

Okay, Deanna, I thought, now's the time.

She thought so too.

Click.

"Fuck," she said.

"What the—" said the guy. His light snapped off. In my head I saw him turning, saw him and his Night-o-Vision tuning in on Deanna, shooting her dead, coming back to do me.

I got a hand free and took hold of his ankle and pulled. He jerked his leg away. I said good-bye to Gina. To Aricela too, while I was at it, and my father and Elaine and—

An enormous noise rent the darkness. I smelled fire and brimstone. I thought, This doesn't seem that bad. It hadn't hurt a bit. Unless the fire and brimstone were indicative of where I'd—

The guy fell on me.

He didn't land exactly on top of me. It would have been impossible, given that my mercifully-unriddled body was partially shoved under the chassis. But some of his parts ended up on some of my parts. And he had me wedged in so I couldn't get out. I knew that right away, because I tried to get out right away. He had to be a big man. He didn't budge. And, just for grins, one of his bodily fluids was soaking my midsection.

"Joe? You okay?" It was Deanna.

"I'm fine."

"Let me see if I can find the flash."

The light snapped back on. It shined in on me through a little gap between the shooter's body—I assumed it was a body; he didn't seem to be breathing—and the bus's bottom.

"I'm fine, I think. You scared the shit out of me. With that first shot. Thank God you tried again."

"I didn't."

"What?"

"When I pulled the trigger and nothing happened I freaked out and froze up."

"Then who shot him?"

"Maybe he shot himself."

"Suddenly overcome with remorse? I doubt it."

"Then who?"

"I don't know. Hey! Whoever shot this schmuck! You out there somewhere?"

If he was, he wasn't admitting it.

"He's gone," Deanna said.

"Or playing a game with us. You think you could drag this corpse away so I can get out from under here?"

"You're sure he's a corpse?"

"If he's not, he's doing a damn good imitation."

"What if he comes to life?"

"What is this, *Carrie*? Just pull this cadaver off me, okay?"

She put the light on the ground, pointing at me. She pulled, the body shifted, she grunted and groaned, it inched away. I pushed and Deanna pulled and as soon as I could squeeze through I did. I grabbed the flashlight and stood, then pointed the beam at where I guessed the head was. I came across the night vision goggles first. They'd slipped off his head. Then the end of the rifle. It was still strapped on and he'd fallen on top of it.

Then I found the face. His eyes were open. This I hadn't expected. I looked away, then back. He had fleshy features, a crooked nose, a shaved head. I ran the light along his body and came to the place he'd been shot. There wasn't much to see. Just a hole in his jacket and, when I pulled the jacket away, a hole in his shirt. I didn't pull at the shirt. "Bullet went in here, I'm guessing. Then out his back, which landed on me, which is why I have blood all over me." I shined the light up and down my front. "What a mess."

My jacket and shirt were sodden. The top half of my pants too. I stripped off the jacket and shirt and tossed them aside. Then undid my jeans and pulled them down. They wouldn't come off over the boots, which were a bitch to get off. I pulled the pants back up.

"What do we do now?" Deanna said.

"Go find the cops."

"Do we have to?"

"You think we should just leave him and drive away?"

"Who would know?"

"The cops, once they checked the registration on the bus."

She took the light from me and carried out her own inspection. "His eyes are open."

"I know."

"Can we close them?"

"You want to put your hand on his face, go ahead."

"Can't you—"

"Get in the van. Now."

"But—"

"Deanna. He's dead. He doesn't care if his eyes are open. Now get in the van and let's get the hell out of here. In case whoever shot him decides to shoot us too."

She just stood there. She was in shock, something like

that. I picked up the guy's handgun. I tried for the rifle too, but it didn't want to come out from under him and I didn't want to argue. I took Deanna's arm, led her around to the passenger side, seated her, belted her in. I went around to the driver's door and got behind the wheel. I managed to get the keys from her, find the one I needed, and stick it in the ignition. I flicked off the light, found a secure cranny, and tucked it away. I turned the key and nothing happened.

"There a trick to this?" I said. "It's not starting."

"It always starts. I've had it twenty-three years, and it's never not started before."

"It's not starting now." I tried the key again. Nothing. "One of the bullets must have hit something."

"Can't you fix it?"

"I know nothing about fixing cars."

"Please try." Her voice quivered.

"All right."

I took the flashlight around to the engine compartment, got it open, did a quick scan. It was quick because I saw the problem right off. One of the bullets had severed the cable from the coil to the distributor. I went around to the passenger door. "This thing's not going anywhere."

"So what do we do?"

"His car must still be up there. We'll borrow it."

I took the flashlight, got her out of the bus, started back around it toward the dead guy.

"What are you doing?" Deanna said.

"Getting his keys. Stay here. Don't move."

"All right."

Someone started shooting again. I yelled, "Down," and hit the dirt. There were three shots. Four. Five. Then silence.

"You okay?" I said.

"Yes."

"We better get our asses out of here."

I ran to the dead man. Going through his pockets was only moderately appalling. The keys were in his pants. I trotted back to Deanna and we started up the road again. We came to the car a couple of minutes later. It was parked half in the bushes by the side of the road. No one was in it. It was a New Beetle, this one bright yellow. Someone had pumped bullets into it. Five of them, forming a neat pentagram on the driver-side door, matching the number of shots we heard after the bad guy was dead.

•

I told the police the story half a dozen times, some with Deanna, some without. After the first runthrough they took away my pants, let me get cleaned up, gave me a Ventura PD T-shirt and gym shorts. I had them call Kalenko in L.A. and he more or less convinced them Deanna and I were more or less on the level. Eventually somebody checked out the scene down by the beach and reported back. Deanna couldn't tell them who made the holes in the VW, and I wouldn't. They took copious notes and filled out a ream of forms and did everything in triplicate.

Four and a half tedious hours later the lead questioner, a tall, handsome man named Ruiz, said we could go.

"Go where?" I said.

"Home."

"Home's sixty miles away. And our transportation's indisposed. Or should we take the Beetle?"

"Hang on." He left and came back a few minutes later. "One of our officers has to go down to L.A. to testify tomorrow morning. You can catch a ride with him."

"When's he leaving?"

"Little after nine."

"It's a quarter to six. What do you suggest we do till then?"

"There's a Bob's Big Boy down the street. We'll have him pick you up there."

"You ever spent three hours at a Bob's?"

"It's Bob's or the Greyhound station. Or a bench in the lobby."

Bob's won. We walked the two blocks over, dropped into the darkest booth there, ordered tea and toast. I kept Deanna talking. She did the same for me. Three hours passed like six. Deanna nodded off half a dozen times. So did I, but I was too amped up to sleep more than a few minutes.

Our ride showed up right on time. A young guy, barely old enough to be out of the academy. He quickly figured out that we didn't want to be chatted up. Deanna fell asleep somewhere around Camarillo. Somewhere around Thousand Oaks, so did I.

Talk Dirty

Our escort detoured off the Hollywood Freeway to drop us at Deanna's place. We said a woozy good-bye. She sleep-walked upstairs, and I stumbled to my truck. I got home at ten-thirty, took a shower, and was headed for bed when I remembered to check the machine. There were three calls. The first two were from Gina. One from the night before: "It's almost eleven and you're not home. Very weird. Call me." Then: "You weren't there at eleven and now you're not there at seven in the morning. I hope you're okay. Call me."

The last message was from Elaine, at nine a.m. A callback for AT&T Broadband. There'd been a screwup, and she hadn't gotten the message when she was supposed to. I had to be in Hollywood at a quarter to twelve.

I called Elaine and assured her I'd make the audition. Then I tracked down Gina in her car. "Where the fuck have you been?" she said.

"I love when you talk dirty."

"Get serious, Portugal. I've got to meet a moronic client in ten minutes and I'm stuck on the 405. I'm in no mood for frivolity."

"I was involved in more gunplay."

"God, no. You okay?"

"Uh-huh." I gave her the *Reader's Digest* version.

"You're sure you're all right?"

"More clothes ruined, but otherwise everything's fine."

"Come over tonight. I want to check you over, see you're really okay."

"Deal."

I made myself presentable for my callback. I got there late, but I'd known the casting director a long time and she let it slide. This time around they had a real parrot. His name was Rollo. They told me he'd been a regular on a sitcom for the past six years. Rollo and I got along famously. Sometimes it's like that. Instant rapport with the other actor.

Before I left they let me feed him a cracker. He thanked me, they thanked me, and I drove home again. I dragged myself into the bedroom and flopped on the bed. And lay there, unable to drop off. Too much running around inside my head. And a lot of noise from next door. Various shrieks of delight, lots of giddy laughter. Someone yelled, "Cool beans." It reminded me of Aricela. Poor Aricela, lost in the cogs of bureaucracy. Or reunited with her parents, the ones she loved so much she refused to admit they existed. Eventually the mental gibberish calmed down and I felt blessed unconsciousness coming on. I heard Ronnie yell, "It's all over my shorts," and then I was asleep.

•

I was a homicide detective, working on a gang shooting at some generic beach. The essential clue was the DNA from whatever was all over Ronnie's shorts. I went to interview her. I knew it was Ronnie, but it looked like Deanna. Then I was having sex with Ronnie/Deanna, but I knew it was all right because Gina was going through menopause.

The phone woke me. "Joe?"

"Mmph."

"It's Bonnie."

"Hi, Bonnie."

"Detective Kalenko called."

That got me out of my stupor. "What'd he say?"

"He told me about what happened to you last night. You're all right?"

"I'm fine."

"He said the Ventura police have identified the man who was shooting at you."

I read the news today, oh boy. "Anyone we know?"

"Someone I know," she said. "Name's Vinnie Mann. He was the bass player in Darren's band."

Slip Kid

I got some of the story from Bonnie, who got it from Darren. Some when I called Kalenko, and the rest, oddly enough, from a Terry Takamura report on Channel 6's six o'clock news.

His name wasn't really Mann. He was Vincent Manson. The manager of a band he was in well before Changing Its Spots insisted that Manson wasn't a good name for a rock and roller and made him change it. This was well before Marilyn Manson happened.

He was the longhair in the group photo I'd seen, but according to Darren, who was still in touch with him now and then, he'd recently whacked off his mane and started shaving his head.

Unlike Darren, music wasn't just a phase for him. He'd been in one band or another since junior high. One I'd even heard of, a group called Fuzzbox, who'd had a semi-hit single, an AC/DC knockoff called "In Bed with the Devil," in '91 or so. He was a fantastic bass player, according to Bonnie, a reasonable backing vocalist, a decent songwriter.

The other significant element in Vinnie Mann's life was getting into trouble, at least up to 1997, when he knocked over a liquor store, got caught, and got thrown in jail. He

had the good sense to choose as his partner in crime someone the cops were really interested in, and was able to plea-
bargain his sentence down to two years in exchange for
ratting on the guy. He'd kept his nose clean since he got
out. Or so everyone thought.

Kalenko said they were checking into Mann's recent
movements. No one knew why he—and presumably the
other man who'd escaped when they went over the side of
the freeway—were going around hunting Platypuses.

•

I finally made the flower stop at Moe's that I'd missed the
night I followed Woz home. I got to Gina's at six-thirty. She
opened the door with a shit-eating grin on. "Are these for
me?" I told her they were and the grin got wider and she
said to go into the guest room. I asked what was going on,
and she said to just go look. I walked down the hall and into
the room. Lying on the bed, wearing a grin that eerily
matched Gina's, was Aricela.

"Hi, Joe," she said.

"Hi, kiddo." I sat on the edge of the bed. Gina followed
me in and stood just inside the door. "How you doing?"

"Okay." Aricela put down the magazine, sat up, and
threw her arms around my neck. I wrapped her up in my
own. We broke it at the same time. She sat lotus-style on
the bed.

I looked over at Gina, then back to Aricela. "So how did
this happen?"

"I got away from them."

"How?"

"It wasn't hard."

Gina came over, sat on the other side of the bed. "She
was waiting for me when I came home."

"Was she, now?"

"So what could I do?"

"Not much choice."

"Nope. And don't worry, there's plenty of dinner for all of us."

"That's not what I'm worried about."

"What *are* you worried about?" Aricela said.

"Just some stuff that happened last night. Nothing, really. Read your magazine, kiddo. I'm going to help Gina in the kitchen."

"'Kay."

On the way to the kitchen Gina said, "What's this 'kiddo' stuff?"

"It just feels right, you know? Like calling you 'babe.' So what do you think about all this?"

"Thanks for the flowers, by the way. Very pretty. TJ's?"

"Moe's, and don't change the subject. Nothing's changed. She's not a puppy."

"Last time you said kitten."

"We have to take her back."

"Can we talk about this later?"

"What's wrong with now?"

"There's nothing we can do about it now. Later, when she goes to sleep, we'll talk. For now, can't we just enjoy ourselves?"

"I suppose." I went to the stove, uncovered a pot, peered in. "This tortilla soup?"

"Uh-huh." She came over, dipped in a spoon, took a taste. "Pretty good. Might need a little more seasoning." She put down the spoon, joined her hands behind my neck, looked up at me. "How come you keep getting mixed up with people with guns?"

"Don't know."

"Do you think there are more of them out there?"

"In general, yes. There's a limitless supply of people with guns. If you're asking about this particular crew, I don't know the answer."

"It didn't end last night."

"I don't know."

"So how do we tell it's over?"

"I don't know, babe. I just don't know."

•

After dessert we watched *Rush Hour* on TV. Jackie Chan was as entertaining as usual. Chris Tucker gave me a headache. They kept running Make 7-Up Yours commercials. It unnerved me that there was a whole ad campaign based on the words *up yours*. Same way those Victoria's Secret ads were unnerving. Not that I minded all those lush young bosoms. But it was unnatural having them splashed all over my TV.

I watched Aricela watch the movie. She was sitting on the floor, too close to the screen. She had her hair in a ponytail, tied with a pale yellow ribbon. It was gorgeous hair, shiny and lustrous. I wondered what would happen if we took her back. Would she escape again? Would they do something awful to make sure she didn't? Post some Nurse Ratched type outside her room or dorm or whatever they had so she didn't make another run for it?

I turned to Gina. She'd been watching me watch Aricela watch TV. She had a somber smile on. She took my hand, sighed, and turned her attention back to the television.

•

At ten we watched the Channel 6 news. The way we figured

it, none of the local stations was worth a hill of beans, so we might as well watch the worst of them all and get some outrage value out of it. Aricela had moved up to the sofa and sat between Gina and me, shoes off, feet drawn up in front of her.

They started with ten or twelve minutes on the Lakers' latest playoff victory. Shaq and Kobe had scored thirty-five apiece. The opposing coach complained about the officiating. Someone said it was a seven-game series and it wasn't over till it was over, and someone said they had great respect for the other team, and someone asked if it was okay to wave to his little girl at home, got permission, and wiggled his fingers at the camera.

Then they had Terry Takamura, repeating almost verbatim her Vinnie Mann report from six o'clock.

With the important stuff covered, they moved on to other matters. India and Pakistan were on the brink of nuclear war. Washington was strengthening the FBI's powers to spy on us and no one was putting up a stink. Israeli soldiers had managed to stop the latest suicide bomber before anyone was killed. She was fourteen. I thought of the kid who'd put a hole in Alberta Burns's leg. Kids were alike the world over.

More local news. The latest on the secession efforts by Hollywood and the Valley. Relations between African Americans and Korean Americans up and down Vermont Avenue were just fine. A cocker spaniel saved a man's life by biting his ankle and keeping him from walking in front of car.

And another update on the big murder-suicide in Hollywood. The old couple, Cecil and Maria Richardson, were the parents of famous radical Elizabeth Baker, who, along with her husband Quentin, had been on the run from the police since '69 for supposedly knocking over a bank. Over footage of the Richardsons' tiny Craftsman house, the anchors speculated about whether the axings had anything to do with the Bakers' underground activities. Then they showed the obligatory neighbor with the obligatory graphic saying NEIGHBOR, saying nothing meaningful. A shot of flowers in front of the house, required in all domestic tragedy stories. Wanted posters showing the grim faces of the Bakers.

I glanced down at Aricela. She looked up at me and burst into tears.

Gina and I both threw arms around her, both asked what was wrong. Aricela buried her head in Gina's chest. "*Abuela*," she said between sobs. "*Abuelo*."

Gina, her face stricken, turned to me and mouthed a translation.

Grandmother. Grandfather.

Run Run Run

As delicately as we could, we got the story out. The important parts. The rest got filled in later.

Aricela had been telling the truth about her parents being dead. Her mother, Lorena Castillo, was the sister of Elizabeth Baker, the famous fugitive. Her father, Ralph Castillo, had worked at Home Depot. When Aricela was six, Lorena got cancer. She was dead within a year. A few months later Ralph left Aricela with his in-laws and jumped off the end of Santa Monica Pier. Aricela wasn't supposed to know about this. She was told her father had gone back to Guatemala to take care of some family business. She found out the truth, but never told her grandparents.

The Richardsons battled constantly. Over big things and little things and nothing at all. Every once in a while Maria would throw something. On occasion Cecil would slap her around. Things were worse when one of them had been drinking. Far worse when both of them had. Those were the times when one or the other might give Aricela a whack or two.

They let her grow up more or less on her own. They fed her and made sure she had clothes to wear and that was about it. She spent a lot of time by herself and a fair amount with the people who lived in Las Palmas Park. When she was ten she got caught shoplifting a bag of pork rinds. After the cops brought her home her grandparents told her she was lucky. That the police were very bad people who would act like your friends when they really weren't. That her Aunt Betsy and Uncle Quentin had been running from them their whole lives, and they hadn't done anything wrong at all.

Then, one night about a week previous, things between Cecil and Maria got out of hand. It was after midnight, after Aricela had gone to bed. Both her grandparents had been drinking since early afternoon. The cursing and yelling woke her up, as it always did. She scrunched herself into the corner, like she always did, and waited for them to finish.

Then she heard screams. She was terribly scared, but she had to see what was going on. She put on her shoes and tiptoed to where she could peek into the living room. She saw her *abuela* lying bloody on the floor with an ax in her chest and her *abuelo* pointing a gun at his head. He didn't see her. He pulled the trigger once, twice, cursed, threw the gun against the wall. He turned her way. She was sure he'd spotted her. She shrunk back. She wanted to go back to her room, but she was mesmerized by what she was seeing.

Cecil turned back to his wife's body. He jerked the ax out of her chest, laid his arm across the table, and brought the ax down. He screamed, dropped the ax, and held his spurting wrist with his other hand. He wheeled around the room, howling in pain.

Then he spied Aricela.

He said her name, and at first she thought he was going to come after her, let the blood pulsing from his arm get all over her, or snatch up the ax again and use it on her. Instead his face got very sad. He sank to the floor and whimpered and moaned. After a while he didn't make any sound at all.

Aricela walked very slowly into the living room. She looked at her grandparents, one dead and one either dead or very close, and at all the blood splattered everywhere, and she fled. She ran a block or two away and hid in a yard until dawn. Then she stole some clothes someone had forgotten to take in off the line. She spent the day wandering around, scared, hungry, not knowing what to do, sure of only one thing: that she couldn't go to the authorities, because they would act like your friends when they really weren't. She didn't go see her friends in Las Palmas Park because just a couple of days before those same police had made them move somewhere else.

That night she fell in with a bunch of older kids. She didn't know if they were runaways or what, and she didn't care. She just knew that they gave her food and that they too didn't want anything to do with the police. They lived in an old empty building and slept on dirty, smelly mattresses. She stayed with them a few days, until one night one of them, a big strong boy with long blond hair, snuck over to her bed and tried to touch her private parts. She told him to stop. He wouldn't. Her friends in the park had told her what to do. She kicked him between the legs. While he was busy calling her names she escaped.

She spent another night and day alone and hungry. The next night she was walking down an alley and suddenly there was a man shooting at her and another man who was in the alley, and the other man picked her up and ran away from the alley and the man with the gun, and saved her.

I Was Just Being Friendly

Midnight. Aricela was asleep in the guest room. Gina and I had just gotten into bed. We turned out the lights and lay there and didn't say anything. A car alarm went off outside, cycled through its repertoire of absurd noises, turned itself off. I heard another sound, a loud hum. "That the refrigerator?"

I felt her nod. "It's been doing that on and off. Going to have to have someone look at it." She pressed herself closer to me and said, "What a tough kid."

"She's been through so much," I said, "and she seems to be in pretty good shape. I'm thinking after a while whatever defenses she's put up are going to break down and she'll become a basket case."

"Post-traumatic stress syndrome."

"Sort of, yeah," I said. "So what do we do?"

"Whatever it is, it doesn't have to be right away. The only living relatives we know about are God knows where. They may be dead too, for all we know."

"Agreed. They're not a factor. But answer this for me. Why haven't we heard anything on the news about a missing child? The cops have been all over that house. Wouldn't they have figured out there was a kid living there?"

"You think she's lying?"

I thought it over. "I think what we've heard is pretty much what happened. There's got to be some other reason why the cops aren't letting on there was someone else living there. Maybe I should ask Burns if she can find anything out."

"Maybe."

The refrigerator stopped its groaning. "Maybe I'll call her in the morning," I said.

"Okay."

"So should we go to sleep now or what?"

"I vote for 'or what.'"

"You're certainly horny lately."

"It's this midlife business. My biological clock ticking and all that."

"Honey, your biological clock wound down years ago."

She poked me in the ribs and rolled on top of me. "You have to keep quiet. We don't want to wake the children."

"No," I said. "We certainly don't want to do that."

•

I woke in the middle of the night and heard sounds from the living room. I threw on a robe and found my way out there. The hall closet was open and the battery-powered light was on. Aricela was sitting on the floor in front of the closet. She'd found an old Solvang cookie tin full of photos and was browsing through them. I had a couple just like it at home that I was going to organize someday.

She acted like I'd caught her with her hand in the cookie jar, which in a way I had. "I'm just looking," she said.

I nodded. "Don't stay up too much longer."

She said okay and returned to the photos. After a few

minutes I heard her making her way back to the guest room. After a few more I was asleep.

•

"Breakfast is ready."

I felt Gina beside me. Which meant …

I opened my eyes. "Good morning, kiddo."

"Morning. I made some of the bagels. And oatmeal. And I bought grapefruits."

Gina sat up, yawned, ran her fingers through her hair. "You really should ask before you take money from the drawer."

"I didn't take money from the drawer."

"Oh?"

"I took it from Joe's wallet. I thought that would be fair, because you paid for everything else."

There was a chair in the corner of the room. My shirt was hanging on the back, my shoes were under it, and my pants were folded on the seat just like I'd left them. I looked over there, then at Aricela. She gave back an innocent smile, said, "Come on, it's gonna get cold," turned, and disappeared.

"She took it from my wallet," I said.

"Uh-huh."

"Quiet as a mouse, that one is."

"Sure is. Come on, it's gonna get cold."

Eating breakfast with Gina and Aricela was starting to feel natural. Like we'd been doing it for years. I found it disturbing. The last time anything like that had happened was when I started sleeping with Gina again. We just picked up where we'd left off over eighteen years before. The comfort level scared me then, and it scared me now.

We were nearly through breakfast when Aricela said, "I have an announcement."

"Oh?" Gina and I both said.

"It's that you shouldn't take me to Family Services again, because I'll just get away again."

Gina said, "What makes you think ..." It trailed away because she saw the way Aricela was looking at her. Couldn't put anything past that kid.

"I know you did it because you think it's what's best," Aricela said. "But it's not. Those places suck. So I'm just gonna stay here for a while. I know you like having me around. So you see, it's the best for everybody. 'Kay?"

"'Kay," I said.

"Okay," Gina said.

"Cool beans," Aricela said. "Now go in the other room while I clean up."

We followed her orders. In the bedroom, Gina said, "Now what?"

"I'll call Burns. You get to play mommy another day at least."

"'Kay. You want to play daddy?"

"Kind of. But there's still at least one wacko with a gun out there. I don't want to be attracting him to you and Aricela. Just in case."

•

I called Burns when I got home, but got the machine and didn't leave a message. I had a short chat with the canaries, made tea, went out to the greenhouse. The plants needed water. I got the hose, turned the spigot, started back for the greenhouse.

"Hey, Mr. Gardener." Ronnie was lurking on the other

side of the fence. She had her hair piled atop her head and wore a pair of sunglasses with DayGlo green frames.

"Morning," I said.

"When can we get started?"

"With?"

"The ropes."

"Maybe tomorrow. Got a lot to do today."

"I read in the paper that Matt Damon is starting a new movie. Or project, that's what they call them, right?"

"Right."

"And I thought, it would really be great if I could get a part in that, because I'm a *huge* fan of his."

"I think this is all going to be a lot harder than you're expecting."

"I know. I'm gonna have to pay some dues for a few months maybe."

A few months. Kid had a lot to learn.

"But in the meantime, I thought maybe lightning could hit me, and I could get in to audition for this movie. I'm a *huge* fan of Matt's. You know what I'd like?"

"What?"

"I want to be your protégé."

"My what?"

"Isn't that the word? You'll be the wise older man, and you'll help me become a big star."

"I will?"

"Uh-huh. Say you will, okay?"

I knew I'd regret it later. And that "older man" business wasn't very pleasing. But here I was running around getting shot at because I wanted to realize my dream, and she just wanted my help in achieving hers. "Sure, Ronnie. You can be my protégé."

"Great!"

"I've really got to get to work now."

"We'll talk later, okay?"

"Okay."

I killed a couple of hours in the greenhouse. It was good spending time with the plants again. They'd let me go off on my musical interlude, knowing I'd return, and when I came back they didn't say a word. I watered, removed dead leaves, and plucked out the oxalis that always sprang up when I wasn't looking. I banged in a couple of nails that had worked their way loose from the benches. There was a cracked panel in the roof that I'd bought a replacement for the previous summer, then never gotten around to putting in. It seemed like as good a time as any. I was almost done with the panel when a wasp wandered in, and I freaked out trying to escape it. While I waited for it to evacuate the premises I went inside for apple juice. Thus fortified, I called Woz.

I'd gone back and forth on it since returning home the morning before. Half the time I wanted to leave well enough alone. Just accept that he'd been trailing Deanna and me, or the man who'd been following us, and was in the right place at the right time to save our asses and assassinate another car.

The other half wanted to insist he tell me everything. Who he'd been following, and why, and for how long. And why, if he'd been on the scene, he'd taken so damned long to take Vinnie boy out.

As usual, I dithered. I decided to call him and see where the conversation went. If it didn't lead to the latest shootout I'd let things be.

I usually let the phone ring six times before giving up.

With Woz I gave it four extra. He just beat the ten-count.
"Yo."

"Hey."

"Joe? How the hell are you?"

"Alive and well, thanks to you." So much for vacillation.

"What're you talking about, man?"

"The other night."

"What happened the other night?"

"So it's that way, is it?" I was a regular Edward G. Robinson.

"What way? I was sitting home watching the tube night before last."

"Who said anything about night before last?"

"You did."

"Uh-uh. I said 'the other night.'"

"You did?"

"Trust me. I did."

"Huh." He was quiet so long I thought he'd nodded off. "Woz."

"We're not having this conversation," he said.

"My lips are sealed."

"No, I don't mean you keep it a secret. I mean we're just not gonna have it. Less you know, the better."

"Tell me one thing, then. What took you so long?"

"What do you mean?"

"If you were following—let me start over. If a person were somewhere and saw something going on he was going to try to stop, why would that person wait long enough for a couple dozen rounds of ammunition to be fired."

"It might be because the person's fucking fuel pump went out on him and he hadn't got to the somewhere yet and he had to do some walking. All that's if the person were doing what you're saying, which I don't know nothing about, so let's talk about something else."

"Fine. How's Squig?"

"Little bugger's getting better by the minute. He's over at Bonnie's where the housekeeper can wait on him hand and foot. And maybe dick, far as I know. Anything else you want?"

"Not today."

"Then I'm getting off."

He hung up. I hung up. The phone rang. I stared at it like it had never made noise before. The machine kicked in. My voice did its spiel. Elaine's came over the speaker. "Pick up the goddamned phone. I know you're there. I just called you and it was busy."

I picked it up. "Hi."

"You have *got* to get call waiting."

"Soon as I get a beeper, cousin dear. What's up?"

"You got the AT&T job."

"Cool beans."

"Where'd you get that from?"

"A Jackie Chan movie. Let me get a pencil."

Rollo the parrot and I were booked for the following Monday at one of the new studios in Manhattan Beach. I wrote down the details and got off the phone. I made a grilled cheese sandwich to celebrate. My new favorite, though I took the lazy man's way out and stuck it in the toaster oven. I took it outside, made sure the wasp was gone, and ate the sandwich while I finished with the fiberglass. Then I poured more apple juice and took the newspaper out front.

I'd been there half an hour when Ronnie showed up. She was dressed relatively sedately in tank top and denim shorts, and carrying a translucent blue plastic glass. She climbed the two steps and sat in the other wicker chair, sucked some of her drink through a straw, and said, "Want an ear?"

"No, thanks, I've already got two."

She smiled, not convincingly. At first I thought she didn't get the joke, such as it was. I was wrong. "That was funny the first time I heard it in junior high," she said.

"Sorry."

"You're going to help me."

"Please. Not now."

She shook her head. "That's not what I meant. I meant … you're the only friend I've got here."

"What about Theta?"

"She's my cousin."

"She can still be your friend. My cousin Elaine's my friend."

Another headshake. "Theta's too weird. The whole gang of them, they're all weird. I didn't know I had such a weird family."

"None of us do."

"So you're my only friend here, and friends don't work just one way. Something's bothering you. Maybe I can help."

I took a sip, watched a mockingbird chase a crow, turned to Ronnie. "You're not as—"

"Dumb?"

"I was going to say 'naive.' You're not as naive as you seem."

"Some of it's an act."

"Thousands of pretty young actresses do that same act. Those who don't stand out."

"Is this a rope that you're showing me?"

"I guess so." I smiled. "Yeah, consider it your first rope."

"That's some rope." She sipped her whatever-it-was and I my juice. "How long have you been at it?"

"Coming up on thirty years. I fell into a job managing a theater and ended up doing some plays and Elaine, who's an agent—and, yes, I'll introduce you to her—decided one day I'd be good in commercials."

"You didn't want to be an actor when you were a kid?"

"No. I wanted to be a musician."

"I heard you playing. You're a heck of a guitarist. You must have been playing a long time."

"I just got back into it. Then I ran into a couple of guys I was in a band with back in the day."

"Tell me more."

I spent the next hour doing just that. I told her about Mark and Ginger's and the Platypuses, past and present, and about my troubled youth. She said her mother thought the sixties were overrated, and I expounded on that for a while, eventually reaching the conclusion that they were everything they were cracked up to be. I got off into the band's reunion and the search for Toby Bonner and the gunmen. I told her what little I remembered about the road trip I took with Toby out to the desert, and how Deanna thought he might be where we'd gone to.

Ronnie had never heard of Toby. I went inside and put his last record on and opened the front window so the sound came through. After a few tracks she said Toby's singing and playing made her sad, but in a good way.

Eventually I said it was her turn for this-is-my-life.

"Me?" she said. "I'm not very interesting."

"Rope number two: never tell anyone you're boring."

"Okay."

"And here's another, free of charge. This one you can take or leave, because there's lots of people in this town who would disagree with me. Stop dyeing your hair. Young blonds are a dime a dozen."

"I thought it looked real natural."

"It does. But I've seen that it isn't."

A moment of confusion, then she got it. She was embarrassed for all of three seconds. Then she broke into a stunning smile. I knew casting directors who would kill for that smile.

"How come I haven't seen that smile before?" I said.

"I guess I've been using my sexy gal smile. Like this."

A lot of guys would have liked it. Lips full, eyes slightly hooded.

"The real one's going to get you commercial work. Trust me on this."

"Okay."

"You were going to tell me about yourself."

"Like what?"

"Like, I don't even know how old you are."

"I'm nineteen. How old are you?"

"Forty-eight."

"That's how old my mom is."

"The one who says the sixties are overrated."

"Uh-huh. Course in Bonesaw, we didn't get the sixties till the seventies."

"And your real name? Veronica?"

There was that smile again. I started a mental list of casting people I would get her in to see. "A lot of people don't know that."

"Like in the comic book."

"That's right. I used to read those Archie comics all the time, and I rooted for Veronica, even though she was a snooty stuck-up bitch and Betty was a nice girl. I would read the stories over and over, and visit the drugstore every day when there was a new one due. I got in trouble once in Brownies because I was reading a comic when I was supposed to be making a lanyard."

"I don't think I know anyone who was a Brownie. Or at least who admits it. Were you a Girl Scout too?"

"Uh-uh. When I finished Brownies I had enough of that stuff."

"Why were they called Brownies, anyway? Were they supposed to be like elves?"

"Sure, that, and the brown uniforms. Though now that I think about it we probably had the brown uniforms because—Joe? Joe, what's wrong? You look like you've seen a ghost."

I reached over and gave her a fatherly pat on the knee. "Maybe I have," I said.

Go to the Mirror

I use my parents' bedroom for storage now, except for the chicken-wired-off corner that the canaries live in. A couple of them chirped a greeting when Ronnie and I came in. I made for the closet while Ronnie occupied herself peep-peeping at them. I pushed aside my father's army coat and my mother's wedding dress and whatever else was on the rod and pulled out the hatboxes and other junk piled up in the back. I was pretty sure what I was looking for was some-where in the closet. I pulled off lids and undid strings and breathed dust for several minutes, finding nothing of interest except the little plastic submarine I'd gotten by sending away to a cereal company. You put baking powder in it and it sank and surfaced, sank and surfaced. Fun for all ages.

The top shelf was full of shoeboxes. I reached for one and another fell on my head. It was full of report cards and other souvenirs of my youth. I got a chair from the dining room and stood on it. Ronnie'd tired of her new friends and stood by while I scouted things out. The next box was filled with old paperback books. *A Bell for Adano*, *The Prisoner of Zenda*, *The Day Lincoln Was Shot*. A couple of Westerns, which I put aside for my father. He used to love them. Then a couple by someone named Fredric Brown, and finally the prize, the tattered copy of *The Carpetbaggers* I used to sneak out of my parents' dresser when they weren't home. I put that one aside too.

The next shoebox was full of model train cabooses. The one after that, salt and pepper shakers inscribed with the names of tourist traps. Then one with, strangely enough, a pair of black high-heeled shoes.

"Mind telling me what you're looking for?" Ronnie said.

"Pictures."

"Why are you all of a sudden looking for pictures?"

"We were talking about Brownies."

"So?"

"So I remembered back when I was a teenager I had a Brownie camera."

"A what?"

"A Brownie. It's what Kodak called some of their cameras back then. And I think I took it with me when I went on the road trip with Toby."

"What good will that do? It's not going to tell you how to get there."

It had seemed a good idea when I thought of it. But she was right. What good would pictures of the secret place do if they didn't come with directions? "As long as I've made this much of a mess, I might as well keep looking."

We went through the rest of the shoeboxes and found nothing. That left a cardboard carton that had originally held boxes of Girl Scout cookies. That came down too. I opened it and found three round, colorful cookie tins from Solvang. I pried the lid off the first and was rewarded with a slew of photos. Mostly black-and-whites. Pictures of my grandparents and of my parents' wedding and of me when I was a kid. I looked at my mother in her gown and at it hanging in the closet and for a moment I couldn't look at anything else.

When I snapped out of it I picked up the tins and took them into the living room. I went through every photo in the first one, and found a lot of old memories, but none of them was Toby. Same with the second tin, except a lot of the shots were in color. They were from my pre-teen years. In one I was standing behind the three-speed bike I got in lieu of a Bar Mitzvah.

In the third cookie tin, I started to look like me. There I was helping my father paint a chair. There I was proudly holding up the first record I ever bought, the Marketts' *Out of Limits*. There I was with my first guitar.

But there was nothing remotely resembling Toby. Nothing that would help find him. Nothing except my childhood.

Until, maybe a dozen pictures from the bottom, I found a photo that sent me back to 1968.

Two girls in 1960s two-piece bathing suits. One with light hair, tall and slim, holding the end of a garden hose. The other dark-haired, buxom, her eyes caught in the middle of a blink.

I sat back on the couch, holding the picture in front of me.

"What?" Ronnie said.

"I did have the Brownie when Toby and I drove to the desert. I remember taking this picture. The girls were at a car wash. Toby stopped the car, they came over, I got the picture. Then they ran away. I—never mind."

"What?"

"I fantasized over them for weeks afterwards."

She stifled a laugh. So did I. Then I sat up and went through the rest of the box. "Nothing."

"Maybe you missed something."

I ran through them again, checking for pictures stuck to the backs of others. Still nothing.

"Where haven't we looked?" Ronnie said.

We went through every box in the house, then hit the garage. I found a lot of junk for Goodwill, but no more photographs. Then I remembered a carton of crap on the top shelf of my bedroom closet. It had been there so long it was part of the architecture. I pulled it down, put it on the floor, undid the flaps.

"It's empty," I said.

Ronnie was leaning against my dresser with her legs crossed at the ankle. "Looks like it," she said.

"Why have I had an empty carton in my closet for thirty years?"

"Drugs?"

"Probably." I looked in it again. Nothing had materialized. "This is stupid. I'm looking for a picture I don't know exists, and if it exists there's no reason to expect it would show anything useful."

"Don't give up. You'll think of something else." She pushed off from the dresser, turned, caught her reflection in the mirror. "You really think I'd look better with my natural color?"

I moved over next to her. I looked at her reflection.

I remembered.

Cache Cache

We started with my sock drawer. Took out all the socks, checked under the shelf paper, put the socks back. I managed not to reveal what I had wrapped up in the fabric sample.

It wasn't there, nor in any of the other drawers.

"Maybe it slipped behind," she said.

We pulled all the left-hand drawers out. We found a couple of rubber bands and a nickel. We moved to the right side. No rubber bands, but several paper clips, another nickel, a Mercury-head dime.

And a photograph.

I reached in and pulled it out. I looked at it, showed it to Ronnie, and stared at it some more.

AND WHATEVER
COMES MY WAY

Underture

They were cruising out toward Palm Springs in Toby's Triumph, with the wind blowing their hair and the sun hot on their faces. Their second joint hung from the corner of Toby's mouth. They had KBRK on the radio, and Jim Ladd was dishing out Cream and Vanilla Fudge and Moby Grape. Their guitars were jammed in behind the seats. A dozen candy bars filled a bag by Joe's feet. He reached in and came out with a Snickers. He undid the wrapper and tossed it on the floor with all the other junk and held it to Toby's mouth for him to take a bite. How he could do that and not lose the joint, Joe never could figure out. After Toby chewed some off Joe swallowed the rest of it and washed it down with a Coke. Then he snatched the joint, took a hit, and coughed his guts out.

Toby grabbed the roach from Joe's fingers. "You okay, man?"

"Yeah," Joe said. "Just had some Snickers in my throat." He coughed some more, then suddenly sneezed, blowing snot onto the dash. He stared at it, amazed at the color. Toby glanced over and said, "Far out, man."

"Far fucking *out," Joe said.*

Around Pomona there was a big wreck, and they had to get off the freeway. They came up on some girls in bathing suits running a car wash. Toby drove real slow to get a good look. Two of the girls started waving. One was short with big tits and the other tall with little ones. Toby stopped the car, and Joe said, "Hold on, girls," and dug out his Brownie camera and hopped out of the car and snapped their picture. Then the girls got giggly and ran away.

After they got started up again Joe said, "How'd you like to get a piece of that?"

"Man, I'd like to get a piece of anything."

"That's the truth."

They got back on the freeway. Joe said, "How far we going?"

"A ways yet."

"I gotta piss."

"Why'n't you piss back there?"

"Didn't have to then."

"Hold onto it. We're almost there."

"How much is almost?"

"A few miles. Sixty, maybe."

"Too far. I really gotta piss."

"So finish your Coke and piss in the bottle."

"Fuck, man. You just want to see my cock."

"Seen it. Little tiny thing."

"Least I got two—"

"Hey, just shut up, okay?"

"Sure, man, whatever you say. But I really gotta go. Stop this fucking thing, okay?"

"Okay, okay."

Toby pulled off at the next exit, and Joe jumped out and down into this sort of ravine and let it out. It was cool watching as the piss pooled up on the ground and then started soaking in.

"You jerkin' off down there?" Toby said.

"No, shithead."

"Then get yourself up here."

Joe shook off the last drops and zipped up and spit on his hands to wash them. He climbed back up to where the car was, and they got back on the freeway. After a while he said, "Hey, man."

"Yeah?"

"How come you're taking me to your secret place?"

"Why you asking?"

"Because you won't even let anybody else know where it is."

"I don't know, man. It just feels right, you know what I mean?"

"No."

"You're like my brother, *man."*

"Right on. You mean it?"

"Yeah."

"I never had a brother," Joe said. "Or a sister, even."

"Only thing is, you gotta promise not to tell anyone where it is."

"Why would I tell?"

"By accident, maybe."

"I won't. I promise."

"Far out."

Somewhere along the way KBRK faded out. Joe fooled with the radio to get another station. All he could find was some country and western shit. "This's all I can get," he said, and turned it off.

"Man, put that back on."

"That country crap?"

Toby flipped the radio back on. "This's Chet Atkins. Guy's fantastic."

"You like this?"

"Anybody plays good guitar, I like. You ever hear Segovia?"

"Never even heard of him."

"Spanish guy. Plays classical shit on guitar. Like nothing you ever heard."

Somewhere near Palm Springs Toby drove the Triumph down

a ramp. He turned left at the stop sign. They went back under the freeway and headed for the mountains. After a while the road got rough. Over to the sides were some neat-looking flowers, orange ones and yellow ones, and behind them lots and lots of tall grass. If it hadn't been for the road and the electric poles and the wires between them, you wouldn't have known anyone had ever been there.

After a while they made a couple more turns. Joe had no clue where he was or even which way he was going. He looked up at the sky to find the sun, but when he did he couldn't figure out how to get it to tell him anything.

"Wow, man," he said. "It's beautiful out here."

"Even better where we're going."

They drove some more and all of a sudden pulled off to the side. There was a little path leading off through the grass. "This's it," Toby said. He grabbed the bag of candy bars and told Joe to take the drinks and got out of the car.

"I don't see anything," Joe said.

"You dumbfuck, when I said this is it, I meant in the car. We gotta walk some." He pulled his guitar from behind the seat. "Come on. What're you waiting for?"

Joe got the drinks and his own guitar and followed Toby down the path. It curved off from the road and went down a hill and ran into another path. When they got to the end of the other path you could see the tops of a bunch of palm trees way off.

"This it?" Joe said.

"Nope. We got a way to go yet."

Toby started climbing down another hill that was all covered with big rocks. Joe went slow, because he was still real loaded, and because the rocks were hard to find a place to put your foot in, and because as soon as he started down he banged his guitar case on one of the rocks. He still didn't know why they'd brought the guitars. There couldn't be any power out there in the middle of nowhere.

He clonked his case a couple more times on the way down, but he didn't think it'd been hard enough to fuck up the SG. When he got to the bottom Toby was already half a football field away. The rocks went up on both sides, and as you went along they got closer together, so you ended up in the shade and felt all closed in. Joe ran after Toby, but he saw something funny in the rocks and stopped to look at it. He thought maybe it was a fossil. A long time ago there'd been all sorts of weird animals running around out there, dinosaurs and mammoths and maybe cavemen. No, that couldn't be right. The dinosaurs happened a jillion years before the mammoths and the cavemen.

Except he saw a movie once where dinosaurs showed up in modern times in a place not a whole lot different from the one they were in. He felt a weird tickle on the back of his neck and ran like hell to catch up with Toby. They kept walking down the valley thing.

"The fuck you doing back there?" Toby said.

"I had to tie my shoe."

"Which one?"

Joe looked down. Left or right? Oh, yeah. He'd just made up the thing about his shoe. "Both of them."

"You're so full of shit your eyes are brown," Toby said.

"Are we almost there yet?"

"Soon."

He wasn't lying about that. The path curved around and all of a sudden they were out in the open. They went up another hill, this one nice and easy. But Joe banged his guitar case anyway. "Shit, man, I'm gonna break this thing."

"Thing's a piece of shit anyway."

They climbed up the rest of the hill. And there they were.
"Outta sight," Joe said.

It was like one of those places you saw in desert movies. An
oasis. There was a pond in the middle, smaller than a backyard
swimming pool. It was dark, like it was real deep. A little in back
of the pond was a cliff. You could see all the different layers of rock
in it. The cliff ran off to both sides, as far as Joe could see.

They went down the path until they were right by the pond.
There were five palm trees around it, two together, and two
together, and one all by itself. Joe figured they were the ones he'd
seen the tops of a while back. He imagined a monkey up in one,
throwing coconuts down at them.

"I didn't know there were palm trees out here in the desert,"
Joe said. "Or water either."

"Why you think they call it Palm Springs?" Toby said.

"Huh. Never thought about it that way. Far out."

There were a bunch of cacti around too. There were some of
those with flat pieces, like his next door neighbors once gave him to
eat. A kind with long red spines that looked like they'd cut you
up if you fell into one. And some covered with spines like little
daggers. Joe bent down to look at one, and Toby said he'd better
watch it, because the stems would jump out and stick themselves
into you if you got too close. Joe thought what Toby said was
probably a bunch of bullshit, but he steered clear of them anyway.

On the other side of the pond was a shack. It was made of old
wood that looked like it had been there a hundred years. They
went around the pond and walked up to it. There was a big old
padlock on the door. Toby pulled out his keyring and opened the
lock. Joe saw a couple of old kitchen chairs in there, and a low
table, and a tarp covering something up.

Toby reached up for something, and a light came on. "What the
fuck?" Joe said. "Did you slip acid in my Snickers?"

"Fuck, no."

"How the hell'd you do this?"

"I didn't. It was all out here already. Come look."

They put down their guitar cases and walked around back of the shack. Toby pointed up the cliff. Joe'd missed the electric line coming down from a pole up there, attached to a metal pipe on top of the shack. He went round front again and stuck his head inside. The line came into the shack and through some more metal pipes. One went across the ceiling to the light and the other went down the walls to a metal electric outlet boxes like in his garage.

"Why's this out here like this?" Joe said. *"With electric and everything."*

"Guy who showed me this place said there was a scientific station out here."

"Who was he?"

"Friend of my dad's. Name's Brad, neat guy, nothing like my dad. Long hair, and he's gotta be forty. He worked here until they shut the place down. He said they were studying rocks and stuff, but he got a funny look when he said it, like there was something he wasn't saying."

"Like what?"

"I think it was a spy station. That's why they ran electric out here. They wouldn't've done it for a crummy science station, but for a spy station I figure they'd spend whatever they had to."

"Who were they spying on? Russians?"

"That's what I think. I think there was a commie spy ring out here and they were checking them out. There were other buildings here, but they fell apart after they stopped using the place."

"When was that?"

"In '62, right after that shit with Cuba where they were gonna set off A-bombs. Story is the government cut off their money. I

figure after the Cuba thing the spies went home. But my dad's friend, he kept coming, 'cause it's such a cool place."

"Why'd he show you?"

"He was balling my mom after my dad ran off, so he was around a lot. And you know what? He was more like a dad to me than my real father. And one day he said, I got something cool to show you, and he drove me up here."

"He still around?"

Toby shook his head and said, "Went off a while back. He was mixed up in some bad shit and had to leave town."

"So you're the only one knows about this place?"

"Me, and you, now."

"Far out."

"And I suppose the other guys that worked here, but Brad said none of them ever came back."

"So the power was still on after all this time?"

"Nah. They shut it off. I got it going again."

"How'd you do that?"

"Wasn't very hard. Come on. We gonna play, or what?"

Toby went in the shack and lifted up the tarp. There was an amp underneath, a big Fender Showman with two speaker boxes. He plugged in the amp, and then he got his guitar case and put it on the table and got his Les Paul out. He picked a real long cable off a hook on the wall and stuck it in the jack. He turned on the amp and played one of those runs of his like Joe knew he'd never be able to do. The whole time Toby had this big shit-eating grin on.

After all that he looked at Joe and said, "C'mon. What're you waitin' for?"

Joe got his SG out too and grabbed another cable off the wall and hooked himself up. They took the guitars and a couple of fold-

ing chairs that were stacked against the wall outside and to the edge of the water. Toby gave Joe his guitar to hold, which made Joe feel good because Toby hardly ever let anyone touch his ax. Then Toby went back to the shack and kind of swung the amp around so it was in the doorway. And then he came back and they started to play.

They were out there all afternoon. Toby taught Joe a lot of stuff that day, showed him how he was fingering a couple of things wrong, and some riffs that ended up a lot easier than you would have thought, and how to use his whammy bar better. The last one was weird, because Toby didn't have one on his Les Paul, but he took Joe's SG and he could use the thing better than anyone Joe'd ever seen, except maybe Hendrix.

Along the way they finished up the candy bars and the drinks and had another couple of joints. A lot of the time they just sat there with their guitars on and talked. Toby was Joe's best friend at The House, except of course for Bonnie, and he'd told Joe a lot, but that afternoon he told him a whole lot more. Stuff he said he'd never told anyone before, about his family mostly, and how fucked-up it was. And about his brother, who he got along fine with but who was in the Army in Vietnam, and how he worried about him. And how if Toby got drafted he would go to Canada. He asked Joe what he would do, and Joe told him how his dad knew someone who had something on someone on the draft board, and had told him not to worry. Then Joe told him about how his dad was in jail for murder, which he hadn't told anyone else, not even Bonnie.

When the sun got pretty low Joe said how the sunset was really going to be out of sight, but Toby said they couldn't stick around for it, because you couldn't walk back in the dark, you'd get lost or eaten by coyotes. Joe got a little scared, but Toby told him he'd *never actually seen a coyote, and he figured as long as they got back to the car before dark they were okay.*

They packed up their axes and Toby covered up the amp and made sure everything was where it belonged, and they left. Joe did a lot better on the way back. He only tripped once or twice.

They were almost back to the car when they came to a really big rock sticking out of the ground. One side of it was flat, and there was a gigantic peace symbol painted on it. The peace symbol was painted in white paint and was about ten feet tall. Joe didn't know how he'd missed it on the way in, until he looked at the angles and saw that the way the flat side of the rock faced, he wouldn't have seen it if he wasn't looking for it.

"I wanted to use DayGlo," Toby said, "but the guy at the store said the white would last a lot longer."

"You did this?"

"Year or so back. Nearly broke my fuckin' neck doing the top part."

"How'd you get way up there?"

"I was so high I fuckin' floated, man."

"I gotta get a picture of this."

"You need a camera to get pictures, dumbass."

"I got the Brownie with me, remember? I took those two girls' picture, 'member?"

"The one with the big tits."

"Her, and the other one too. I think I left it in the car. Stay here, okay? I'm gonna go get it and take a picture."

"You can't show it to anyone."

"Sure, sure."

"And hurry up. It's gettin' dark."

"Don't worry. I got flashbulbs."

It only took a minute to get back to the car and another to get back. They walked across the rocks to where the peace symbol was. Joe made Toby stand in front of it. He told Toby to give the peace sign. Toby gave him the finger instead, and Joe thought that rocked. He tried to line up the picture just right and Toby made howling noises, like a coyote would. Then Joe snapped the picture and the flashbulb went off and Toby said, "Can we get the fuck out of here now?"

They picked up KBRK again on the way back. They played some Beatles and some Stones and some of everybody else Joe and Toby wanted to hear. Partway home Toby asked if Joe wanted to smoke their last joint. Joe said he didn't think he needed it, that the day had been so fucking fantastic he didn't need any more dope, and Toby said he thought the same but just thought he'd ask.

When they got back near Mark and Ginger's, Joe told Toby thanks for taking him out there. Toby said he'd really wanted to and he was glad he did, and that they'd do it again soon. But just a few days later he and Bonnie got discovered and Joe never saw either one of them again. Joe thought about going to the place without Toby, but he wasn't sure he could find it. And besides, without Toby it just wouldn't be right.

A couple of months later Joe got around to developing the film in his Brownie. The picture of the girls was pretty good, except the one with the big tits was blinking. The one of Toby wasn't so good. He looked kind of like a zombie. And with all the time Joe took, he still cut off the top of the big peace sign.

Empty Glass

"It was the only photo of Toby I had," I said. I touched the surface of the mirror, a couple of inches up from the lower left corner. Then I slipped the picture between the frame and the mirror, right where it had been way back when, just below the Who ticket stub that had been there since '71.

"How do you think it got where it was?" Ronnie said.

"One day Elaine said my room was a pit and I had to clean it up. I was working on the dresser and I looked at the picture. I wasn't sure why I still had it up there. I took it out and threw it in a drawer. Somewhere along the line it fell behind, I guess."

•

I showed up at Gina's well after nine. I ate reheated Pollo Loco and a dish of Ben and Jerry's. The three of us sat on the couch watching a *Buffy the Vampire Slayer* rerun. Gina and I put Aricela to bed at ten-thirty and went back out to the living room. We sat silently, side by side, leaning on each other. After a while I said, "Guess what I found."

"The holy grail? A lottery ticket worth a million dollars?"

"Actually, I should've said 'we found.' Ronnie and I."

"If you're trying to get a rise out of me, I'm too tired."

"A photo of Toby."

"Where?"

"It fell behind the drawers in my dresser I don't know how many years ago."

"And this is significant why?"

"The peace symbol. I forgot all about it. But there was a giant peace symbol painted on the rock on the way into his hideaway."

"So?"

"So all we have to do is find that, and we're on the way to finding the hideaway."

"We."

"Deanna and me."

"Right, her. I have trouble keeping track of all your new girlfriends. There are two problems with your scheme."

"Only two?"

"First, knowing there's a peace symbol on a rock doesn't tell you where the rock is."

"I know. But there are only so many turnoffs from the freeway in the area, and so many turns off each turnoff, if you know what I mean."

"Sounds tedious. Here's the second problem: What makes you think it's still there?"

"Why wouldn't it be there?"

"Thirty-however-many years of sun and wind."

"I don't know. What about that big rock off the Pasadena Freeway? The one with all the fraternity letters and things painted on it. Some of that stuff has been there as long as I can remember."

"Pasadena isn't the desert."

I thought about it. "There's still a chance."

"A very small one."

"I really want to be in this band."

"And I really want you to. But if it depends on finding Toby Bonner, you might as well forget it." She took my hand. "You're not going to forget it, though, are you?"

"You know me so well."

"So be careful out there. Drink plenty of liquids. Wear sunscreen. Take a snakebite kit."

"Yes, ma'am."

The Channel 6 news came on. I muted the TV. They made as much sense with the sound off as on.

"How's our little girl?" I said.

"For one thing, I caught her going through my dresser."

"She have an explanation?"

"I didn't let on that I'd seen her. The way she was doing it. Sort of reverently. She'd touch something and run her finger over it, pick something else out and hold it to her face."

"She's a snoopy one, all right. I found her going through the pictures in your closet last night."

"I think she's auditioning us for parents."

"Boy, did she use the wrong casting director."

"Be serious for once. Living with Gran and Gramps clearly wasn't a walk in the park. I think she sees us as a chance for some stability. Maybe some love too. God, listen to me. I sound like a fucking Junior Leaguer." She looked back over her shoulder, like she was watching Aricela through the wall. "That little girl's going to have a lot to deal with. I think she's buried what happened that night with her grandparents. It's going to come out sometime. She's going to need lots of therapy, I'm afraid." She turned back and stared at the TV. "Did you call Burns?"

"I did, but she didn't call back."

"Did you leave a message?"

"No."

"That would explain it, then." She picked up the remote. "Let's drop it for now."

"I do wonder why they still haven't said anything about her on the news. I caught a report just before I left, and they just talked about the one daughter. Not Aricela's mom, the other one."

"The Basque separatist, or whatever she is. What part of 'Let's drop it for now' didn't you understand?"

"I'm sick of that expression. That 'what part didn't you—'"

"I knew what you meant."

A minute or two went by. The skeleton of a bus smoldered on the silent screen.

"Why are we getting snippy here?" I said.

She clicked off the TV. "Mental exhaustion. Also PMS."

"I don't have PMS."

"You should try it sometime." She moved up to the edge of the sofa. "Don't take it seriously, babe. I'm still dealing with my stuff." She stood and held out a hand. "Come, let's go to bed. I need my beauty sleep."

"That," I said, "would be gilding the lily."

I got a smile out of it. "Smooth talker," she said.

•

I got out of there early. Gina was still dozing and Aricela was watching Katie Couric make thirteen million a year. When I got home I poured a bowl of cereal and read the paper. I checked out who had died, how many were over eighty and how many were under seventy. Some World War I veteran had kicked the bucket at a hundred and four.

A spate of centenarians had moved on lately, the supposed oldest man in the world among them. Guys like that gave me hope that my life wasn't more than half over. Which was something that had been bugging me lately.

I checked out the comics. In *Zits*, Jeremy's friend Pierce had taken Jeremy's guitar apart. The pieces were scattered all over a table. Pierce said Jeremy looked more like a keyboard player anyway. I knew this related to my situation. I just didn't know how.

On to the sports page. The Lakers were storming through the playoffs. The purple and gold flags were appearing on cars again, supplanting the Stars and Stripes that sprouted on September 12. I'd been waiting for the nationalistic fervor to calm down and for all the instant patriots to return to their regularly scheduled programs. In the days after the attacks, everyone kept saying everything had changed. They were wrong. Nothing had changed. Not really. Especially my life. Everything was as it had been for the last decade or more, except that I was sleeping with Gina. I lazed around the house, went out on auditions, booked the occasional job, sold bugs at shopping malls. I watered my cacti and watched Jackie Chan movies and ate takeout. I'd probably do the same things until I dropped dead. Thoreau said most men lived lives of quiet desperation. I didn't even do that. I led a life of quiet apathy.

I didn't want to do it for the rest of my life. I called Deanna and told her about the photo.

Going Mobile

We were just past downtown when the sun began to break through, bathing us in that peculiar light L.A. gets when most of the overcast has burned away. A few minutes later the last of the clouds boiled off, and we were under a hot blue sky. The 10 was as clear as it ever gets, and we were making good time. It was a quarter after eleven, just more than an hour since I'd called Deanna and been told that Mott had wandered off again, and that she was raring to wander around in the desert. I picked her up in Hollywood, stopped for supplies at Mayfair, and jumped on the freeway.

I let Deanna rave about Mott until we got over the big hill before Pomona. Then I said, "Enough."

"Excuse me?"

"I gave you forty miles worth of bitching. You're starting to repeat yourself. The guy's a loser. Get over him."

"Asshole."

"No. I'm not. I'm just a friend who wants to remind you you're over fifty and the rest of your life doesn't have to suck."

"Well, la-de-da."

No conversation for a couple of miles. KLOS started crackling and was gone half a minute later. I shoved Tom

Petty into the tape player. Tom let it be known that he didn't want to live like a refugee.

"Okay," Deanna said. "I'm done."

"Good. Tell me why you really want to find Toby."

"I told you why."

"That something-I-have-to-do business? That you might feel your life is complete if you see him again?"

"Did I say those things?"

"You did. At my house."

"I probably could have done better, couldn't I?"

"Probably. You could have said, say, a friend of yours was doing a documentary on the sixties. Or that Toby had a child he'd never seen who wanted to get to know him before going off to be a missionary in darkest Africa."

She didn't say anything. She just stared out the side window.

"Is that it?" I said. "Something about a child?"

She turned to me. I took a quick look. Her eyes were wet. "Yes."

"You want to talk about it?"

"No."

More miles unspooled. Neither of us spoke. I created a fantasy. We'd get to where we were going, find or not find Toby, drive all the way back without either of us saying a word.

Just past San Bernardino she blew that scenario to shreds. "The part about not sleeping with Toby? That wasn't quite the truth."

"Oh?"

"I did. Just that once."

"Why tell me you didn't?"

"I don't know. Maybe it made a better story. I was mixing fact and fiction and that part came out fiction."

"Why lie to me at all?"

"I didn't want you to know the truth until I was sure I could trust you."

"And now you trust me?"

"Yes. Actually, since the business up near Ventura. When I did my little death scene and you were genuinely concerned I'd been shot."

"Good. Okay, let me guess. You slept with Toby and you got pregnant and had a kid. And now the kid's in his thirties and wants to see his father."

"The kid never reached thirty. He never even reached ten."

"What happened?"

"A playground accident. He got hit in the head with a baseball bat."

The image blew my mind.

"He was old enough to wonder why most of the other kids had daddies and he didn't. He'd started asking about his. I let it slip that his father didn't know he existed. He wanted to meet him. When I lost him I felt horribly guilty. I decided to at least tell his father about him, show him a picture, something."

"You keep saying 'his father.' Not 'Toby.'"

She smiled, barely. "When I got pregnant I had a boyfriend. He and I fucked like bunnies, two, three, four times a day. You know what those days were like. Free love and all that."

I didn't tell her I'd missed out on that aspect of the sixties.

"When I got pregnant—I was on the pill, but with all that

sex the odds were against me—I assumed Roger was the father. The odds on it were so in favor. A couple of months later he took off."

"Didn't want to be a father."

"He didn't know I was pregnant. He was just moving on. I knew where he was, more or less, and probably could have found him, but I chose not to. Not until Chris died. Then I looked him up and told him the whole story. He looked at the pictures I had and said the whole thing was a trip and that was that."

"But there was always the chance Toby was the father."

"Right. I tormented myself with that. Eventually I convinced myself I was over it."

"And now, just in case, you want to make sure Toby, if he's even alive, knows about the kid."

"Sort of. I ran into Roger a couple of months ago. He became a grownup somewhere along the line, runs a restaurant, respectable businessman, all that. He was with his family, a wife and two daughters. The wife was much younger, blond, big boobs, you know the type. Not a big surprise. The kids were the surprise."

"How so?"

"They were Chinese. Roger's family's from Denmark."

"He adopted them."

"Give the boy a stuffed bear."

I thought I knew where she was leading. I wanted to hear it from her. "Lots of people adopt Chinese babies. It's a big thing nowadays among guilt-ridden liberals."

"The wife went off with the kids. Roger and I went for coffee, to get caught up. Soon as we sat down he told me they adopted because it was the only way they would ever have kids. They'd tried and tried, gone to doctors, found there was a problem. His problem. He couldn't father a child. And according to the doctors, he never could have."

I Can See For Miles

We found him on the second day.

On the way out to the desert Deanna told me how, now that she knew Toby had to be Chris's father, she'd obsessed on finding him, or at least finding out if he were alive. The trail led nowhere. Then I came along, all bright and shiny-eyed and ready to go looking for him.

We tried Highway 62 that first afternoon. It came off the freeway before Palm Springs, but neither of us had more than the vaguest memory of where we'd gotten off the road all those years ago. It came first, we investigated it first. We went down a lot of side roads, walked down a lot of trails, breathed a lot of dirt, and emerged each time wondering whether if we'd just gone another twenty yards we would have found the right place.

When it got dark, when we were more tired, dirty, sweaty than we could stand, we found a motel. We rented rooms, got ourselves cleaned up, had dinner at a Red Lobster, returned to the motel. We got a drink in the lobby bar and went to our rooms. I called Gina, brought her up to date, found out she'd taken Aricela to Universal Studios, where they both had a blast. We chatted a little more, love-you-love-you'd, got off the phone. I channel-surfed and found pro wrestling. It was just the kind of mindless entertainment I needed. When it was over I turned off the TV and reached into the gym bag I'd used for luggage. I took out the two photos, the one of Toby and the one of the two girls. I'd tossed them in the bag just before I walked out the door. I looked at the one of Toby, asked him whether he wanted to be found, didn't get an answer. Then I checked out the one of the girls. I wondered what had happened to them, whether they still lived in Pomona, whether the big-breasted one had gotten fat, whether they had kids of their own, grown ones, ones who would make me feel old if I knew about them.

•

We got an early start in the morning. We had a quick break-fast and planned our strategy. We weren't sure we'd exhausted all the possibilities up 62, but decided to try something else. Dillon Road seemed the best choice. It formed a big loop starting in North Palm Springs and returning to the freeway a little south of Indio. We opted to take the freeway south and follow the loop back.

The morning was much like the day before. Drive, turn, drive, walk, turn back. Repeat as necessary. We stopped for a lunch of sandwiches and fruit at noon. Even in the shade of a tall date palm it was hotter than Salma Hayek. The previous afternoon we'd used up our water by four. This time we brought five gallons of Sparkletts. It was almost half gone.

After lunch I let Deanna drive. We dismissed several more possibilities. We were both tired and cranky. I was questioning my sanity and sure she was uncertain about hers. Around our fifth post-lunch expedition I was begin-ning to doubt I'd make it through the afternoon.

We drove up a narrow dirt road that ended in a *T*. We

chose to go right. A dusty mile later we hit a dead end. We turned around and drove past the crossroads. A couple of miles on the other side was another *T*. Again we went right. In a couple of minutes we saw a trail. We got out and followed it until it stopped at a big outcropping. Somebody had done some painting there, but it wasn't Toby. It was Julio, and he wanted the world to know he loved Celia.

We retraced our steps, got back in, followed the road some more to another trail. We stomped off down it and followed it as it went around a couple of huge boulders. Deanna was a little behind me. I turned my head to say something and saw a chunk of rock sticking twenty feet out of the ground. One side of it was flat.

"I want to take a look at that big rock," I said. "Coming?"

"Wherever you go, I go."

We navigated our way to it. By the time we were ten yards away we knew we were there. The peace sign was vague and parts of it were gone altogether. But if you squinted ...

We threw our arms around each other and jumped up and down like *Wheel of Fortune* contestants. This wasted half the energy we had left. We returned to the trail and followed it. It went down a hill and spliced into another path. At the end of this one, we saw a clump of palm trees off in the distance.

The second trail ended at the top of a rock-strewn slope. A little beyond the bottom was a vague path that went into a gap in some rocks. We picked our way down, holding onto each other for support. Grit and stones sifted out from under our shoes. We half-walked, half-slid to the bottom and made for the opening between the rocks. We entered a narrow corridor, like a mini-Grand Canyon. The farther we got in the higher the walls went. For some reason I thought of *The Lost World*, that movie where latter-day dinosaurs inhabited an area not unlike the one we were in. My neck hair prickled. I stepped up my pace.

The good thing about the canyon was that it put us in shade. It was cooler, though just barely. We kept going and going and began to wonder if we were wrong about the whole thing. The path curved around and the walls on either side abruptly ended and we were thrust into the glaring sunlight. There was nothing to indicate which way to go. We went straight, up a shallow slope. Three steps after we reached the top we could see Toby's hideaway.

There was a pond in the center, and five palm trees, one of them dead, spread around its periphery. The whole setup stood in front of a tall cliff. A decrepit wood shack more or less stood directly across the pond. A cable led from a pole on top of the cliff to a pipe sticking out of the remains of the roof. Another structure was alongside the shack, a backyard utility shed. Another length of pipe went from the wood shack to the metal one. To the left of the utility shed a backyard barbecue sat with its orange lid open. Further to the left was a ring of stones with the remains of burnt logs scattered within. More items were scattered on the ground, a dead beach chair and a portable cooler and a couple of empty orange crates.

We moved down the last slope, circumnavigated the pond, came to the skeleton of the shack. "This is where he kept his stuff," I said. "He had an amp in here, a big Fender I think. I don't know how the hell he got it in here." I pointed at the metal shed. "Or that either. It's new. Wasn't there when I was here."

"Look around," Deanna said. "What impression do you get?"

I scanned the immediate area, then farther out, to the far edge of the pond. "That no one's been here lately."

She nodded. "I think he's long gone."

"I think so too. But it was a hell of an idea while it lasted." I rapped on the wall of the metal hut. "Maybe we'll find something in here."

"Can't hurt to look. I'm sure Toby won't mind."

The door was latched. I opened it a couple of inches, then cautiously swung it the rest of the way. I didn't want to waltz into a nest of rattlesnakes.

It took my eyes several seconds to adjust. When they had, I saw a cot-size mattress taking up half the floor. Someone was on it, lying very still. I inched aside to let Deanna look.

"He's not moving," she said. "If it's him."

"I've had more than my share of stumbling over dead bodies," I said, "and I'm not eager for this to be another. But I suppose we ought to be sure." I stepped closer and knelt by the mattress. I leaned forward to see if it was Toby. I didn't know if I'd recognize him, but what else could I do?

When I got close enough to get a good look I closed my eyes. When I opened them he didn't look any different. I stayed there staring until Deanna said, "Is he dead?"

I turned to look at her over my shoulder. She stood outlined against the rectangle of blue sky a million miles beyond the doorway.

"Dead?" I said. "He's more than dead. He's a mummy."

Say It Ain't So, Joe

We found a flashlight in the shed. We didn't expect it to work, and it didn't disappoint us. We found a couple of batteries with an expiration date several years back. But the Energizer Bunny was working overtime. There was enough juice to get the flashlight lit. I pointed it at the mummy for a closer look.

Picture a big piece of beef jerky with arms and legs, clad only in the remains of a pair of thin cotton shorts. The skin was stretched close over his bones, so tightly it was shiny in some places. Looking at him wasn't as bad as you might have expected. He resembled an alien artifact more than a dead person.

Only the eyes were repellent. They looked like raisins, creased and sunken in their sockets. You think of mummies, you don't think of eyes. Not until you've seen some.

"How could this happen?" Deanna said.

"I guess if you die out here in the heat and dryness … maybe it's too dry for the bacteria or whatever that usually turn dead people to mush."

"How long do you think he's been here?"

"Got me. A month? Ten years?"

"If it's him, who's been showing up to play those gigs?"

"Some clever impersonator."

"You really think that?"

I stood to relieve the ache in my knees. "I don't know what I think." I turned her around and gave her a nudge to get her outside. I took one more look at the thing on the mattress and walked out too.

"What do we do now?" she said.

"Build him a pyramid?"

"That's not funny."

"Then why are you laughing?"

"I'm not laughing."

"Giggling, then."

"I probably have heatstroke. Though it is funny, in a way." She let loose a final snicker. "We wander around in the desert for two days, and all we come up with is a mummy."

"Stop complaining. The Israelites wandered in the desert for forty years."

"But at least they had that golden calf to eat. What am I *talking* about?"

I put a hand on her shoulder. "It's a shock, finding him dead. More of a shock finding him looking like Lon Chaney."

She placed a hand atop mine. "What do we do now?"

"We could carry him out of here. I'm sure he doesn't weigh much."

"You're not serious, are you?"

"No." I turned back to the metal mausoleum. "I think the best thing is to leave him here. Just get the hell out, pretend we never came, leave him be."

"I suppose you're right. After I tell him what I came here to tell him."

I took back my hand. "I'll be around somewhere. Take your time."

"Don't wander too far."

"I won't, I promise."

I turned and walked away. The door squeaked as Deanna went back into the shed. I walked around the pond, stopping directly opposite Toby's lonely settlement. I snatched up one of the rocks at the water's edge and tried to skim it across the surface. It sank like a stone. Not surprising. I'd never skimmed one in forty-eight years of trying. There was no reason I should succeed now.

I tried another, with the same result. I picked up one more, but held onto it. I closed my eyes and tried to imagine myself at fifteen, high as a kite, a city boy out of his element. It was no use. I had no connection with the place. I couldn't imagine why I'd come.

I took out the two photos. I looked at the one of Toby first, but found I'd wrung all the memories I could from it. Then I looked at the other, the two car-wash girls. I wondered what would have happened if Toby and I had gotten to know them. Maybe we wouldn't have even made it out to the desert.

I wandered away from the pond to take a leak. It was the first time since breakfast. Most of the water I'd taken in had been sweated out. My urine was deep yellow, almost orange. The ground was too dry for it to soak in, and it flowed into a depression and pooled up.

It's funny what kicks off a memory. A photo of a couple of teenage girls, a puddle of pee …

Deanna was in the shed half an hour. I didn't ask what she did in there, and she didn't volunteer the information. I was waiting outside when she emerged. I told her she'd inspired me to say my own private good-bye. I assured her it would only take a few minutes. She told me to take as long as I needed and walked away.

I went in and closed the door behind me. It only took a couple of minutes to do what I needed to.

Deanna was surprised when I came out so quickly, but she didn't say a word. She just turned and started back, and so did I. Partway through the narrow passage there was a noise above, something skittering around, a coyote, a ghost, I don't know. She squealed, I yelped, we wrapped our arms around each other and looked up. Nothing there. We exchanged foolish grins and started back again. She hung onto my hand the whole way.

•

I pulled in at a hydrant in front of Deanna's place. She said she'd call in a couple of days, after we'd both soaked every-thing in, and we could talk about it then. I didn't think she'd call and I didn't much care. Nothing personal; we'd just been two people with a common goal, and now there was nothing to connect us. We shared an across-the-seat hug and she got out. I watched her safely in the door of the building and found a 7-Eleven. I called Gina, told her I was back, said I was coming over.

It took longer to get there than it should have. There was a disturbance at Hollywood and La Brea. A Disney cartoon was opening and someone was protesting, Arabs or feminists or Arab feminists. I had to skirt around and got stuck at every light.

I found a spot, went upstairs, rang the bell. The door opened. Gina stood there, squirming, with an arm wrapped around her from the back. There was blood all over her cheek and some trickling from her mouth.

The arm belonged to Darren Chapman. The hand at the end of his other one held a gun.

Cat's in the Cupboard

"You son of a—" The gun was suddenly six inches from my face. I shut up.

"Get over there," he said. "You too, bitch."

Bitch was Gina. *Over there* was the living room.

We followed orders. The next one was to get on the sofa. We followed that one too.

"I'm sorry," Gina said. "I shouldn't have opened the door for him. I thought it was you. You called and the timing was right and—"

"Shut up." He was standing in front of the television, right where Aricela had sat watching Dick Van Dyke think aliens had invaded.

Aricela?

Stay best friends with someone enough years, you develop a kind of telepathy. I turned an inch toward Gina. She knew what I was asking. A slight eye movement told me Aricela was on the premises and that Darren Chapman didn't know it.

"Okay," he said. "Who should I do first?" The gun went between Gina and me, back and forth, back and forth.

"Why do you have to do either one of us?" Gina said.

"Oh, no," he said. "Not that old trick. I've seen it in too

many movies. The hero keeps the killer talking, the killer explains everything, the hero figures out a plan." He came around the back of the couch, poked the gun behind Gina's ear, nuzzled it through her hair. "I think I'll do you first. Spare you seeing your boyfriend get shot. You, Portugal, get to see her brains blown out before—"

"I'm your father," I said.

"What the fuck are you talking about?"

"I slept with your mother the last time I saw her. I'm your father."

"Really."

"Uh-huh."

"And what year was this?"

"'70."

"Really."

"One. '71."

"I was born in '74. I knew my mother was capable of some weird shit, but carrying me for three years ... nice try."

He stepped back. If I was going to do anything—anything better than pretending we were Luke Skywalker and Darth Vader—this was the time. If I could just—

"Please put the gun down, mister."

He froze. But only for an instant. My chance had come and I'd blown it. Because I was as surprised as he was.

He looked toward the hall, smiled, and walked around the sofa so he had all three of us in his line of sight. Gina. Me. And Aricela. Who he'd already shot once, most likely. Woz had said the guy he chased had a shaved head. Vinnie Mann, probably. It was Darren in the alley.

She was at the end of the hall, holding the gun Woz gave

me in the alley. It was pointed at Darren, though her hand was shaking so much it was hard to tell. How had she found it? Did she see me put it away?

No. It was her snooping. Like in the drawer for the money, and in the closet for the photos, and in Gina's dresser for God knew what. She'd been poking around the closet and got up on a chair and found the shoebox. And now she was dashing to the rescue.

Too bad I'd taken the bullets out.

"Leave her alone!" Gina started for Darren. A quick wave of the gun sent her back.

"Put it down," Aricela said. She was clearly scared to death. Just as clearly, ready to do what she had to.

"Or what, little girl? You going to shoot me? You going to shoot the big bad man before he shoots your friends here?"

"If you make me."

"Stop it," Gina said. "She's just a kid!"

"You're right," Darren said. "Wouldn't want to shoot a kid. Not first, anyway."

Now or never.

I pushed off the sofa and flung myself at him. The gun wavered, moved toward me.

I tripped over Gina's feet.

"Okay," he said. "That's it. You win. You get shot first."

I closed my eyes.

The gun went off, incredibly loud in the confines of the living room.

I opened my eyes.

It was getting old, this business about thinking I was going to get shot, and it not happening. With Woz in the record store. With Vinnie Mann on the beach. And now, with Darren. Speaking of whom …

He'd staggered back against the wall. Now he was sliding down it. I expected him to leave a smear of red as he sank, like in the movies, but he didn't. The bullet must not have gone through. It was a little bullet. From a little gun. A girl's gun. She must have hit something vital.

Like animatronic dummies, Gina and I swung our heads toward Aricela.

She stood with her hands loosely at her sides. The gun dangled from one. The fear was gone. So was the determination. What was left was mostly sadness. At having her precious youth drain away, maybe. Or maybe that was making too much of it. Maybe she was sad because she'd just gone through more in a week or two than any child should have to go through in a lifetime.

She tried to focus on Gina, on me, on anything. Then she looked at the man she'd shot, sitting leaning against the wall like he was just taking a nap. She dropped the gun and began to cry.

The Song Is Over

I spent five seconds wondering where the bullet had come from. Another ten or twelve trying to figure out why Darren Chapman had been, one had to assume, behind the Platypus hunt. At the moment, that was all the thought either was worth.

Aricela cried until the first knock at the door told us the law had arrived. Then she put on a tough guy act. Gina took her in hand and led her to the bedroom. I didn't see either of them for a while. Then one of the cops insisted on talking to her, and she sat on the bed with Gina holding one hand and me the other and calmly answered questions.

When they put it together that Aricela wasn't our kid, somebody called the Family Services people. Their representative showed up, a tall skinny guy in a tall skinny suit, and made noises about bringing charges against us for endangerment. I put up with him until he used the word *kidnapping*, at which I went off at him, shouting how none of this would have happened if his people had been able to keep a thirteen-year-old girl in custody. I almost got physical, but Kalenko wrapped me up from behind and dragged me away.

A couple of dozen people came through altogether. Lots of cops, both uniformed and un-. Even my old friend

Hector Casillas, who'd heard my name bandied about in the station and came to see what new mischief I'd gotten into. Someone with an FBI ID flashed it in my face before getting involved in a jurisdictional disagreement. A series of crime scene people arrived, coroners and technicians and a guy whose only function seemed to be waiting until everyone was done and zipping Darren into a body bag.

About two hours in, I saw Bonnie outside the door, talking to a couple of cops. She looked my way and we locked eyes and it was clear there'd been some things she hadn't told me. Then another policeman blocked my view and when he moved she'd gone elsewhere. That was the last I saw of her that night.

After that, it took another hour and more for things to calm down. The body was gone and so were most of the crime scene crowd. Kalenko was still there, plus one uniformed cop standing outside the front door, a final technician with a fine-tooth comb, and an FBI agent standing silent in the dining room. Kalenko'd told me why the FBI had such an interest. They'd been trying to use the situation to flush out Elizabeth and Quentin Baker. That was why they'd kept quiet about the unaccounted-for child who'd lived at the ax murder site. It didn't make a lot of sense to me, but the FBI seldom does.

The tall skinny Family Services guy had been joined by a short skinny woman. They'd closeted themselves with Aricela, no doubt quizzing her on the miserable treatment she'd gotten at our hands. Finally they came out, the woman guiding Aricela by the shoulder, the man following behind. The kid looked like she hadn't slept in days. She shook off the hand and ran to us. Gina took her in her arms.

I told the Family Services people I wanted to talk to

them. They eyed me, then each other. "What can we do for you?" said the woman.

"In here," I said, and led her to the bedroom. The man stayed behind, guarding against Aricela making a break for it, avoiding me lunging for his throat.

"What's going to happen to her?" I said.

"It's hard to tell. She'll be in our custody until the investigation's finished."

"Custody? What in hell for?"

"Since there's no family, we'll keep her until we know what to do with her. It's clear she acted to save you and Ms. Vela. Nevertheless, there are procedures."

"There always are. And when all that's done?"

"We'll probably find a foster home for her."

"How will you do that?"

"There are—"

"Procedures, I know. Will we be able to see her?"

She produced a business card. "Call me tomorrow. We'll know more then. Right now we need to get Aricela out of here and settled in."

She walked out. I followed a few seconds later. Aricela broke from Gina and ran to me. I got on my knees and hugged her. "What's gonna happen to me?" she said.

"I'm not sure, kiddo."

"Can't I stay here?"

"I'm afraid not."

"Can I come back here?"

"I don't know that either."

"Do you want me to?"

I looked into Gina's eyes. She came to us, put one hand on Aricela's shoulder, the other on mine. "Of course we do," she said.

Aricela looked up at her, managed a smile, turned back to me. "How about you?"

"Me too, kiddo."

"You mean it?"

"Course I do."

"Cool beans." She broke free and said to the two skinnies, "We can go now."

They ushered her out. She didn't look back. The FBI guy decided there was no point in hanging around and followed. The door closed behind them.

I went to the window and looked out on the street. Several figures, one smaller than the rest, appeared out of the building. I turned away. I didn't need to see more.

A quarter hour later we were alone. I went to Gina. She was staring at the wall, where Darren Chapman and his bad end had gotten acquainted. "I can't be here," she said.

She went in the bedroom and gathered up some stuff, and we went down to my truck.

Happy Jack

We didn't say much on the way to Culver City, and even less when we got to my place. We didn't even brush our teeth, just stripped down, got into bed, and went to sleep. I woke up a little later and dug the fabric sample with the bullets out of my sock drawer. There were five of them. Aricela had interrupted me when I was emptying the gun, and I didn't notice that one stayed put. I'd hadn't had a reason to look at them since. We'd had a one-in-six chance when she pulled the trigger the one left was in the right place.

I woke up alone in bed the next morning. I found Gina out in the Jungle, tending a glass of apple juice. I took the other wicker chair. After a while she said, "It wasn't about the kid, you know."

"I know."

"It's about getting old."

"I know."

"The kid, she was just a handy outlet. As long as I had her to worry about, I was able to back-burner this, this …"

"Existential dread?"

"Yes. This existential dread I've been feeling."

"I know."

"Stop saying, 'I know.'"

"I know."

She smiled and slapped my forearm. "Asshole."

"Bitch."

The squirrel was back next door. He ran up the birch tree. A mockingbird dive-bombed him. He held his ground, chittering maniacally. The bird went off in search of something easier to scare.

"Did you mean it?" I said. "About Aricela coming to live with us … you … whoever."

"I did at the moment."

"What about now?"

"I don't know. You?"

"The same."

A car pulled up in front. A beat-up old sedan, a Monarch or Concord or something equally faceless. The engine dieseled when the driver turned it off, making sounds not unlike the squirrel's. When it stopped he got out, nodded to us, and came up the walk.

He was of average build, with nondescript looks and unremarkable clothing. He didn't look like a cop, but he didn't exactly look like a civilian. He stopped in front of us. "Mr. Portugal?"

We looked each other over. Neither was very impressed, but neither was very unhappy either. "We don't want any," I said.

He smiled, as if people mistook him for a salesman all the time. I didn't think he was one. It was just the first thing that came out. "My name's Jack Liffey," he said.

"You don't look like a Mormon or a Jehovah's Witness."

"Far from it."

"Then what do you want?"

"I find lost children."

"You're too late," Gina said. "She's not lost anymore."

"I know that, Ms. Vela."

"Then why are you here?"

"To bring you both a message."

"From who?" I said.

"From Elizabeth and Quentin Baker."

"Aricela's aunt and uncle."

He was happy not to have to explain who they were. "They hired me to find her."

"You have some interesting clients, Mr. Liffey."

"Always," Jack Liffey said.

"Are they off the lam?"

He smiled and shook his head. "No."

"Then how—"

"I've known them for a very long time."

"Are you a dangerous radical too?"

"A retired one."

"I see." I caught myself smiling. Guess I liked the guy. "So what's the message?"

"They want to thank you. Both of you. For taking care of their niece after, well, you know what it was after."

"Yes," I said.

"That's it."

"Not much of a message."

"No," Jack Liffey said, "But it's the only one I've got. And now that I've passed it on, I'll be going. Good to meet you both." He shook our hands, said, "See you around," and walked back to his car.

Too Late the Hero

Darren's funeral was two days later. All the male Platypuses
and our old ladies sat together near the back of the chapel at
Forest Lawn. Squig and Woz had geeky ties on. Frampton
looked just swell in a suit. I had one on too, my only one,
the one I only wore to funerals and the occasional audition.
I doubt I looked as good as Frampton did.

We were all there for Bonnie's sake. You do things for
your bandmates that you don't really want to do, even if
you're pretty sure they're not going to be your bandmates
for long.

It was a nice enough ceremony, I guess, with a solemn
minister and flowers and sappy music I'm sure Darren
would have hated. The minister said some things about fate
and faith and the mysteries of life. God looked down upon
us all. Then we left, and they cleaned up the chapel to do it
all again, amen.

The second we hit the sidewalk Squig and Woz tore off
their ties. Goldie reminded them we still had to go grave-
side for further festivities, and they clipped them back on.
We piled into Frampton's van, drove up to the burial spot,
listened while a few more nice things were said. A distant
cousin began to wail uncontrollably and had to be led away.
That was about it as far as displays of emotion.

Before we got back in the van Bonnie came over and asked us all back to her place. No one knew how to say no. We returned to the parking lot. Gina suggested the four guys all go together in the van. She would drive June in her car, and Goldie could take Chloe in the Barracuda. We guys all looked at each other and agreed. I think we knew it was going to be our last chance to all be together.

No one said much of anything for the first couple of minutes. I think we were all savoring the irony. A bunch of guys in a band driving around in a van. Like in all the how-they-became-rock-stars stories.

"Fuck," Woz said.

I turned around in my captain's chair. "You want to expand on that?"

He jerked off his tie again and tossed it on the floor. "Fucking kid," he said.

I watched him. It made him uncomfortable. He looked away, back at me, then at Squig. He grabbed Squig's tie and snatched it off too. I glanced at Frampton and saw that he wanted to know the same thing I did. "What's your story, Woz?" I said.

"What's that supposed to mean?"

"You used to be a troublemaker, but basically an okay kid. Somewhere along the line you became a psychotic thug. When?"

He looked over at Squig, but there was no help from that quarter. He turned back to us. "Where do you think?"

I'd been fairly sure all along. "Vietnam," I said.

He didn't say anything. He didn't have to.

"Want to tell us what happened?"

"Guys died."

"I need more, Woz. I need—"

"Joe?" It was Squig.

"Uh-huh?"

"He's never even told me. He sure as shit isn't going to tell you."

"You asked?"

"About a thousand times. The prick won't tell me anything. After a while, you get it that he's not gonna. You just get it that he's a prick, and either you hang out with him or you don't." He shrugged. "Being a prick isn't any worse than being a dumbhead like me."

"You're not—"

"Course I am. And Frampton here, he sold out. He's a fucking *engineer*, for shit's sake. I mean, what's that all about?"

Frampton kept his eyes on the road.

"And you, Joe," Squig said. "You're just waiting for something to turn your life into something. You're gonna wait forever, brother, is what I suspect."

Everyone, me included, waited to see what I would say. I tried a few things on for size. They were all feeble. After a while everyone gave up waiting. Frampton flipped on the radio. K-Arrow was playing "Stairway to Heaven." I stabbed a button. 95.5 lit up. KLOS. They had Zeppelin on too, the song about squeezing my lemon till the juice ran down my leg. We listened until it ended and a commercial for satellite TV came on. Frampton snapped off the radio, and we drove the rest of the way in our own individual funks.

•

A woman I'd never seen before let us in at Bonnie's. Eight

or nine people were scattered about inside. The only one I knew was Detective Kalenko. He was over by a window, talking to a perfectly coiffed man in a perfectly cut charcoal suit. Kalenko spotted me and we nodded hellos. He returned his attention to the suit. Someone's lawyer, I would have bet.

Squig and Woz made for the bar, Frampton for the bathroom. The woman who let us in came back and said Bonnie wanted to see me. She led me through the entrance hall and the living room. We walked by the kitchen. A young woman who'd been on the cover of the Sunday *Calendar* a couple of weeks before was in there, pale, disheveled, leaning on the center island, gripping a huge green mug. She was, according to the *Times*, the next big singer-songwriter thing. We locked eyes. I wanted to say, run away, quick as you can. She'd wouldn't have listened.

A pair of French doors opened onto a big brick patio studded with potted plants. My guide opened the door and closed it behind me. The landscaping was as handsome as the palm garden in the front. More scheffleras, huge philodendrons with finger-thick air roots. About a million impatiens. My father would have been ecstatic.

Bonnie was seated at a wooden table halfway across the impeccable lawn. She occupied one of four chairs, atop a green-and-white-striped cushion. A furled green umbrella poked up through a hole in the middle of the table. A pitcher and a couple of glasses sat on the table. There was a brown liquid in the pitcher and in one of the glasses.

She saw me, stood, waited for me to come across the lawn. When I got to the table she stepped in to hug me. It was a good hug, an old friends hug. When we got untangled I held her at arms' length. She was wearing a dark blue suit with a cameo pinned on, one of those ivory things, like my mother had, like Gina's mother had, like every other mother I'd ever known had. A graduation present from mother school.

We took our places. "Some iced tea?" she said.

"Sure."

"It's spiked."

"What with?"

"Gin."

"Fill me up."

She picked up the pitcher, filled the empty glass, topped up her own. She pressed her finger onto a drop that had fallen onto the table and rubbed it into the wood. Then she held up her glass. "To … something," she said.

I took my glass and clinked it with hers. "To something." We each had a slug, put our glasses down, sat there silently, picked them up, drank some more. It was a while before either of us said anything else.

"Shit, Joe."

"That about sums things up."

"Why did he do this?" she said.

"I suspect you know."

She eked out a frown, drained her drink, poured some more, looked at me. My glass was half full. Or half empty, the way I was feeling. I nodded and she topped it off. "One thing I don't get," she said. "If he was so pissed off at me, why go after the band? Why not just kill me?"

"Because then you'd have been dead, and you wouldn't have suffered. One of us is whacked, you feel it's your fault, and you carry it with you the rest of your life. Some people might consider that worse than themselves getting killed."

A jay was shrieking in a tree nearby. We both watched until it flew away over the house.

"You still haven't told me anything," I said.

She nodded. "Remember the two reasons I told you why his band wasn't with Hysteria?"

"They wanted to make it themselves, and they weren't good enough anyway."

"Only one of them is true."

"The second."

"Yes."

"Why'd you lie to me?"

"I'm not sure. Maybe I didn't want you to think I was a shitty mother."

"So he did want you to record his band."

"Of course he did. This business, you have connections, you use them."

"And you told him ..."

"That I couldn't. That I'd never signed anyone who I didn't think had a good chance to make it, and I wasn't going to start with him."

"How'd he take it?"

"How do you think?"

"He was pissed."

"Very much so. But he got over it. Or so I thought. I mean, things were pretty miserable between us for a few months, but after a while it wore off. Just a few months ago he told me he realized I'd been right. That they weren't that good. Have you listened to the CD?"

"I don't have a CD player."

"Everyone has a CD player."

"Not me."

The jay was back. It landed on the lawn a few feet away, gave us the eye, squawked and winged away.

"It's competent," Bonnie said. "There are a few moments where they show some flash. But in general … after you've seen a couple of thousand bands, you know which might be something someday and which won't ever. They wouldn't have ever."

"Then why did he—"

"I don't know. I don't think it was all his idea. I think Vinnie was behind a lot of it. Then when Vinnie got killed … shit, I don't know. I'm guessing at a lot of this." She picked up her glass, put it down again. "Fact is, Joe, most of this is conjecture. I'm not really sure why he did it." She took up the glass again, and this time downed a good portion of it. "Pretty sad, huh? When a mother can't even figure out why her son wants to kill her friends."

"Is that what we are? Friends?"

She looked toward the house, like there was a cheat sheet printed on the stucco. Then back at me. "You think we're more, you and me?"

"You and me, and Squig and Woz and Frampton. I think we're less."

"If we keep playing together—"

"That's not going to happen."

"But we could—"

"Without Toby?"

She shook her head. "I've been thinking about that. Maybe we could get—" She saw my expression. "Who am I kidding? Even with Toby, it was a fantasy. And without him …" She stood, finished her drink, put the glass down a bit too hard. "I've got to go be sociable. You'll make sure you see me before you leave, won't you?"

"Of course I will."

Another hug, more perfunctory than the first, and I watched her head for the house.

"Bonnie."

She turned and waited.

"Did you know?" I said.

"Know what?"

"That it was Darren."

She frowned, chewed her lip, shook her head. "Of course not."

"Should I believe you?"

"Yes," she said. "You should." She turned and went inside.

Within seconds Papa Cass appeared from around the side of the house and lay down beside my chair. I got the feeling he'd waited until she was gone, that he didn't want to be around her just then. I rubbed his ears and shared my worldview with him. He didn't say much, merely giving me the bloodshot eye every so often to make sure I knew he was listening.

But after a while he got bored with me and, as dogs will, twisted around to lick his nether regions. It made me think of what I'd told Woz a while back, of how I'd said I had as many *cojones* as anyone. Which wasn't quite true. Poor old Papa Cass didn't have any. I wondered if he missed them, or if there wasn't room in his dim doggy memory for anything that far back.

And then there was Toby. Who made the mistake, one day not long before we drove out into the desert, of telling me that he had only one testicle, the other being a casualty of a bicycling accident when he was seven. I teased him about it more than I should have, a stupid teenage defense mechanism. He may have been ten times the guitarist as I was, but at least I had both my balls.

As did—though they were dried and shrunken, like a couple of dried garbanzos inside his parchment-like scrotum—that mummy out in the desert.

Love Is a Heart Attack

Gina and I spoke to Aricela on the phone half a dozen times over the next couple of weeks. They finally let us see her early on a sunny Thursday afternoon. She was doing fine, it seemed, and it was clear she had the staff at the shelter wrapped around her little finger. We expected her to ask when we were going to take her away from there, but she never said a word about it. I don't know if she realized we wouldn't really be fit parents, or if she was just biding her time, knowing sooner or later things would work out for her. They did, eventually. But that's another story.

We were on the Hollywood Freeway, driving back to Gina's from the shelter, when the DJ on KLOS said that John Entwistle had died, on the eve of yet another Who comeback tour. I had to pull to the shoulder.

Over the next several days they kept referring to him as the group's founding bassist. I guess that was as good a term as any, for the world at large. To me he was a hero, one of the ones who survived and was still kicking out good music thirty-five years down the road. I loved watching him. While Pete would wreak havoc on his guitar, while Roger would swing his mike like a buzz-bomb, while Keith would savage his drum kit, John—The Ox—would stand like an anchor, with his fingers flying up and down the fretboard, playing the most astounding bass anyone had heard before or since.

First George, then The Ox. With George, we'd at least had some warning. We knew he was sick. And when he left us, it was easy to believe he was simply going on to a higher plane.

But John … John was fifty-seven when he died. He'd had a heart condition, we found out afterward, but it wasn't that serious. It shouldn't have been enough to kill him.

Fifty-seven, for Christ's sake.

•

That night, after we were settled in bed, Gina said, "I put the condo on the market."

I'd made half a dozen runs over there for clothing and her computer and interior design paraphernalia. She hadn't been back. "Oh?"

"After what happened, I'll never be able to live there. I gave myself enough time to see if I'd feel different, but I don't."

"Where will you live?"

"I was kind of hoping I could move in here."

We'd never discussed it. There never seemed a reason to.

"You hate this place," I said.

"I think 'hate' is too strong a word."

"Dislike with a passion, then."

"That's closer."

"So how could you live here?"

"Real estate market's way up."

"You're suggesting I sell this place and we buy one together?"

"You can't."

"Of course I can't."

"No, I mean you can't. You don't own it. Your father does."

"Right. I knew that."

"Anyway, I'd never ask you to leave. I know how much you love it here." She leaned over, licked my ear, said, "I was thinking home improvement."

I shivered. "Explain, please."

"I've got a ton of equity in my place. We could use it to add on. There could be a Gina area and a Joe area and an us area. The bedroom would be in the us area."

"This is pretty overwhelming."

"Think about it."

I thought about it.

"Okay," I said.

"Okay? Just like that?"

"Just like that," I said. "Things change. We're changing. The house can change."

"I didn't expect an answer so soon."

"Only one thing."

"What's that?"

"Your mother."

"You want her to live here?"

"Of course not. Yick."

"My feelings exactly."

"What I meant was, I don't want to upset her. By having her daughter live in sin."

Several seconds floated by. "Are you saying what I think you're saying?"

"Think about it."

She thought about it.
"Okay," she said.
"Okay? Just like that?"
"Just like that," she said.

acknowledgements

My sincere thanks to:

UglyGuys Tom Fassbender and Jim Pascoe, for letting Joe make a comeback, for giving me a long leash, and for being the future of crime fiction publishing.

John Shannon, for letting me borrow the character of Jack Liffey. If you haven't read John's books, please do. He captures Los Angeles better than anyone.

D.P. Lyle, MD, for information on mummification, and especially for the raisins.

Sean Doolittle for his most excellent comments on the manuscript.

The folks at the Guitar Center, for the use of the cover shot gear and site.

Janet Manus, the best agent a guy could have, for standing behind me no matter how many wrong alleys I've wandered down.

Andrea Cohen, my wife, who has indulged my moods, nudged me when I needed it, and been my compass over the last couple of very strange years.